Mr. Francis' Wife

PROMISES
A ROMANCE

Mr. Francis' Wife

SANDY GILLS

Chariot Victor Publishing
A Division of Cook Communications

Chariot VICTOR Publishing,
Cook Communications, Colorado Springs, Colorado 80918
Cook Communications, Paris, Ontario, Canada
Kingsway Communications, Eastbourne, England

MR. FRANCIS' WIFE
Printed in the United States of America

All Scripture references are authorized (*King James Version*).

Editor: LoraBeth Norton
Designer: Bill Gray
Cover Illustration: Matthew Archambault

1 2 3 4 5 6 7 8 9 10 Printing/ Year 01 00 99 98

Library of Congress Cataloging-in-Publication Data

Gills, Sandy.
        Mr. Francis' wife/Sandy Gills.
            p. cm.—(Promises, a romance)
        ISBN 1-56476-689-6
        I. Title. II. Series: Gills, Sandy. Promises, a romance.
PS3557.I417M7 1998   97-48910
813'.54—dc21   CIP

Dedicated
to my husband and children
whose lives are the
heart of my treasure

One

*H*annah glanced over the papers that lay scattered across the kitchen table, as though by staring at them she could will a logical solution to appear. But no matter how hard she tried to juggle the figures, she could not deny the fact that it had been a bad year for cattle on the Petersheims' Wyoming ranch.

Even if sales were good, she told herself as she paced the dimly lighted room, she hadn't enough steers to market to pay a hired hand throughout the winter. And yet without that extra help, how could they manage? She and the children couldn't care for the cattle alone.

She thought again about working in Saratoga to bring in the money to pay Francis Allison his wages. It was a modern, moderate-sized town whose main attraction was the hot springs within its limits. But the prospect of a thirty-mile drive through winter cold was daunting, to say nothing of the extra burden her absence would make for the older children. And the chances of finding a job this time of year were slim, anyway.

Hannah glanced through the kitchen window to the darkness outside, drawn once again to the trailer where their hired hand—"Mr. Francis," the children had always called him—slept. If she was going to do this, she thought, it would have to be now—now before the reality of what she was thinking could really sink in.

Quickly then, she reached for the long, black shawl that hung on the hook beside the kitchen door. Wrapping it around herself, she hurried into the night.

The cold air rushed across Frank's bare feet as he opened the door of the trailer. It was dark, but he could see the clear outline of Hannah Petersheim as she stood huddled outside his doorway.

"Mr. Francis," she said haltingly, "I—need for you to marry me." Her eyes were misty from the sting of the cold night air. She shuffled her feet and pulled the shawl closer around her.

"I am losing the ranch," she continued. "I cannot pay you throughout the winter." She peered at him from beneath her shawl and said quietly, "And I am with child."

Frank Allison blinked at her, speechless. It was 2 A.M. and the late October wind was promising an early freeze. He fought the look of incredulous astonishment that threatened to spread across his face.

Frank had worked for the Petersheims for nearly five years now, ever since their move from southern Illinois. He had liked Eli, who was an honest, if a little eccentric, man with a natural gift for working with animals. He had always liked Hannah, too, and their ever growing family. But to take on a widow and her twelve—almost thirteen—children . . . !

"Mrs. Petersheim," he said, opening the door wider, "you'd better come in."

Hannah shook her head. "You know the testimony of my faith," she continued, as though listing her prime asset. "The ranch is without debt and would offer you security. The children know you and are comfortable with you. I—" She paused and glanced hesitantly at him, the crystal blue of her eyes meeting the paler shade of his own. "I . . . respect you, and I . . . I trust you."

She lowered her head, as though ashamed of the rejection her heart was anticipating. Clearly it was a long gamble asking him, but it was the only way she could think of to keep her children together in the home she had worked so hard to build.

Frank scratched at his thermal shirt. He could see what the woman was thinking. Still, friendship went just so far. "Don't you have any relatives back East?" he questioned.

"No, Mr. Francis," she told him. "Eli and I left our homes and families more than fifteen years ago. We have not been welcome there since."

She looked at him again, directly and without emotion. "You needn't answer now," she told him. "But think it over."

Frank nodded his head, then watched as she turned and disappeared into the darkness.

Frank could have easily imagined that the vision he had seen in the darkness had been a figment of his imagination. But when he joined the Petersheims at his usual place at the breakfast table the next morning, the look in Hannah's eyes left little doubt as to the reality of the situation.

He stared into the coffee cup she set before him as three-year-old Leah climbed happily into his lap. The household was busy, clamoring with the rush of children as they hurried to meet the school bus.

Frank looked around him with new eyes. The house, as well as the people in it, was a contradiction of cultures. Eli and Hannah's Amish background was reflected in the plain and simple furnishings. The stove that served for both heat and cooking burned wood instead of propane, and on the walls and shelves there were knickknacks and stitchery that bespoke their love of family.

Yet Eli had a fancy for electric gadgets. Having been denied these in his youth, he had indulged in the purchase of electric can openers and pencil sharpeners, a trash compactor and a dishwasher. And though large oil lamps still graced each table and burned throughout the winter, the small fluorescent light above the sink was the one that stayed on most days and nights whenever anyone was in the house.

The boys, though they wore blue jeans and gym shoes, also still wore suspenders—yet these might be brightly colored or printed with the Levi's label!

The five girls had long hair, just as their mother did, and

at home often covered it with scarves. Here they went barefoot and wore long skirts of plain, solid-colored material. Dressing for school, however, the older girls wore the same clothing as their peers.

And though the family spoke English fluently, at home they often fell into the familiar dialect of their ancestors. It was a habit Frank had grown accustomed to over the years, and he just smiled to himself when they would absentmindedly include him in the conversation, not stopping to think that he hadn't a clue as to what they were talking about.

As the children left for school that morning, Frank set Leah on her feet to play, then rose from his chair. He gulped the last of his coffee quickly and met Hannah's gaze. "I'll be out by the barn if you need me," he said, returning the empty cup to the table.

Hannah nodded and silently continued clearing the dishes.

TWO

*D*espite the chill of the previous evening, the day warmed quickly beneath the autumn sun. Hannah wondered as she glanced out her kitchen window how many days were left before the cold set in.

She thought, then, how unlike the East it all was. There, the autumn was often wet and breezy. When winter came, a sort of dark and gloomy sky hung over the land for months on end. But here in her adopted home in the West, the sun shone brightly, despite the cold, bringing hope for a time of planting and harvest again.

The sound of metal clinking against the flatbed trailer drew Hannah's pensive thoughts to the yard where Frank worked. He was busy repairing the equipment before storing it for the winter. He was good about things like that, always careful with the machinery and tools, always conscientious and conservative.

It would be a good union, she thought. And yet she frowned. She didn't love him. He was tall and thin and at forty-two, not unhandsome to look at, with his dark brown hair and misty blue eyes. His manner was quiet and pleasant; never once had she heard him curse. He had been raised just outside of Butte, Montana, and was as devout a Christian as she could ever hope to find. But he was not Eli.

Eli had been a big, boisterous man, and before that a big, boisterous boy who had wooed her from the time she was a little girl in braids and pinafores, carrying a lunch pail to school. A brawny blond, he could lift her from the ground with one arm and tote a sack of grain with the other, and all the while he was gentle and filled with laughter and the fullness of life.

How could it be that he was gone from her now? Their plans were unfinished, their children not yet raised. And within her a new life stirred. Hannah knew she could not handle the responsibility of raising these children alone, of guiding them spiritually and physically.

If only Eli would walk through the door. If only she were somehow dreaming this terrible reality. When she closed her eyes, she could hear his voice and feel the tickle of his graying beard near her face, she could feel his broad arms close around her to keep the fear and sorrow away. There had never been any doubt that he was the only man for her. Hadn't God created them for this purpose? Hadn't they left their homes to find His pathway in the world together?

Hannah blinked the tears from her eyes and folded the drying towel she had hung on a chair close to the stove. She wondered, then, if asking Mr. Francis to join with her had been wrong. Was she any more than a simple whore, willing to sell her body and her servitude in an effort to keep the land that she and Eli had worked so hard to make their own?

After all, she didn't love the man. And she wasn't sure she ever could.

Mealtime that evening was filled with chatter about school and friends and church activities. Throughout it all, the children were oblivious to the brief and troubled glances exchanged between the adults who sat with them.

When the meal was finished and the prayer of thanksgiving said, Frank rose from the chair and took his hat from the hook on the wall beside the door.

He stepped to Hannah and waited for the children to leave momentarily with a stack of dishes. "I made an appointment for our blood tests for tomorrow morning," he told her quietly, a hint of shyness entering his voice.

Hannah stared at him, surprised; he hadn't told her he'd agreed yet, nor had she expected his answer at the passing of one day.

"We can get the license by Friday," he continued, evading her eyes.

This was, after all, marriage he was talking about. Marriage! And he was relating it with all the fervor of the six o'clock stock report!

Fumbling with the brim of his hat, he rushed onward. "Would you like me to make arrangements with the minister for next Monday morning after the bus leaves?"

Silently Hannah nodded in agreement. A part of her sighed in relief that he had not rejected her, that she would not lose her home or the land or the privilege she'd had of raising her children all these years. And a part of her trembled in fear and screamed out in anger that she was committing herself to a lifetime agreement that in truth she wanted no part of.

She quieted her mind and went to wash the dining room table.

"Stephen and Henry," Frank called to her nine- and eight-year-old sons, "don't forget we're cutting wood right after school tomorrow."

"All right," Stephen answered.

"I remember, Mr. Francis," Henry added, his smile revealing his pride at having been included in the task.

Frank smiled back at the boy, recalling how Henry had helped to give him that name. Eli had always called him Francis instead of Frank. Henry, just three years old and jabbering up a streak when Frank arrived at the ranch, was soon imitating his father's call. Eli corrected the boy several times for what by Petersheim standards was disrespectful and a grave breach in courtesy, but little Henry couldn't seem to remember "Mister Allison." At last Eli compromised by putting the "mister" in front of Francis, and soon no one in the household could imagine calling him anything else.

"Should I feed the heifers hay, Mr. Francis?" asked Samuel, interrupting Frank's reverie.

Samuel was fourteen and eager to drive the tractor or anything else with wheels and an engine. The heifers were in the field farthest from the feedlot—a journey somewhat difficult to make with a flatbed full of hay in tow.

And yet he had watched Samuel grow from an inexperienced, shy farm boy to a young man who had served well at his father's side. Samuel had suffered deeply at the loss of Eli, and it was perhaps that reason that caused Frank to give in to the boy's pleading eyes.

"All right," he told him, "but Ben, you ride Captain out with him."

Ben, only twelve, frowned at the thought of taking the aged, graying draft horse out to the pasture while his brother drove the tractor. Though he said nothing, his eyes expressed his disgust as he turned from the room to empty the pan of ashes from the cookstove.

Frank glanced at Hannah before placing his hand on the door. Ever so slightly, he nodded his good-night. For a brief moment, Hannah smiled.

On Saturday evenings, after chores were finished and baths taken, Hannah usually read to her children. They would gather in one of the bedrooms, clad in pajamas and nightgowns, the girls braiding each other's hair while their mother read. It was a time they all enjoyed and looked forward to throughout the week.

It was eleven-year-old Emma, her light brown hair shimmering in the light of the oil lamp, who pointed out the obvious. "Mom, you forgot the book."

Hannah pulled the chair from the desk in Sam and Benjamin's room, where the children were sprawled across the two single beds and floor. Stephen and Henry played quietly in the corner, a row of brightly painted Matchbox cars split evenly between them. She spoke hesitantly. "There's something I want to talk with you about."

The children all looked up at once, alarmed by the uneasiness of her voice. It was the tone that told them trips had been canceled or new shoes would have to wait. It was the voice that explained loss and illness and the sacrifices necessary in so large a family.

Only six-year-old Amos, his thick auburn hair drooping lazily to cover the brown of his eyes, mumbled his objection. "But, Mom, we're supposed to read."

"Hush," Samuel said. "What is it, Mama?"

Hannah spoke quietly. "Mr. Francis and I have decided to marry."

She glanced at their faces, expecting perhaps betrayal or shock, surprise at the very least. Yet she owed them no explanation. Marriage, she had been taught, was a very private decision. Once a couple were of legal age, not even their parents need be consulted beforehand. Announcements to the church community were sometimes as brief as two weeks before the actual wedding day. This sacred joining that bonded two people for life was not meant to be a topic for speculation or gossip. In truth, though, Hannah knew that rumors ran rampant in the Amish community, just as they did everywhere else. The young girls whispered about buggy rides to the Sunday afternoon singings.

Hannah's older children understood this reticence and felt honored that their mother had chosen to confide in them. They knew, too, that the burden of raising them was never meant for a woman alone.

But Stephen, always impulsive despite his parents' attempts to instill in him a sense of caution, got to his feet and faced his mother. "Mr. Francis!" he exclaimed. "You can't marry him!"

"Stephen!" Rebecca nearly shouted, her dark eyes glaring into his—a lighter shade of blue. "It's none of your business who she marries!"

"It is, too!" he argued. "I've got to listen to him." He turned to Hannah, pleading. "Mama, we don't need another father. You've got us. We can run the ranch."

Hannah stood and held up her hand to cease the anxious words of her son. "We cannot run the ranch," she corrected firmly. "And you are to respect Mr. Francis," she told them all, meeting their eyes with a look they knew not to disobey. "He is your elder, as he always has been," she reminded them. "And now he will be your stepfather as well.

"Without Mr. Francis, I would not attempt to keep this ranch. It's a great responsibility he's taking on, and we will all do everything possible to show our willingness to cooperate."

"That's right." Samuel voiced his support, followed by a nod from Benjamin. The two eldest boys knew the responsibilities of running the ranch since the death of their father. Mr. Francis had helped them shoulder those responsibilities, helped them make decisions they couldn't possibly have made alone. He allowed them the freedom to remain boys instead of men, trying to fill the position their father made look so simple.

They heard their mother's news and felt primarily relief. Though they grieved for the companionship of the man they'd known as Father, they welcomed the presence of another whom they'd trusted and worked beside for many years.

"You children go on to bed now," Hannah told them. "Say your prayers." One by one they filed past her for a hug and kiss good-night.

The lights in the room that Emma and Rebecca shared had long since been extinguished, but Emma turned in the darkness toward the bed where her sister lay. "Do you think he'll be strict, Becca?" she whispered.

Rebecca did not answer right away. Then, "I don't know," she said quietly. "He never has been."

"He never was our father before!" Emma replied.

Rebecca sighed. What difference did it make, she wondered; the decision was already made.

"I don't think Mama even loves him," Emma continued, her voice straining to remain calm. "How could she marry him?"

"She doesn't have to love him," Rebecca chided, as though the idea of it was ludicrous. "They're grown-ups; they don't have to be in love."

Emma leaned against the edge of her bed, her hands propped beneath her chin. "Why not?" she questioned. "Didn't she love Father?"

"That's different," Rebecca told her with the wisdom of a fifteen-year-old. "Mama and Father were young when they met. It's different when you're older. It's more practical."

"Practical?" Emma repeated in disbelief. "How can it be practical?" At the word *wedding*, she conjured up visions of flowers and romance and music. How could two people intending to marry not somehow be in love?

"How should I know?" her sister snapped. "It just is. Mama's pregnant, and it doesn't look good to be with child when you're alone. Anyway, I'm glad they're getting married."

"You are?" Somehow it hurt to think that her closest sister was actually happy to see their father replaced so quickly. It made Emma's own pain more secret, more intense.

There was silence between them, and for a moment Emma thought that perhaps Rebecca had fallen asleep.

"I was afraid that Mama would return to her people, to the community," Rebecca finally said.

"You mean to Grandma's?"

Rebecca turned toward her sister, barely able to see her outline in the dim light that peered in from the window. "Yes," she whispered. "I thought maybe she wouldn't be able to feed us anymore. I thought she would go back to being Amish."

Emma began to sense the same doubts that had gripped her sister. She had heard many tales of their relatives back East, none of whom she'd ever met. "Would we all have had to become Amish?" she questioned.

"No," Rebecca answered. "I'd have run away. This is my home. I'm not one of them, and I don't belong there. I wouldn't go."

Emma's imagination drew grave images of Rebecca's staunch struggle for independence, of the battle and separation that would have followed. Suddenly she was not as set against Mr. Francis as she thought she'd been.

"Maybe he won't be so bad," she said.

Rebecca lay back on her bed and smiled as she stared up at the ceiling. "No, maybe not."

Three

*T*ime, which had up till then trickled painfully by, suddenly flew. Before Hannah wished for it to be there, Monday morning came.

She waited until the older children had left for school, then dressed herself and the three youngest in their Sunday clothes and waited for Mr. Francis.

He arrived in a dark brown suit that he had bought for the occasion and handed her a small bouquet of flowers. From his pocket he withdrew a blue velvet box and opened it for Hannah to see. Inside were two gold bands, one wide and one thin, with a finely etched design on them. "I had to guess at the size," he said apologetically.

Hannah stared from the delicate-looking rings to Mr. Francis. She and Eli had been married in a church where rings were looked on as frivolous and showy, certainly not a necessary part of marriage. But it was clear to her by the look in Frank Allison's eyes that he considered these rings neither trite nor ostentatious.

Before she could speak, he closed the box and returned

it to his pocket. He lifted one-year-old Isaac from the floor, and with his other hand held the door for Hannah and Leah and Gideon to pass through.

Gideon, with his auburn hair and scattered freckles, had always had a strong attachment to Mr. Francis, following him around the ranch for the four years of his life. He imitated the way that the hired hand walked and the low grumbling he made when his horse stumbled into a gopher hole or rubbed too close to a fence post. As they seated themselves in the van, Gideon chattered away, oblivious to his mother's worried brow.

Befitting Hannah's mood, the day was overcast with a wind that swept unceasingly across the hillside.

Josh and Sara Conners, members of their church, joined them to serve as witnesses. Sara was also from an Amish community in the Midwest, though her dress and dialect were different from Hannah's. Yet the women were bound by a common struggle to leave their past behind and come to terms with the rest of the twentieth century.

Fully understanding the desperation in Hannah's situation, Sara and Josh could only hope to offer their neighbors a supportive hand and a fearful blessing.

The ceremony that bound Hannah for a lifetime to a man who neither spoke the language she was born to or knew a glimmer of her past lasted all of five minutes.

The ring was slipped onto her finger, its mate put onto Frank's. He kissed her cheek briefly to seal the minister's words, then they turned and, with the children and their friends, left the church.

Josh, a carpenter by trade, had already committed himself to oversee a cabinet-making seminar in Rawlins that day, so the couples parted company. Frank drove his family into Saratoga to the Wolfe Hotel where he had reserved a quiet corner table.

There he ordered steak for himself and Hannah, and a rather expensive cheeseburger for each of the children. They returned home after a brief stop at the hardware store for nails and were back in their everyday work clothes by chore time.

The boys helped carry over the few belongings Frank had accumulated over the years. His shaving things he put in the cabinet in the bathroom. His clothing, although Hannah had provided space for it in their bedroom, he placed in an old trunk at the foot of the couch in the living room. "I'll move it later when there's more time," he told her.

Uncomfortable with his presence, the children went to bed early, without their usual round of squabbling or delays.

Hannah dug through the boxes at the far corner of her closet until she located one with yellow twine tied around it. Carefully she set it on her bed.

In the quiet of her room, she opened the box that held the wedding dress she had worn at eighteen, some sixteen years ago now. Also inside were the cards she and Eli had received that day and the flowers her sister had given her, which Hannah had pressed between the covers of her Bible.

She smiled, remembering how timid she had been,

unable to eat or drink the entire day, nervous that she would say the wrong thing or shame Eli who was from a far wealthier family than her own. But it was Eli, who had brought the crowd of 200 to laughter, by tripping and spilling an entire bowl of punch down his front.

Hannah reached further into the box and removed a soft, white nightgown with delicate pink ribbon interwoven at the sleeves and collar. She smoothed it against her and glanced in the mirror. With her other hand, she unpinned the clip that held her long, dark brown hair and let it spill across her shoulders and down her back.

She was no longer young and innocent and unknowing of the ways of a woman. God had blessed her with twelve children and another who, by spring, would make itself known to the world. Her body bore the scars of her labor, and in her face was a tired sorrow—not the blush that should accompany a bride on her wedding night.

Still, she thought, she must do her best to please Mr. Francis. He had, after all, taken on a tremendous responsibility at her request, and he was due the respect a husband expected from his wife.

With a deep breath, she rose determinedly from the edge of the bed and set the nightgown on the dresser before returning the box to its place in the closet.

Frank, who had spent all the time he could showering and shaving and brushing the dust from the suit he had worn so briefly that day, entered the dimly lit bedroom.

He stepped to the closet, his suit in hand, and then hesitated. "I'd like to put this in here," he said, turning to her.

She smiled and nodded her approval.

Frank hung his suit quietly on the rack. He thought how lovely she looked, her hair shining in the reflection of the lamp that was lit on the bureau beside the bed.

The room smelled vaguely of roses, though he couldn't imagine how she'd accomplished that in the middle of October. The sheets were clean and crisp, and the quilt thick and fluffed, quiet evidence of the efforts she was making to merge their lives into one.

He walked to the side of the bed and sat beside her. "Hannah," he finally began, running his fingers along the stitched pattern of the quilt. He looked into her eyes, hoping his words would not offend her. "It isn't that I don't want to be here," he said. "It's just too soon."

Hannah did not speak. A great relief spread over her, and at the same time a small panic entered the back of her mind. Perhaps he had changed his mind, and she would awaken to find him gone.

Rising, he turned to leave.

"Mr. Francis," she said. He turned back. "Mr. Francis, there are extra blankets in the front hall closet. You are welcome to them."

Frank nodded in gratitude. Barefoot, he walked down the hallway and made his bed on the couch, prayerfully certain that his decision had been the right one.

Four

*F*rank returned from morning chores to the smell of pancakes and the voices of children. He was greeted by the five-year-old twins, Malinda and Miriam, who were clean and dressed, their dusty blond hair neatly combed and braided.

"Mornin', ladies," he said with a smile.

The girls burst into a fit of giggling, which stopped suddenly as their mother called them to the table.

Gideon was not as shy as his sisters. Sticky and with a distinct odor of maple syrup about him, he charged into his newly acquired stepfather with a roar.

For a moment they wrestled for possession of the hat that Frank was holding. Twice Hannah called the boy to be seated and finally, with a swat from Frank to hurry him along, Gideon complied.

Soon all but the youngest group had left for school. Predictably, someone had left a lunch bag on the counter.

Oh, well, thought Frank. *No one ever died of starvation from missing one lunch.*

Isaac was sitting in his high chair, eating the bits of pancake Hannah had set on the tray. To Frank's surprise, she actually smiled as she turned to him. He had not seen her features brighten so since before the logging accident that took Eli's life over three months ago.

"Would you like some coffee, Mr. Francis? Gideon, find him a plate," Hannah said.

Gideon, anxious to please, set a clean plate at the table for Frank.

Hannah, bearing a steaming platter of pancakes, stopped and stared from the place setting to Frank, who stood beside it. She blinked suddenly, searching his features for signs of disapproval. *What must he think,* she wondered, *when I've placed him outside the head of the table? He's no longer a hired hand here, to work for wages and the surplus of our meals. It's his place to manage what we're provided and to be served the best from what he's earned.*

And shifting the hot platter to one hand, she moved the clean plate to Eli's empty chair at the head of the table. There she filled his plate and returned to the next batch of pancakes that were simmering on the cookstove.

Now Frank surveyed the situation. How could he sit in Eli's place, despite Hannah's well-defined sense of propriety? *Vows or not,* he thought, *no piece of paper is going to replace those kids' father. Doesn't matter what "rights" it might entitle me to.*

Shaking his head, he took the straight-backed chair at the head of the table and exchanged it with Isaac's high chair, scooting it close to Hannah's usual seat.

He then set his plate of pancakes in the place opposite hers, close to the four- and five-year-olds.

Gideon was delighted with this new arrangement and eagerly joined Frank as he ate heartily.

Hannah, apparently pleased by his understanding, again graced him with her smile.

On this morning he did not hurry through his meal. He caught himself watching Hannah as she worked about the kitchen. Feeding and cleaning such a large family was no easy task, and he admired her ability to keep up with it.

Before, he had been cautious around her. After all, she had been another man's wife. He had to remind himself that those barriers no longer existed. *You're a married man now,* he told himself as he stood to leave for the day's work. *And that is your wife!*

When evening came, Frank questioned Hannah about the books that Eli had kept on the livestock and finances.

She went into the pantry and got out a large cardboard box. While she and the girls washed the supper dishes, Frank began sorting and stacking receipts and documents on the dining room table.

"It's nine o'clock," Hannah told the children finally. "Time for bed."

"Mama, is my blue sweater clean?" Emma asked anxiously. "I need it for tomorrow; it's the only one that matches my gray jeans."

Hannah had had this conversation many times with her children. "Did you put it in the wash?" she questioned. Not waiting for an answer, she continued. "If you put it in the wash now, it will be clean and dry by Thursday. Monday and Thursday are laundry days," she finished.

As though Emma needed a reminder! She'd been folding laundry on Mondays and Thursdays since she was five years old—yet this last-minute panic over clothing always seemed to surface at bedtime.

Disgruntled with her mother's answer, Emma turned to the stairway with her siblings.

Patiently Hannah directed the traffic that led up and down the stairs toward the bathroom for teeth brushing, toward the kitchen sink for final drinks of water. She doled out second good-night kisses, assisted with buttons that could not be reached, and sorted through the tattling that came her way.

After thirty minutes she climbed the stairs to tuck them in and turn out the lights. She had just returned to her reading at the dining room table where Frank was working when a sudden thud sounded from the upper hallway, followed by the giggling of male voices.

Frank and Hannah glanced at each other. It was understood that once the lights were out, bedtime was strictly adhered to.

"Maybe someone fell out of bed," Frank offered, trying to justify the outburst.

"Perhaps," Hannah agreed doubtfully. She set aside her book and rose from her chair to investigate.

"Are you boys all right?" she called from the bottom of the stairway.

It was Sam's voice that answered. Hannah had relied on

him heavily in the months since Eli's death, and had come to
trust his word when dealing with the younger children. This
evening, however, she detected a note of amusement in his
tone, and she waited until the children were quiet before
speaking again.

"Good-night," she said sternly before turning from the
front hall.

"Good-night," resounded the chorus from the bedrooms.

But once again, as Hannah returned to the dining room,
scuffling could be heard on the floors above, followed by giggling and what sounded like a ball bouncing down the stairway.

Hannah's eyes reflected her disapproval, but Frank
pushed his chair from the table.

"I think this is being done for my benefit," he said. "They
just want to break the ice. I'll tuck them in this time."

Break the ice! Hannah thought as she watched him leave
the room. *Break the rules is more like it!* She listened, curious as
to how he would handle their disobedience, only to hear the
same scuffling she'd heard before, but now accompanied by
the louder laughter of Francis Allison. Shaking her head, she
resumed her reading until he returned.

Frank's face was a ruddy hue and his hair was mussed as
well when he returned. He tucked his shirttail back into the
waist of his jeans and attempted to meet Hannah's eyes with
sobriety. "I took care of it," he told her with authority.

Hannah's look was dubious. "So I heard," she remarked.

Frank suppressed a chuckle, covering it with a cough. He
returned to his chair and the stack of papers he had left
unsorted on the table.

Hannah said no more, but rose to fix herself a cup of tea and to offer him one as well. For a while they shared the evening's quiet together. Then, weary from the day, Hannah closed her book. She stood awkwardly, unsure about disturbing him.

Frank glanced up from his work, looking puzzled, and Hannah felt a heat rise to the tips of her ears. "I . . . would like to retire," she said.

He nodded; it had been a long day.

Nervously she took the cup she'd been drinking from and held it in her hands, but she did not leave.

"Can I get you anything else?" she questioned.

Frank had already returned to his papers. "No, thanks."

Still she stood there. He looked at her, clearly confused. "Is there something you wanted?" he asked her.

The bumbling dolt! Hannah thought in frustration. Of course there was nothing that she wanted! It was his pleasure that she had thought to satisfy, and he was making it so difficult, so awkward and uncomfortable. Did he actually expect her to come out and say it? She tried vaguely to broach the subject. "I wasn't certain if you were tired."

Still Frank was oblivious to her intentions. "Oh, I just thought I'd stay up a while longer and read over these papers. You can go to bed if you want. I'll close up in here."

"You'll be along?" she asked.

He did not answer her but mumbled a sort of *hmmm* instead. Sighing, Hannah bid him good-night and left the room unnoticed.

It was almost one o'clock when she reappeared. Still the oil lamp burned as Frank sat at the dining room table with papers and pencil and a calculator.

"Mr. Francis," she said quietly, "Is there something wrong?"

Startled, Frank quickly removed his glasses—glasses that Hannah had never seen him wear—and set them on the table. "No, oh no," he assured her. "I'm just trying to make some sense of all this." He chose his words carefully, not wanting to offend her.

"I . . . have a hard time reading Eli's writing," he told her. "And some of this is in lower German."

Hannah inched forward. "Would you like me to help you?"

Tentatively Frank rubbed the back of his neck with his hand. *How can I tell her that the man who was her husband, the man who was my boss for over five years, had no sense of business management whatsoever? How can I criticize him without offending her?* The hurt, he knew, was still fresh in her eyes, in her voice when she spoke of him. How could he help her through this transition of grief if he told her how poorly he felt Eli had prepared for her future?

"No," he answered her. "I'll just muddle through."

"Well, shall I fix you some coffee, then?"

"I won't be much longer," he replied. "Thanks, anyway."

Shyly Hannah turned. "Good-night, then, Mr. Francis."

"'Night," he answered. He was watching the waves in her

long dark hair as she started toward the bedroom. Suddenly he called her back. "Oh, Hannah," he said.

She stopped and looked at him.

"I'll be reorganizing most of this for my own files. You don't mind, do you?"

Surely she understood that he was now in charge of running the herd and would need access to the breeding records.

"No, of course not. I don't mind."

She returned to bed and didn't know when the oil lamp finally dimmed and Francis retired to his bed on the couch.

Five

*H*annah expected Frank to sleep late the next morning. Instead, she woke to find the chores done and a note on the table saying he had gone to Rawlins and would be back later that day.

When he arrived home, he brought with him a computer and all the accompanying equipment. He set it up and immediately went to work, sorting and filing the information Eli had kept inside the humble cardboard box.

As soon as the children returned from school, Frank set Samuel in front of the computer screen and began instructing him in its use.

All the children, of course, were interested in the brightly lighted screen. Rebecca and Sam had taken keyboard classes in school and were not totally unfamiliar with it. They saw this new addition as a significant advance for their household into the twentieth century. Hannah saw it as an expensive toy.

Hadn't paper and pencil always been enough? What was the point in such an elaborate record-keeping system when there might not be enough food to see them through the winter?

She did not voice this opinion aloud, but Frank was getting wind of it nonetheless. She avoided eye contact with him, and was silent throughout the evening meal.

After supper, Frank set Benjamin at the computer screen and ambled cautiously into the kitchen where Hannah was slamming plates into the cabinet above the sink. The girls hurried about, avoiding their mother's pathway, eager to leave the tension they sensed but did not understand.

Frank winked and waved them into the other room, taking the dishcloth from Malinda and stepping to the sink to take her place. With one foot he pushed aside the little stool on which the child had been standing, and Hannah turned at the sound.

He couldn't help but grin at the frown that greeted him. Hannah set down the large stainless steel bowl in which she'd mixed their pie dough earlier—set it down a little more firmly than she'd intended, and it rang slightly from the blow.

"Have you decided to take over the women's chores as well?" she questioned.

Frank swished the dishrag inside a pitcher before rinsing it in the clear water in the pan beside him. "Mmmm . . . maybe," he answered casually.

Hannah met his eyes, then dropped hers, ashamed for speaking to him that way, for venting her anger before pausing to think. All her life she'd been taught restraint in the manner of her voice and temper. Amish homes were distinguished in a modern world not only by the size of their families, but by the lack of angry, biting words and shouting.

And yet her temper had been a problem for her from childhood. Like a pressure cooker boiling, she would maintain proper order until one day a small burst of steam would show itself. Even in her marriage with Eli, she had been unable to keep these ill feelings from stirring within her. Sometimes she would close herself in the bathroom to grumble at the towels or toss about the toothbrushes. When she was settled and more rational, she would form her words exactly, using calm and common sense to support her viewpoint instead of anger and bitterness.

But she had used no such caution with Francis Allison. They'd been married barely two days, and she had demonstrated a fine showing of temper without so much as a second thought.

Frank let the pitcher drip for a moment before setting it on the counter with the others. Then he leaned his soapy hands against the sink and turned to Hannah, awaiting their first confrontation. "Are we having a problem?" he asked bluntly.

If she didn't like his decision to purchase the computer, he thought, he'd just as soon get it out in the open now. "Well?" he asked her.

Hannah shook her head. "No," she answered timidly. "Nothing's wrong."

He hesitated a moment longer. "You sure?" he questioned more gently.

"There is no problem," she told him, refusing to discuss the issue.

"All right," he said, "if you're sure there's nothing wrong. Malinda," he called then, "you can finish these pots and pans now."

The little girl returned quickly to the kitchen and Frank

resigned his position to her care, returning the stool for her to stand on.

"I'm afraid your ma doesn't approve of my work," he teased. "You appear to be better qualified."

Malinda smiled at him and resumed her scrubbing.

When the children were finally settled in bed, Frank called Hannah into the dining room. "Sit down," he said, offering her the chair beside him. "I want to explain this to you."

Hannah shook her head. She wouldn't protest the presence of the square machine on the table before him, but she most certainly did not have to touch it herself. "I have too much work to be fiddling with this," she told him. "Besides, I'm sure you're far more capable of keeping these records than I'd ever be."

She turned to leave, but Frank took her hand and held her there. "Please," he requested.

Hannah hesitated. She meant what she had said; she had assumed when she married Frank that he would take over the management of the herd. It only made sense that he would do it in his own way, and if he needed her to understand, then she must listen. Reluctantly, she seated herself beside him.

Frank smiled. He turned to the computer and began showing her the access into breeding records, grain rations, marketing prices, and patterns of calf losses.

Though she had meant to sit in dull and silent obedience, Hannah quickly found her interest sparked as he showed her what their last five years of labor had produced. He pointed out weak areas in cow fertility and undergrazed pastures. He showed her bullish and bearish marketing times and the effect that gluttonous corn yields had on the margin of profit they'd made each year.

Hannah was amazed at the figures he could pull out of one small machine by the press of a button. She had all but forgotten the mending she had meant to do when suddenly the screen changed, and a funny little song began to play. Across the screen, a face began eating dots to accumulate points. She watched disapprovingly as this man—her husband—chased little dots and monsters across the screen.

When he lost the game, he turned to her. "Your turn."

Hannah was indignant. "I will not."

"Why not?" he asked.

"Because it's foolishness," she said resolutely.

"What's foolish about it?" he asked her. "It's just a way of getting used to the keyboard."

"I will not spend my time gobbling little dots," she said stubbornly, crossing her arms in front of her.

Frank grinned. "You're just afraid."

"I am not!"

"Oh yes, you are," he said. "You're afraid you'll be outsmarted by a machine."

Glaring at him, Hannah reached for the keyboard and accepted his brief words of instruction.

An hour later Frank, tired from his previous late night, finally headed for bed, leaving Hannah to her foolish chasing of dots.

For the next week, every moment that school was not in session found Frank, Samuel, and Ben sorting through the cattle to be shipped East. Though prices were not at their best, Frank had decided to cull heavily and invest in some better bulls to upgrade the herd.

As much as he had liked Eli, he had always found him to be a much better farmer than rancher. Eli had understood the soil and had the best stand of hay in the county, but he did not understand rangeland cattle. His corrals and loading chutes were poorly made and inconvenient for handling. His haphazard record keeping allowed for poorly bred cows to be held over year after year and weak strains to continually pull down weights. While some pastures were heavily overgrazed, allowing for excessive parasites and possible poison exposure, other pastures went to seed, doing cattle and grassland harm in the long run.

Frank meant to correct all that. With the money from heavy culling and the little he had set aside, he intended to put the ranch back on track. They would never do more than just make ends meet, he realized—not with all those mouths to feed and shoes to buy. But being rich had never been his goal in life. No, surviving and helping the children get a start in life would be enough to accomplish in one lifetime, he thought. Even with the Lord's help, it was enough of a challenge for any man.

He was pleased with the way the children seemed to accept his new role in their lives. No one spoke of changing his title; he was still "Mr. Francis." But he had moved from hired hand to foreman of the ranch, and he was content with that position. He'd fill it for the present, or forever, if need be.

The older children, exposed to modern thoughts and ways at school, were open to change, even eager for it. Frank used this yearning to ally himself to them as teacher and provider. Yet he knew he must be cautious; he had no desire to upset the delicate balance Hannah had maintained between their past convictions and the present world in which they had to compete.

Hannah, on the other hand, was suspicious of change— and why not, given her upbringing. It was a wonder that he had gotten that computer in as easily as he did!

Frank knew that patience was the key to his success with this woman—his wife. Hannah had taken a great risk in coming to him. She needed more time, he knew, to recover from her grief. He wanted her to come to him freely, not out of obligation or in exchange for his help, but out of the feelings that he prayed would grow between them.

Six

*B*y the time Frank had finished culling the cows and bulls and yearling calves, there was precious little left of the herd—a fact that worried Hannah to distraction.

Her first inkling of what had become of the money came in the form of a stock trailer that pulled into the yard about a week later.

From it, Frank unloaded two new Hereford bulls and a young Angus bull, which he planned to put with the eighteen-month-old heifers come June.

From the other side of the trailer, he brought out a big buckskin quarter horse gelding. Beside it were two small horses of the same breed, which Frank announced at the supper table were the new responsibility of Samuel and Benjamin.

Hannah was livid. Eli had never kept horses other than the drafters on the ranch, for he knew that boys in their foolishness were forever racing here and there and proud of such animals the way that some men were of their cars. The truck and tractor were just as capable of getting the cows into the mountain pasture without all the expense a horse took for feed and equipment, and well Mr. Francis knew that.

Still, he had not asked her opinion, so she did not give it . . . at least not right away. Later that evening she was bathing Isaac. She had been leaning over the tub, scrubbing the slippery one-year-old while he jabbered and splashed at the floating rubber cow Leah had given him to play with.

Frank had stood at the door frame, casually munching a piece of cold pumpkin pie. "Hannah," he began, "now that the bulls are paid for, I think we ought to go into Rawlins and pick up some clothes and grub for the winter."

Hadn't they spent enough money already? she wondered in outrage. "I'm sure we'll be just fine with what we have," she told him, continuing to rinse Isaac's hair.

Frank heard the sense of irritation in her tone, but he didn't know why it was there. "The boys need boots and jeans and coats," he observed. "And we can buy food in bulk in Rawlins; we can't do that in Saratoga."

"I can buy whatever I need as the winter goes along. We can do with very little when need be," she pointed out. She was glad that her back was to him, so that he could not see the angry color that had sprung to her face.

Frank shifted his weight as he straightened from the door frame. "It'll cost a lot more for food if we don't buy in bulk."

"Well," she stated, wringing the water from the washrag in an impatient gesture and tossing it into the corner of the tub, "you should have thought of that before you spent so much on those horses and bulls."

" 'Those horses'," he replied, his own anger rising defensively, "are not pleasure horses, they're cutting horses. They'll get the cattle separated and loaded with a lot less stress and injury than the way we've been doing it. And the bulls," he continued, "are to improve the herd."

"Herd!" she exclaimed, glancing over her shoulder. "What herd? You've sold three-fourths of them!"

Frank stepped forward and then hesitated. "You can't keep breeding bad cows; they can only produce bad offspring."

Hannah said no more, but turned her attention and her conversation to Isaac.

Frank waited until there was a lull in her evasive cooing. "I'm not your hired hand anymore, Hannah," he told her bluntly. "I'm taking the children into town Saturday for winter shopping. They look forward to it every year and they deserve it. You can come if you like," he tried, softening the steely edge his voice had taken. "But either way, please see to it that a list is ready before I leave."

By Saturday morning Hannah had made several lists, all of which she crumpled into small balls and tossed into the burning wood of the cookstove. She would not go to Rawlins with Frank, that was certain. She wouldn't so much as step a foot in the van.

But as she served breakfast and her eyes met her husband's, her determination wavered. Quickly, while he was brushing his teeth in the bathroom, she scribbled a few things on a sheet of paper and folded it in half, placing it in her apron pocket.

Frank mustered the little bit of courage he had as he glanced in the bathroom mirror. He was not used to confronting the female gender; in fact, had avoided such distasteful encounters most of his adult life.

And yet he knew that if he didn't take hold of this issue now, he would never lead the family in anything; he would be a husband in name only for the rest of their lives. *Lord,* he said in silent prayer, *please let my voice be gentle. Let my words show kindness without weakness, guidance without criticism. Let me give the leadership my family needs of me yet remain the servant You've called me to be. In all things, let the love of Christ be foremost in my life. In Jesus' name, I pray.*

He straightened the collar of his shirt as he finished his words and wondered for a moment if he was absolutely insane attempting to take so large a group shopping. But as much as he dreaded it, the fall excursion was a Petersheim tradition that Frank would not omit. It was the last opportunity they'd have, perhaps, to visit with "civilization" before the snows of winter made travel hazardous. And it was the children's reward after harvest, a tangible symbol of the labor they had participated in throughout the spring and summer. It was a visible means of reaping the profit they'd worked so hard for.

Without this journey, their work on the ranch was merely chores assigned by their parents. It made their home and the cattle and the land around them less "theirs," if they had no choice as to where the money went once the cattle had been sold. It was, after all, a tradition that Eli had begun, and

Frank saw it as good and necessary. He would not alter it—
with or without Hannah's blessing. Resolutely then, he
stepped from the bathroom and walked to the stairway.
"You children put your coats on; it's time to leave," he
hollered.

Footsteps sounded throughout the house as the children gathered for their eagerly awaited journey to the city.
But Emma touched her hand to Rebecca's arm as she
turned to leave their room. "Is Mama going?" she asked as
they joined the others in the hallway.

"I hope so," Rebecca answered.

"Me, too," Sam cut in.

"How come they're arguing?" Benjamin asked in a
hushed voice.

Henry poked his head into the group, his eyes wide as
he joined the conspirators. "Are they arguing?" he questioned.

Emma nodded. "Mama said she wasn't going," she
informed them. "I heard her telling Miriam last night."

"Why wouldn't she want to go?" Henry wondered aloud.
Shopping in Rawlins was one of his favorite treats. It included dinner in a restaurant, new clothes, and sometimes even
soda pop and candy. Why in the world would anyone want
to miss all that?

But the others wouldn't answer him, or perhaps they
didn't know, for they went right on talking as though he
wasn't there.

"I'm not going if Mama isn't," Rebecca said defiantly.
"I'm not keeping an eye on all of you."

"I'm not, either," Samuel agreed.

"It's not fair for us to have to spend our whole shopping trip chasing after little ones," she continued.

"Or running to the bathroom every time somebody's got to go," Ben added, thinking of a chore that often fell to him.

"Oh, good," Emma said in disappointment, her arms crossed before her. "You tell Mr. Francis that, and none of us will be able to go!"

Ben gave a nervous chuckle. He'd watched Frank Allison wrestle bulls too many years to step voluntarily into the pathway of his anger. "I ain't tellin' him," he said.

Sam nudged his brother and smiled. "I ain't, either."

But Rebecca's hands flew to her hips as she glared at her brothers. "Well, I will," she told them. "I'm not afraid of him."

"That's fine. You tell him." Samuel patted her dotingly on the back as they started toward the stairway. "And we'll all come to your funeral, won't we?" He winked at Henry and Ben.

"That's right," they agreed.

Rebecca jerked his hand from her. "I will," she promised as they walked. "You'll see. If Mama isn't coming, I'll tell him."

The boys, however, were not the only ones having misgivings about so staunch a rebellion. Hannah was feeling her own moment of indecision as she stood diapering Isaac at the dining room table. Frank approached, and her cheeks flushed in color though she did not meet his eyes.

"Have you made out a list?" he asked her.

Hannah nodded but continued dressing Isaac.

Frank waited a moment longer. "May I see it?"

Somewhat ashamed of her own stubbornness, Hannah took the meager list from her pocket and handed it to him.

Frank took out his reading glasses and put them on before unfolding the small slip of paper.

Quietly, then, he glanced over the rim of his glasses to Hannah, who was busying herself with Isaac's snaps. "Flour and sugar," he read aloud. "Is that all?"

Hannah felt her ears burn beneath his scrutiny. "Yes, Mr. Francis," she answered in a quiet voice.

Frank studied her features, trying to determine if she was being obstinate or if she simply didn't want to burden him with the family's needs. In the end, he couldn't decide. Silently he folded the list and tucked it into the case along with his glasses.

Then he turned to the front hall closet for his coat.

Hannah hurried with the last of Isaac's snaps. She had hoped that he would ask her one more time to accompany them, that she would be able to join in this occasion that meant so much to the children. It was wrong of her, she'd decided, to judge him so harshly before ever giving him the chance to prove his theory right. She had lashed out at him in anger the moment he'd taken his first step in being the head of their family. And wasn't that, after all, what she'd married him for? Wasn't that the very burden she'd felt incapable of handling?

"Mr. Francis?" she called to him suddenly. "Mr. Francis, may I come along?"

Frank grinned warmly in obvious relief. "Of course you may come, Hannah," he told her. "I'd love your company."

Samuel, who'd been standing silently at the bottom of the stairway with the other children, nudged Rebecca. With a grin, he mouthed one word: "Lucky."

Seven

*A*nticipating the long trek into Rawlins with twelve children, Frank had gone to the library earlier that week and copied some pages from a travel game book. He had also made up a lunch list—how many fries, how many hamburgers and shakes it would take to feed them all. And he had written down the size of shirts and pants for each boy and girl, along with their current shoe size.

Having Hannah along made it all that much easier, for when they arrived at the shopping center, he simply ripped off the girls' list and gave it to her while he and the six boys, excluding Isaac, went off to the men's department.

They met at the restaurant for lunch, and afterward they all trooped into a large fabric and craft shop. It was the first time that Frank had ever entered into this realm that he considered strictly women's territory, and he watched in silent curiosity as Hannah walked from bolt to bolt of material. Pausing, he fingered the texture of a royal blue satin.

Hannah hesitated beside him. "Would you—like for me to sew a shirt for you?" she questioned.

Frank withdrew his hand quickly. "No," he answered, clearly embarrassed. "No, thank you."

Hannah turned her head to hide her smile. She walked a little further down the aisle and turned to him again. "And this?" she asked timidly, displaying a sheer fabric of powder blue. "Would this please you?"

He blinked at her as though she'd lost the only sense the good Lord had seen to bless her with. "What would I do with a shirt like that!" he exclaimed.

Hannah chuckled. "Not for you, Mr. Francis," she told him shyly. "For me."

Frank was astonished. "Hannah," he said firmly, "you start wearing clothes like that, and we're gonna have to have us a serious talk."

Hannah could contain her mirth no longer. "It's for sleepwear, Mr. Francis," she whispered, and turning from him, she continued quickly down the row to where the girls were comparing calicos.

"Oh," Frank mumbled in confusion. And then his eyes widened. "Oh!" he repeated, suddenly enlightened. Jostling Isaac in his arms, he hurried to follow the others.

After what seemed like hours of mulling over textures and colors, the women finally had what they needed. And having had more than enough of joint shopping, Frank took the boys to the hardware store while Hannah finished their list by going to the grocery store.

By the time they met again, Hannah and the girls were finished and were loading groceries into the back of the van. Frank looked approvingly at the three full carts waiting to be unloaded. Hannah, caught up in the joy of being so well prepared for winter, didn't notice at first when he stepped up beside her as she supervised the unloading. Then she turned and saw him, a questioning look on his face and a familiar piece of paper in his hand.

"I thought you only needed sugar and flour."

Hannah hardly knew what to do. The groceries were already paid for and put into sacks. Was he angry with her? What if she had spent money that was needed for bills later in the winter? After all that he had done for them that day, had she now ruined it by overspending?

Her worry showed in her dark blue eyes. "Oh, Mr. Francis, I just didn't stop to think. The cereals and juices are so much cheaper here. . . . I just added up what we used each month and . . ."

She paused guiltily. She had been thinking of the holidays and all the baking she and the girls could do. She hadn't been thinking of savings at all.

Frank waited for her explanation to continue. Somehow he wanted to hear her admit that she had enjoyed their day together and say it had been a good idea after all.

"Perhaps we could take some of the jeans back," she suggested. "Or the material, if the store will take it."

Frank thought of all the arguing and cajoling Hannah had gone through to convince him that each piece of fabric was absolutely necessary. The truth was that no cajoling had been needed at all.

Frank gave a roar of laughter. "And go through all that again come spring?" he questioned. "Never! Keep the groceries. Keep the clothes! Load the van! Load the van!" he ordered the children.

Hannah's eyes twinkled as she saw through his guise. "Thank you, Mr. Francis," she said primly before climbing quietly into her seat.

Hannah glanced out the window as Frank and the boys cut the last of the wood with the chain saw and stacked it in the lean-to beside the house. With the threat of a winter storm at any moment, the family was anxious to put up as much wood as possible while the weather still held and before the holidays arrived.

Mr. Francis' sister, Roxanne, was coming to stay over Thanksgiving. She had been to see her brother many times over the past five years, and she and Hannah had always been cordial enough toward one another. But the realization that Roxanne was now her sister-in-law made everything look different.

In her pensive mood, Hannah looked at the walls around her. She and Eli had lived pretty much in seclusion all their lives. She was comfortable with the simple things she owned. Children, she had learned, were forever messing about a place. Before you knew it, one scuffled here and left a black shoe mark on a beige wall. Another tumbled there, pulling down a curtain rod or a window blind or shade.

To worry about every nick and scrape would be an invitation to ulcers and a tension in one's relationship with the children that seemed unnecessary in the short span of a lifetime. Still, Hannah wondered if her laxness in this area would prove to be a disgrace to her husband before his sister.

Later that evening, while Rebecca watched the younger children and Emma supervised the table setting, Hannah took her shawl and slipped out into the darkness to the quiet of the barn.

Ever since he had learned of her pregnancy, Frank had insisted upon milking the cows himself. It was ridiculous, she thought, that here, with her thirteenth child, she should suddenly cease her normal outdoor activities and become a simpering invalid. Nonetheless, to keep peace between them, she had agreed to leave the task to him. Now he looked up from the cow he was milking to find her standing next to the jersey, and acknowledged her with a smile.

"Lovely night, isn't it?" Hannah said softly.

"Yes, it is." Frank continued milking.

"I love the smell of the wood burning," she told him dreamily. "There's something secure about seeing a stream of smoke rising from a chimney on a cold night. It makes the whole world seem a little warmer somehow."

"Guess that's so. Never thought about it before."

"Becca and I finished butting the blocks to the quilt this afternoon," she said.

Frank glanced at her, perplexed. Why was she standing there shivering, talking about chimneys and sewing? He stood up and said, "I'll be done here in a few minutes if you want to go in."

Hannah hugged her shawl closer to her and stomped her feet. "No, I'll be fine."

Henry and Amos ran into the barn, breathless and giggling from their race.

"We're done, Mr. Francis," Henry announced, jostling his brother. Amos was trying unsuccessfully to stand at attention with a sober expression.

"Are you sure you threw down enough hay? We wouldn't want the horses to go hungry," Frank said.

"Yes, sir," Henry answered.

"Yes, sir," Amos imitated, stifling a spurt of laughter.

"Then go wash up for supper. We'll be inside in a minute."

Off the boys ran. While Frank led the cow to her spacious stall inside the barn, Hannah took a shovel and scooped the manure from the milking area into the gutter. Then she hurried to his side as he lifted the bucket of milk and turned toward the house. If she were ever going to say anything, she knew it had better be now.

"Mr. Francis," she began, touching his arm with her hand to gain his attention. "Mr. Francis, do the . . . are the children . . . is the house . . . an embarrassment to you?"

Frank set the bucket down on the soft, clean straw of the barn floor and turned to her in puzzlement.

"I mean," she said, "I'm not deaf. I know that people say you are a fool for taking in so many children, and none of them your own. And maybe . . . maybe I don't take care of the house the way I should." She shook her head in frustration. "I don't keep after the children the way I should to make them mind, especially since . . ."

Hannah was near tears now, and Frank put his hands on her shoulders and then raised her chin to meet his gaze. "Hannah," he told her, "I don't really care what people say."

He waited until he was certain she was hearing him. "As

far as the house goes," he said with a warm grin, "I think it's a wonder you can figure out your own name with all the rushing around you do. If you want help cleaning before my sister comes, I'll be glad to lend a hand. Just tell me what needs doing."

Hannah was shocked. "Oh, my no," she said. "I didn't mean to have you—it wasn't my intention, Mr. Francis—"

"Hannah, Hannah," he interrupted, smiling at her flustered state, "I've been a bachelor for most all my life. Who do you imagine kept the trailer clean? I'm not exactly foreign to a vacuum or a mop."

"Well—I—wasn't thinking of having you do the work—not that you aren't capable of it," she added quickly. "I just didn't want to shame you in front of Roxanne."

Frank was touched by her thoughtfulness. "You could never shame me, Hannah."

She smiled gently and pulled the shawl more closely around her. Looking down, she said quietly, "I . . . have put your things away." She turned quickly to leave the barn, but Frank was faster and seized her arm to stay her flight.

"Wait a minute. What, now?" he questioned. "You put my things where?"

Hannah would not meet his eyes. She stood very still and quiet before him. "Away," she repeated timidly.

Frank stooped down, but she would not face him. "Away—" he tried again. "Away—in the attic. Away—in the trailer," he guessed. "Away in the manger!"

Hannah laughed despite herself and looked up to find him smiling at her. "Away in my bedroom—in our bedroom," she answered.

He removed his hand from her arm and stepped back, studying the ruddy hue that had rushed to color her face. Leaning against the heavy post within the barn, he crossed his arms before him and asked her gently, "Why?"

Hannah covered her hands with her shawl, crossed her arms, and gestured with a shrug. "It's been a month now," she said, "and we have not been—together."

"I wasn't counting."

Hannah kicked at the dirt beneath her feet. "But it's not binding," she explained. "The marriage isn't binding."

"Is that important?" he asked her. "You think that's all that makes our vows valid?"

"Of course not, Mr. Francis," she said, her shyness suddenly lost as she rushed to explain her meaning. "But it isn't right, your sleeping on the couch. It isn't good for the children or your sister to see us that way. They may think—well, that we don't—"

He swallowed a smile, sensing that she wouldn't find it well timed. Still, he wasn't convinced that her sudden rearrangement of the furniture had anything to do with some noble sense of propriety. "You're worried about what the children and Roxie will think?" he questioned dubiously.

Hannah's hands were suddenly on her hips. "And shouldn't I be?" she demanded. "Shouldn't we both be?"

Frank rubbed his hand along the back of his neck. "Is that it?" he repeated, a smile showing in his eyes even while he kept it from his mouth. "You're concerned about—public opinion?"

Hannah was nearly livid as she glared at him. He was deliberately trying to embarrass her! "No," she answered boldly, stepping forward. "I thought that since we were married, it was high time we—got on with life!"

Quickly then, Hannah seized the front of his jacket and pulled him from the post he'd been leaning against. She kissed him intently on the mouth before releasing him, and before he could speak she had turned and run from the barn.

Eight

*R*oxanne Allison's arrival was heralded by the beep-beep of a shining green Jeep pulling into the drive-way. Out came a boom box, six pieces of matching luggage, and Roxanne. She was twenty-six and the tail end of the family, Frank had told them.

There was an older brother, Jack, who had taken off up toward northern Montana when he was seventeen, leaving behind a sixteen-year-old brother, Frank, and a baby sister, Roxie. They never heard from him again, not even when their parents had died ten years ago. They'd had no way of contacting him, though they placed notices in several news-papers in Montana, Wyoming, and Utah.

Frank figured Jack was dead or in prison somewhere, or he'd have heard from him by now. He was always kind of mad at Jack for taking off and leaving him with all the work. But he was glad, too, because in his loneliness he had wandered into a Bible tent meeting that summer and become a Christian.

But Roxie was a different story. For several years after

their parents had died, Frank "raised" her. She challenged him every step of the way, claiming that Frank had been brainwashed or drugged into believing the Bible was the true authority on life, given by a living God. Frank sent her to college in Laramie, and she now worked as a legal secretary at a small law office outside of Medicine Bow.

Roxie may have found her brother's ways and beliefs contrary to her own, but he was all the family she had, and she visited him several times a year. She'd taken her meals with the Petersheims, never offering to set a table or wash up, but Hannah hadn't given it much thought . . . she was, after all, just the hired hand's sister. Observing the girl's breezy style and unnaturally blonde hair, Hannah had assumed they'd had very little in common and hadn't exactly gone out of her way to get acquainted. Now that Roxie was her sister-in-law, however, she could hardly avoid it.

With help from a couple of her new "nephews and nieces," Roxie moved her belongings into the house. She promptly found a chair located near the cookstove and buried her nose in a magazine, her radio playing much too loudly for Hannah's taste, while she munched idly on a bag of sunflower seeds that she did not offer to share.

Hannah gritted her teeth as she rushed about the house doing the usual tasks: cleaning spills, peeling potatoes, picking up dirty laundry. She served Roxie her supper and washed her dishes and made the bed where she was to sleep, and still the young woman had not moved from the chair where she'd been sitting.

At long last, when the children were in bed and the lights were dimmed, she stood and stretched. Turning to Hannah she said, "No offense, but I don't know why anyone would want so many children. No one could possibly take care of them all." She yawned and smiled briefly. "Good-night," she concluded.

"Good-night, Miss Allison," Hannah answered curtly, and went down the hallway to her room.

"So many children indeed!" Hannah mumbled to herself. She unpinned the scarf she wore and set it on the corner of the dresser. She removed the clips that held her hair in place and nimbly began to unbraid it. "What would she know of children? She never took her nose out of that magazine long enough to meet one."

Angrily she took the brush from the dresser and began to smooth the curls from her braid in swift, harsh strokes. "Of course it's a lot of work, if one person does it all while everyone else just sits around and watches! No wonder—"

"It must hurt when you pull that hard."

Hannah started, and the brush flipped from her hand and clattered to the dresser. She glanced at her husband's reflection as he lay in bed, propped against the pillows, watching her.

She wondered if he'd understood what she'd said. Would he be angry that she had criticized his sister? Well, even if he was, everything she'd said was true! More slowly this time, she resumed brushing her hair.

Frank watched her in silence for a moment, then he spoke. "Roxie's never been much help around the place when she's visited, has she?"

"No, Mr. Francis," Hannah answered honestly. "She has not."

Frank scooted up higher on his pillows and patted the space beside him. Hannah came and sat down.

"I'm afraid she never really had to share anything," he said. "The rest of us were so much older that we just naturally did everything for her. And she was the only girl in the family. We treated her like a pet cat or something."

Their eyes met and they smiled.

"But you know what?" Frank continued. "I don't think she ever liked herself too much because of it. And sometimes"— he ran his hand along the curls Hannah had just brushed— "I don't think she joins in women's things and babies and all because she doesn't know a thing about them. She's afraid she'll make a fool of herself trying."

Hannah had never thought of it that way. She had just assumed that the girl was spoiled and lazy and looked down on those who worked hard for their living.

"If you really think so," she told him in a new resolve, "then I will try in patience to show her."

"Good," he said and scooted further into the covers again. "Now we'd better get some sleep; there's a lot to be done when the sun comes up."

A scream pierced his dreams, waking him with a jolt. Frank tumbled from his bed, disentangling himself from the covers, and charged into the hallway, grabbing a pair of pants as he went.

Bedroom doors burst open as Roxie shrieked, "That

thing! That thing is after me!" Her pronouncement was punctuated with a generous sprinkling of cusswords. She stood in the hallway, barefoot and just tolerably decent in a pastel pink nightshirt. Excitedly, she pointed toward the room she had just come from. "Look!"

Standing in her doorway, his neck arched and his tail feathers, what there were of them, spread in lovely display, strutted an old tom turkey that had lived at the ranch for as long as anyone could remember.

Roxanne screamed again as it waddled toward the family, understandably confused by its surroundings and the commotion.

"Jolly!" Frank said in relief. "Jolly, how did you get in here?"

By then the entire family, except for Isaac, was standing in the hallway. Henry gently stroked the head and feathers of the enormous white bird.

"Maybe he wanted to join us for Thanksgiving dinner," Hannah speculated. She turned into the small nursery beside her room where Isaac, awakened by the noise, had begun to cry.

"Or maybe," Roxie said viciously, glaring at the faces around her, "just maybe, one of you sneaky little *brats* put him in my room!"

Frank looked around at the children, but they all seemed fascinated by the same invisible speck on the floor. He looked for clues, for a guilty glance or a trace of outdoor clothing beneath a housecoat, but found nothing to incriminate anyone.

"Who did this?" he finally asked.

No one spoke.

Hannah rejoined them in the hallway, holding Isaac.

"I want an answer," Frank demanded, but again he was met only by silence.

"You can stand here all night if you like," Roxanne snarled. "You'll never get an answer out of them! I'm going back to bed. It's freezing out here!"

By now Jolly was at the other end of the hallway and safely blocked by the gathering of people, so Roxie could retreat to her room, still storming as she went. "Frank, you must be nuts to live in a place like this! Kids everywhere! Animals running up and down the ha—"

She interrupted her own harangue with another scream, followed by a rush of curses. She lifted a foot, then wiped it on the hall rug, stalked into her room, and slammed the door.

Nine

S ilence hung in the hallway. No one moved. Then, unable to contain himself any longer, Benjamin snorted a chuckle.

"Ben!" Frank snapped, bringing the boy to quick attention. "You brought that bird in here."

"No, Mr. Francis. I don't know how he got in here."

Hannah shifted the fussy Isaac in her arms. She was leaving this to her husband. "I need to go feed the baby and start the stoves," she said quietly, and slipped away.

Frank nodded, not taking his eyes off the brood of mavericks before him. He wondered what Eli would have done about this outbreak of rebellion. Then he thought of the little sapling that hung above the door frame of the mudroom, and he knew just exactly what his friend and former employer would have done. Somehow he wasn't quite ready for that.

"Very well," he said finally. "Since Jolly invited himself in for Thanksgiving dinner, he can stay for the meal. Samuel, get my ax from the workshop. Come on, Jolly. It's to the woodshed with you."

Malinda blinked at him with fearful eyes, then suddenly grabbed his hand. "No, Mr. Francis," she pleaded anxiously. "I let him in. Please don't kill Jolly."

Frank looked into the innocent blue eyes of the five-year-old. She couldn't possibly have maneuvered that bird onto the second floor. Nonetheless, he took her hand. "Very well, Malinda. I guess it's you who needs to go to the shed."

Rebecca stared at them aghast. She knew exactly who had let that turkey in. But it had served Roxanne right to be scared by that silly bird—looking down on them the way she did. Why, Mr. Francis had been more than honorable to take on such a family, and her mother due with child again. And all Roxanne could do was make snide remarks about his playing daddy to half the state of Wyoming. Had it been up to her, it wouldn't have been a turkey turned loose in the room—but there were no grizzlies handy.

Now she thought about the sturdy switch her father had placed in the mudroom and used often. He was a stern man, her father, seldom repeating an order twice, and yet she remembered his smile far more than his frown. Disobedience was always dealt with swiftly, without a lot of warnings or yelling or lectures.

"There are consequences whenever you step beyond the limits of the law," he would say. "Better you learn that from my hand now than from the hand of God later." Rebecca remembered how, when it was over, he held her close to him and hugged her. He said he knew that she would try harder and that whatever she'd done wrong would not be repeated.

But she was not about to let Malinda be punished because of some misguided affection she held for the bird whose life she had just saved. Boldly she stepped directly into Malinda's and her stepfather's path. "It wasn't Malinda," she said. "I let the bird in the house."

That was too much for Samuel, who lunged forward to come to his sisters' aid. "No, Mr. Francis. I did it."

Chivalry was contagious, until at last even Gideon had admitted to the deed.

"All right," Frank said, "since you all let the turkey in, you can all get dressed and meet me out in the barn in half an hour—everyone over the age of six."

Somberly and in silence, the group turned to their rooms.

"Oh, and you older boys," he told them, "see to it that you get this turkey back outside. Emma," he added, "you can clean up after it."

Frank returned to his room to quickly dress and tend to morning chores before the children came out. It was a quiet gathering that met thirty minutes later. The children seated themselves on bales of hay.

"We're sorry, Mr. Francis," Ben told him. "It was a mean trick to play."

But Rebecca stood defiantly. "I'm not sorry," she declared. "I'm glad I put Jolly in her room."

Stephen stood beside her. "Me, too." But as Frank turned toward him, Stephen quickly seated himself, blushing beneath his stepfather's gaze.

"As Christians," he told them, "it's up to us to be an example of Christ to Roxie. If she doesn't see Christ working through our lives, she won't see Him anywhere. How many Christians do you think she finds at the bars where she parties or even at the office where she works?"

Henry and Emma nodded while the older boys hung their heads, but Rebecca lowered her eyes. "I don't care," she said, but her tone was less determined now. "She *deserved* it. She's never helped Mama when she comes to visit—and she doesn't like us."

Frank smiled weakly. "And you think putting a turkey in her room will win her over?"

Samuel chuckled. "No, sir," he answered. Standing, he joined Rebecca and put his hand on her shoulder. "Come on, Becca," he told her, "we'd better apologize. Mama isn't gonna like it if we don't. Besides, Mr. Francis is right."

Rebecca's chin rose slightly. *Coward!* she thought. *You're just afraid to stand up to him, that's all.*

But there was merit to her stepfather's words, she had to admit. He had only echoed what the minister and her parents had taught them all their lives. If Roxanne were ever to find salvation, it would most likely be through her contact with Christian people. And putting Jolly in her bedroom in the wee hours of the morning probably hadn't helped to lead her in the right direction.

"All right," she agreed reluctantly. "I'll apologize"—she glanced at Mr. Francis—"this once."

Frank placed his hands on his knees and leaned forward. "This once?" he repeated. "There isn't going to be more than once, is there?"

The other children stood quickly and began pushing one another toward the open door of the barn. "No, sir," they answered meekly, eager to leave the barn and the incident behind them.

"Is there, Becca?" Frank repeated.

Pushed along by Samuel, Rebecca paused and glanced over her shoulder, her eyes smiling merrily in what she considered no small victory. She had, after all, spoken up for herself and come through the Mysterious Turkey Caper unscathed. "No, Mr. Francis," she answered lightheartedly. "Not this weekend."

In the kitchen, Rebecca hesitantly approached Roxanne and waited to be acknowledged. "I'm sorry to have played such an awful trick on you, Aunt Roxanne. I hope you can forgive me."

Awkwardly, she leaned down to hug a startled Roxie.

One by one, Emma and the boys followed Rebecca's example until at last, they all had a turn and the family was seated and eating the hot cereal Hannah had cooked.

Roxanne stared at them in disbelief. "What'd you do?" she asked Frank, disturbing the silence that had settled upon them.

Frank shrugged lightly. "Oh," he said. "We just talked."

Ten

The remainder of the day was far more pleasant than its beginning had been. Soon the incident of the morning was forgotten, and the children were caught up in busy preparations for Thanksgiving dinner.

While the stove kept a steady heat that brought a comfort to those near it, Hannah and Emma baked pies and Rebecca entertained Isaac and Leah in the living room.

Malinda and Miriam were allowed a small corner of the table where they made "little pies" from scrap pieces of dough.

The boys worked outside with Frank in the machine shed, making a hayrack on skids to be put with the new bulls.

Soon the aroma of baked turkey, a twenty-pounder that Hannah had purchased during their shopping extravaganza in Rawlins, began to fill the house and arouse the taste buds of its inhabitants.

Cherry pie and baked squash and hot, buttered peas added to the delights of cranberry sauce and fruit salad Jell-O molds that awaited them on the table.

As they seated themselves, Hannah felt a sudden empti-ness. It was the first holiday without Eli—Eli who had brought her to this place in what had seemed to her a wilderness. Hannah looked sorrowfully at Frank as the children held each other's hands around the table.

He looked at her, questioning the sadness before such bounty, then turned his attention to the blessing, which his sister grudgingly sat through.

Soon the clatter of plates and knives and forks made a pleasant background to the lively conversation around the table. They talked about the football season and Carol Henning's baby, whose foot had gotten stuck in the crib's metal springs beneath the mattress. They talked about adding cottonseed meal to the feed ration and whether or not the State Highway Department would be able to keep the roads near Medicine Bow free of snow that year.

Somewhere between Frank's blessing and her last bite of turkey, Roxanne admitted to herself that she was rather glad to be a part of this odd but boisterous gathering.

Finally, when they were all too stuffed to eat another bite and pie was set aside for later that evening when they would have room to enjoy it, Hannah wiped Isaac's hands and face and lifted him from the high chair.

"Roxanne," she suggested amicably, stepping beside her sister-in-law, "would you like to watch the baby while we clean up in here?" She placed Isaac in her arms. "We won't be too awfully long."

Roxie picked the baby off her lap, reached over, and forced him into her brother's arms. "Nope," she refused bluntly. "Let Frank watch him." She stood and brushed the wrinkles from her slacks. "I'll help clean up."

Rebecca and Hannah cleared the table and put the food away. Henry and Amos soon took the table scraps out to the barn cats, while Roxanne and Emma worked on the pots and pans and serving dishes at the sink.

"Reminds me of the restaurant where I worked during college," Roxie said. "Only this is a lot more fun and a lot less work."

Eleven

The holiday was over, the family had returned to its usual routine, and snow began to fall. It was not the icy, bitter snow of deep winter, but a calm, lighthearted snow that reminded them of all the things they had forgotten to do in order to be ready for the more serious bite of the northern winds to come.

The younger children eagerly put on boots and scarves and mittens and carried kindling to the wood box in the dining room, while Frank tended to the last-minute details of insulating the water pipes.

With Isaac napping and the dishes done, Hannah dressed warmly and stepped outside, enjoying the bright blue of the sky now that the snow clouds had passed.

Frank had been stacking bales of straw around the henhouse in an effort to keep out drafts. Like everything else, it too needed repairs he hadn't gotten around to yet.

Suddenly a slush of snow hit the back of his neck and slipped down his shirt collar. He wiggled to evade its icy touch and whirled about to find the guilty party, but no one so much as looked his way.

Gideon was playing with a wooden tractor—its front end sporting a new blade that Stephen had fashioned for him. Leah was busily making snow pies with her toy dishes beside her mother, who was pulling dead stems out of the marigolds that had once graced wooden boxes outside the living room windows.

He glanced at the roof of the chicken coop. *Sun must be melting the snow already,* he thought. Tightening the collar of his work suit, he returned to the barn for another bale.

No sooner had he set this one in place than another slush of snow struck his shoulder and splattered itself along his neck and into his ear.

He turned quickly enough to find Hannah, blue eyes ever soft and gentle, with a mischievous smirk tugging at the corners of her mouth. He looked at her in surprise. She just stood, waiting for him to do something about her blatant challenge.

"So," he said, stooping down and scooping a handful of snow into his leather work gloves, "you want to do battle, eh?"

But before he got the snowball made, his wife had bombarded him with the row of Leah's neatly packed snow pies. His only defense was to charge full force through the onslaught and tackle her to the snowy ground.

Hannah shrieked, and suddenly Frank remembered the baby she carried and moved quickly away from her.

"Are you all right? Are you hurt?" he asked in great concern.

Hannah smiled, her cheeks rosy from the cold and her attempted escape. "Oh, I'm fine," she assured him, brushing the snow from her woolen cap.

"But the baby—" he said. "I forgot—I didn't mean—"

"You mustn't worry, Mr. Francis," she told him. "It would take a lot more than tumbling in the snow to dislodge this baby. It's well protected in there."

"You mean he—doesn't mind all this?"

Hannah chuckled, propping herself up on her elbows. "No. The snow is quite soft," she pointed out.

"Good," he said, and quickly shoved a handful of snow down the collar of her coat. "Then this shouldn't bother him at all!"

Frank paced outside the bathroom door. "Please come out and let's talk about this," he pleaded.

"There is nothing to talk about," Hannah insisted from within, followed by a loud sniffle.

"Hannah, it's just for three days," he reasoned.

Rebecca and Emma squeezed past him on their way to the kitchen through the narrow hallway. Embarrassed, he leaned closer to the door and sighed impatiently.

"I've always gone coyote hunting this time of year," he reminded her.

The door opened just a crack. Hannah's hair was down and she'd been brushing it again. Her eyes were red and swollen from crying.

"You were a bachelor then," she pointed out.

Frank stepped forward, and the door slammed shut

again. He rubbed his nose gingerly. Why hadn't he put his foot there instead of his face?

Samuel and Benjamin appeared in the hallway, quietly waiting to be acknowledged. Their blanket rolls were slung across their shoulders.

"Shall we get the horses ready?" Sam whispered.

Frank nodded and hurried them on their way before turning back to the bathroom door. "You know we need the bounty for Christmas," he said.

"I think we could survive Christmas without it," she snapped.

Frank hesitated. He didn't want to lose his temper out there in the hallway. "I need to get away," he said finally. To himself he could admit that he longed for the solitude of the mountains, for an open campfire and the challenge of sleeping in the wilderness wrapped in the silence of a mountain winter.

On the other side of the door, Hannah thought of a hundred replies. Day after day she worked in a hot and steamy kitchen with demanding teenagers and crying babies. *Who in his right mind,* she wondered, *didn't need to "get away"?* But aloud she said, "Then why take Samuel and Benjamin?"

"The experience will be good for them," he told her. "They'll learn about survival."

"They'll learn to shirk their responsibilities!"

"Doggone it, Hannah, this—"

"Don't you cuss at me, Mr. Francis," she hollered angrily.

"I'm not cussing," Frank insisted, and forced his voice to stay calm. "This isn't shirking. The work's been done ahead, there's plenty of wood inside, and Henry and Stephen and

Amos can do what chores are left. Rebecca will milk the cow," he finished.

There was silence from the other side of the door.

"I hate to leave when you're so angry," he tried gently.

"I am not angry!" she snapped. He heard a hairbrush clang against the cubbyhole in the cabinet as she threw it into its place.

Frank smiled, his mirth shielded by the thick wood between them. "I've got to go now," he told her. "The boys are waiting."

"So, go—good-bye."

He waited a moment, hoping she would soften. "Goodbye," he finally answered.

Frank looked over the kitchen to be certain they hadn't left any supplies behind. Then he bade the children good-bye and repeated some last-minute instructions.

Still the bathroom door hadn't opened.

Sam and Benjamin held their horses steady and handed Frank the lead rope to the packhorse he had borrowed from their neighbor.

He mounted the buckskin, secured his pack, and turned the little group toward the Rocky Mountain range where they would camp that night.

Suddenly Hannah rushed at them from the doorway, her shawl clasped around her nightgown and her slippers sinking in the snow. "Be careful! Have a good trip!" she called to her sons.

She hurried then to Frank's side, dwarfed by the size of the large quarter horse he rode. Reaching up, she handed him a bag filled with biscuits she had baked earlier that morning. "For your trip," she mumbled, avoiding his eyes.

Frank took them and tucked them carefully into his saddlebag. "They'll come in real handy," he said quietly.

His horse swerved impatiently to the side, and Frank brought him up short as Hannah moved to avoid being stepped on.

"I—I—" she stammered, and then looked up at him and placed her hand gently on his thigh. She backed away from him, pulling the shawl around her. "Be careful, Mr. Francis," she said.

Grinning, he touched the rim of his hat with his free hand. "You can bet on that, Mrs. Francis," he told her, and whirling his eager horse around, led him into a trot.

Good-byes flew back and forth between the children until the horses faded from sight and the chill air forced those remaining behind back inside.

Twelve

*B*y the end of the first day, Frank and the boys had bagged five coyotes and caught enough fish to feed themselves that evening.

Frank taught them how to build an emergency shelter from tree boughs, bushes, sticks, and snow. He had them make snowshoes out of branches and twine and evergreen sprigs. Together they followed tracks and identified the scat of porcupines, beavers, and weasels.

They built a platform of small, round chunks of green wood to make their campfires on. The platform kept the dry kindling and smaller branches from sinking into the snow.

Each boy was responsible for his own mount and the pack he'd brought with him. He had to keep track of his food and water and be certain that his blanket and clothing and tinder didn't get wet.

"There are no second chances in the wilderness," Frank told them. "The first careless mistake you make could easily be your last."

With supper cleaned up, the horses well secured for the

night, and their beds rolled out inside the snug winter shelter, Frank and the boys sat around the warm glow of the campfire. There was no wind, and they were lulled by the crackling and popping of the wood. They talked of horses and the elk that lived on the mountain range and blue heeler cattle dogs.

Then Samuel sat up straighter. "Mr. Francis," he said, "how did you learn all of this?"

"All of what?"

Sam gestured about him. "About the mountains and the animals and all."

Frank lifted a stick from the ground and poked at the fire, sending sparks shooting into the darkness of the night. "From my dad," he told him. "He was a trapper—up in Montana."

"Wow." Samuel's hazel eyes widened. "That must have been neat."

Frank stirred the ashes on the outside of the fire and set the stick into the snow where it sizzled and then quieted. "No," he replied, "it was not 'neat.' We lived on a small ranch, pretty isolated. It was lonely and the work was very hard. My parents weren't Christians, and without any guidance from the Lord, they made a lot of mistakes.

"My brother, Jack, and I learned to survive in the wilderness in order to stay alive."

He wondered then, as he spoke of his childhood, if some of his willingness to take on the Petersheim ranch and provide for Hannah's children came from a deep desire to correct his own past . . . to make up for the things that should have been but never were. He felt good about what he was doing, confident, as though all these years he'd been just waiting to take the reins in his own hands and fulfill the ministry God had for him.

"I'm sorry," Samuel said quietly, interrupting Frank's reverie. "I never heard you mention your parents before."

Frank smiled, touched by his maturity and concern. "And what is it you want to do when you get older? Any ideas yet?"

Samuel shrugged his shoulders. "Ranch, I guess."

"What about you, Ben?" Frank questioned. "You plan on having your own spread someday?"

Ben didn't answer. Frank and Samuel turned simultaneously and found the younger boy sound asleep, sitting on the log before the fire just as he had been before their conversation began. Laughing, the two of them awoke their sleeping companion just long enough to bank the fire and crawl into their shelter for the night.

The little group formed its own worship service on Sunday. Once again then, they fished and set up camp. They ate jerky and dried apple rings and spent the better part of half a day building a solid igloo for their shelter.

By early Monday morning the winds began to pick up and the sky took on the gray of snow.

Frank decided not to risk being stuck in a storm that could keep them in the mountains without better provisions, so they packed up their gear and headed directly down the trail toward home.

The snow had already begun to fall when they brought the horses to the barn. It felt good to be home, to know that warmth and food and comfort were only a few minutes away.

They took their bedrolls and saddlebags and carried them into the house. The kitchen was in disarray, with dirty dishes piled on the counter and table. Frank stepped into the dining room and was greeted by greater chaos.

Material and thread and scissors lay scattered among unidentifiable pieces of paper that draped the table and chairs, the desktop, and the wood box. Paper plates, some holding half-eaten pieces of chicken and bits of potato chips, and empty cups sat here and there.

"What in the world . . ." he mumbled aloud.

Samuel and Ben didn't look alarmed. "Looks like Mom's sewing," Sam said matter-of-factly. He and Ben helped themselves to apples and headed toward the stairs.

"Oh." Frank worked his way to the living room, only to find his pathway blocked. Every chair in the house, it seemed, had been used to form a square that filled the entire room and held what looked to be a large blanket made of squares of various shades of blue.

Hannah, her mouth filled with pins and her arms laden with three large folds of cloth, appeared from the hallway at the other end of the room. Her eyes grew wide as she saw him. "Oh! Oh, Mr. Francis!" she exclaimed, fumbling with the material until it unfolded in a heap on the floor before her. Quickly she removed the pins from her mouth and inserted them in the right shoulder of the apron she wore.

"I—you're home early," she ventured brightly.

"And just what have you been up to since I left?" he asked,

holding his laughter in check and gesturing at the room around him. He was rather enjoying the sudden panic his presence had caused.

"The girls and I decided to sew," Hannah offered in explanation.

"Well, I can see that." Frank dropped his bedroll and saddlebags in the doorway.

"We're making Roxanne a coverlet for Christmas."

Frank studied her meek and humble expression. How different from the tears and angry sarcasm he had received on his departure three days ago. Was she play-acting the same as he? He knew she had grown up in a home that allowed little disagreement with the male authority. He wondered if Eli had ruled his wife in the same patriarchal way, despite their change in external appearances.

He cleared his throat and scratched at the stubble of his beard thoughtfully. "I'm going to shave and clean up," he said. "And I expect this room back in order by the time I finish."

He did not look at Hannah again for fear of bursting into laughter, but took one long stride, instead, toward the bathroom down the hallway.

Stealthily then, he slipped down the darkened hallway, attempting to come back into the living room through the other door and surprise Hannah. Halfway there, however, the two of them collided.

Laughing, Frank held her in his arms to keep them both from falling and then lifted her straight up from the floor and kissed her.

"Ow! Ow! Ow!" Frank dropped her suddenly and rubbed

the spot where her pins had jabbed him in the chest.

"Serves you right," Hannah scolded, wagging her finger at him, her blue eyes narrowing. "Pretending to be angry with me."

Frank chuckled guiltily. "Well, I am angry," he justified. "I can't even walk through my own house."

An odd expression flickered across Hannah's face; she had always thought of the house as hers. She wondered if she would ever get used to the idea that it was now as much Frank's as it had been Eli's.

"Then I shall clear you a pathway, Mr. Francis," she assured him, whirling about to do just that.

Frank straightened. "Well, be quick about it," he ordered, and as Hannah turned back to meet his challenging tone, he darted into the bathroom and locked the door.

Suddenly the door opened again. "Hannah," he called.

She paused at the end of the hallway and looked at him questioningly.

"There's a storm coming," he told her.

She nodded. "I'm glad you and the boys are home safely, Mr. Francis."

Thirteen

Christmas was coming . . . and with it, another area of tension between Hannah and her husband. She had been raised in a conservative home where frugality was not only a necessity, but was thought to be one's responsibility as a member of the community and a baptized Christian.

Frank, however, had all too many painful memories of cold and empty Christmas mornings where he and his brother cowered in the corner watching his father "celebrate" with a bottle of whiskey, while their mother silently sat at the kitchen table and pretended not to notice any of them.

This was his first "real" Christmas . . . his first Christmas with a family he could call his very own . . . and he wasn't about to let anyone take that away from him.

"Hannah," he said one morning after the children had left for school and another Christmas dialogue was going nowhere, "go to the bathroom!" He slammed his cup on the table and pointed down the hallway.

Hannah looked at him with an expression that was half

wonder, half laughter. "Whatever for?" she asked, spooning another scoop of oatmeal into Isaac's open mouth.

"Because I'm about to yell," he informed her.

"Oh." She set the spoon aside and handed the boy a training cup filled with milk. Then she got to her feet and wiped her hands on the apron that covered her rapidly rounding belly. "Well, I'm afraid I'll just have to listen from here," she said. "I've far too much work to do to be interrupted." She stepped toward the sink with her hands full of dishes. "Leah, help Mama clear the table, please."

Frank pursed his lips. *Doggone it,* he thought, *how come she never seems to take me seriously?*

"Hannah, you just don't seem to understand how important this is to me," he argued.

"We don't have the money."

"We do," he countered, stepping to the sink beside her. "At least we do this year."

Hannah frowned as she looked at him. *What sort of attitude is that?* Silently she scraped a plate. "You'll spoil them," she said. "They'll expect it every year."

"Just once isn't going to spoil them," he argued. "This is our first Christmas together. I want the children to feel this year is special."

Hannah took the mug he'd been holding and put it into the dishwasher. She shook the water from her hands and turned to face him, leaning against the counter as she did.

"Mr. Francis," she tried patiently, "I know you mean well to indulge the children this way, but it leads them to—well, worldliness."

"Worldliness?" he questioned. "Do you feel worldly

because you own an electric light or because there's nylon in your stockings?"

Hannah toyed with the corner of her apron and her face flushed. "There are some who would say yes," she answered quietly. "Eli was very drawn to that sort of thing. I—couldn't stop him."

"But where do you draw the line?" Frank argued. "With horses? Lanterns? Why not candles, then? If you use the things in this world, how can any of it *not* be called worldly?

"Hannah," he said intently, "worldliness refers to the *sins* of the world, not the things in it. We mustn't think that by avoiding the present we can avoid evil. Anything can be misused for sin instead of good . . . and holiness comes from inside the heart, not outside of it."

Hannah could not argue against such logic. "But, Mr. Francis," she pleaded, "it isn't decent to spend so much money on gifts, simply for the sake of Christmas. We have always kept it plain."

Frank sighed. *She hasn't heard a word I've said.* "All right," he finally conceded, taking her gently by the shoulders and looking right at her. "We'll shop together first and then, if I find something more I feel we really ought to have, I'll buy it. No more arguing, no more questions. Is that a deal?"

Hannah nodded, satisfied. "It's a deal."

Frank and Hannah checked the weather reports carefully before leaving the children in Rebecca and Samuel's care and heading off to Rawlins.

It was the first time they had actually gone anywhere together alone. Frank was pleased by the idea. He had never courted Hannah, never even thought of it, and though she was well into her fifth month of pregnancy, he thought the day ideal to make up for lost time.

Hannah's mind was on other things. What if a storm came up and they couldn't get home? What if little Isaac got sick or one of the boys was hurt during chores? What if Amos and Henry disobeyed and got in with one of those bulls?

"Hannah!" Frank finally said. "Stop worrying so much and start trusting the Lord long enough to enjoy yourself a little. See that Mexican restaurant over there? We're going to sit down in there and have supper, and not say one word about what might be happening back home!"

He parked the van and led Hannah inside to a booth where soft candlelight reflected a decor rich in red and brown and gold. Aztec masks hung on the walls, and carvings of bulls and donkeys accented countertops and shelves.

A painting of a man sleeping beneath a sombrero caught Hannah's attention as she listened to the cheerful music of a mariachi band.

"What would you like to order?" Frank asked as they looked over their menus.

Hannah leaned across the table. "Mr. Francis," she whispered, "I don't know what any of this is."

He chuckled then and gave their order to the smiling waiter, handling the Spanish terms with apparent ease.

Hannah was amazed. "Do you actually know what it is you ordered?"

"Of course I do," he said confidently. "One of the first foods I learned to cook was chili."

Hannah leaned back against the booth and eyed him skeptically. "You call opening a can of chili cooking?"

"I mean to tell you, chili from scratch," he informed her. "No canned foods for me, no sir."

Hannah snorted. "Oh, is that what I smelled burning from the trailer?" she inquired. "I thought you were having an electrical fire."

The waiter brought them a plate of appetizers, and Hannah cautiously sampled the *sopaipillas*, a triangular, puffy hot bread served with a brown sugar syrup.

Frank rolled a small tortilla and dipped it into the spicy salsa. He pointed it at Hannah before taking a bite. "It's a long walk back home, young lady," he warned her.

Hannah smiled. It had been a long time since anyone had referred to her as "young lady."

He continued, "Not that chili is actually a Mexican food; it's from Texas originally."

"I didn't know you were such a connoisseur."

He shrugged his shoulders. "I had Roxie to take care of. My dad was too drunk to help, and Mom was too weak—or had just given up trying. I'm not sure which. Anyway, it was learn to cook or live on shredded wheat for the rest of our lives."

Before long their waiter put before them a smorgasbord of tamales and enchiladas, frijoles and *sopa ranchera*. While they ate, Frank talked about his early days in Montana, of the years he had struggled to hold his family together, being both mother and father to Roxie while he was himself still a boy.

Hannah understood, then, why being such a part of hers and Eli's family had meant so much to him, even before he signed on as head of the household. She realized why he had stayed, even when times were lean and the wages more attractive on the well-established ranches in the area. She understood why he had admired Eli's attention to the children and why he tried so hard now to take his place.

After their meal, Frank and Hannah got down to serious shopping: Hannah bought clothes for Rebecca and Emma while Frank purchased woodworking tools for Stephen. For Henry and Amos and Gideon they picked a new sled, while Samuel got a hat and Benjamin a pocketknife. Malinda and Miriam shared doll dishes and Leah got a set of housecleaning toys. Isaac, Hannah declared, was far too young for Christmas and would have enough fun with the paper and ribbon and boxes to worry about what was in them.

Frank kept to his bargain and did not push, though now and then he would throw in a bag of candy canes or chocolate-covered cherries. And what holiday, he wondered aloud, would be complete without assorted nuts and ribbon candy?

When it was all over and the van was stuffed to bursting, they started on the long journey home.

Unfortunately, Hannah's baby apparently didn't take to Mexican food. Twice Frank had to pull off to the shoulder while Hannah was sick by the roadside. Her feet were swollen and her side ached and try as she would, she simply could not stop the intermittent bursts of tears.

"I'm so sorry," she sobbed. "You planned such a nice evening, and I've ruined it."

Frank comforted her as best he knew how, wondering all the while how in the world Eli had put up with such blubbering twelve times in the span of one short lifetime. The next time he went shopping, he decided, it would definitely be alone.

Fourteen

By Christmas, the house was gleaming with tinsel and ornaments. For Frank, every moment was a treasure that he longed to place in a memory filled with emptiness. Together, the family sang Christmas carols and drank eggnog. They trimmed the evergreen and made sugar cookies and colored paper chains to decorate the railing on the stairs.

Roxanne wouldn't be with them, since she'd made holiday plans months ago, before she had gained an instant extended family. But the Petersheims visited with members of their church family and listened while the high school band played music in the gymnasium and the elementary school choir, of which Emma was a part, sang of Christ's birth on that special day so long ago.

As she watched the children sing, Hannah realized that she had grown to love this little town, nestled at the foot of the mountains. It was the type of place where the fifth-grade teacher threw pajama parties for the girls in her class and the English teacher drove students home from the basketball games. The mayor sold clothing at a Western wear shop and people invited the children in groups for hot dog roasts and sleigh rides. Yes, in this small town where the postman married the lady who ran the grocery store, Hannah felt secure and safe. Parents fought for their children, for their ranches and their way of life. Isolated from the mainstream of the world, they held closely to their faith, to the ideals their parents and grandparents had held onto through the hardships of life and the demands of nature all around them.

She thought on this as they opened their gifts Christmas Eve. *And how well suited Mr. Francis is for raising my children in this country he knows so well,* she concluded, offering a brief prayer of gratitude to the Lord.

Rebecca unwrapped a box of socks and mittens and was excitedly exclaiming over the used sewing machine her stepfather had found at a bargain basement during his last-minute shopping spree.

Hannah smiled in approval, and as everyone's attention went to Samuel, Hannah returned to her musings. *Frank seems to understand the land and weather and the mountains,* she thought, watching Sam fuss over the new hat they'd bought him.

From under the couch, Frank withdrew a Remington Classic rifle and handed it to the boy, along with a stern lecture on the responsibilities of owning such a thing and the consequences of abusing the privilege.

At least he told me about it first, Hannah thought. He'd gone to great lengths to explain the necessity of such an item for a young man in that part of the country. And even she had to agree that as Samuel stepped into manhood, the use of a rifle was as much a part of their society as it was a part of the trade he would one day inherit. And Sam had proven himself time and again to be not only levelheaded under stress, but responsible enough to care for a gun. She'd protested at first that it was too expensive a gift, but Frank saved quite a bit by trading in two of Eli's older and less accurate rifles. To Hannah's way of thinking, her son had earned the honor of owning his first rifle, and she was as proud of him this day as she had been on the day he had taken his first step.

Benjamin was next. As Frank handed him his small package containing a pocketknife, his eyes briefly met Hannah's, and she smiled. Emma happily opened her gifts of clothing and a secondhand pair of ice skates.

Hannah, although she appeared to be fully focused on the merriment around her, turned her thoughts to the way Frank had taken over the business of the ranch. He certainly understood world marketing in a way that she and Eli hadn't even glimpsed. *We thought you just grew your feed, fed your animals, and took whatever they were willing to pay you at the end of the growth period.*

But Frank knew about bullish and bearish markets. He understood how lush corn crops affected cattle markets and how custom feeding, though not a foundation to base one's ranch on, was certainly opening new avenues of income.

Stephen had opened his woodworking tool and a sled that somehow appeared from nowhere. And Henry, she realized suddenly, was admiring a bright yellow plastic dump truck, alongside the sled she and Frank had bought him together. Amos' number of packages, too, had grown. As well as his sled, he now had a fine toy rifle to play with.

Frank had long since stopped glancing in his wife's direction. After all, he had kept his part of the bargain. He'd given her free rein at shopping, and had simply filled in the blanks here and there where he felt something was lacking. No doubt she'd "accidentally" wake him up at some bizarre hour of the night and give him an earful on the hazards of leading children into the clutches of greediness. He'd listen politely, naturally, before going back to sleep.

But for now, he was enjoying the twins' enthusiasm over the brand-new dollies he had added to their collection. After all, he reasoned, if Hannah could have thirteen children, certainly the twins could use a few more additions to their family, too.

While Gideon played with his sled and miniature cars, Leah eagerly opened her housecleaning toys and doll. And last, but not least, Isaac opened a brightly colored plastic horse, which Rebecca willingly helped him play with.

Frank stood from his cramped position on the floor beside the tree and beamed in the midst of the paper and boxes and noise.

"Ben," he called, "give me a hand." Ben had received only a pocketknife, but what Frank knew, and Ben didn't, was that he would receive an even better gift a little later. Frank watched the boy for signs of resentment, but saw none. Bringing him to the pantry, he lifted a basket filled with apples and oranges and tangerines. "Aunt Roxie sent these. There are crayons and coloring books and puzzles buried beneath the fruit. Would you pass them out to the younger ones?"

They went back to the tree and Frank brought some packages to Hannah, who was patiently praising the treasures the children were bringing to show her.

"And now yours," he told his wife with a smile.

Ever so neatly, Hannah unwrapped her packages and found a matching stoneware bowl and platter.

Hannah thanked him quietly. "Go look in the back of our closet beneath the afghan. I—forgot to wrap yours."

In a minute Frank was back, grinning ear to ear and lugging a sixteen-inch Circle buckskin saddle. His blue eyes filled with the tenderness he felt for her. "I can see why you 'forgot' to wrap this," he said happily.

Setting the saddle down between them, he held out his hands to help her rise from the couch and gently pulled her to him, the saddle and her growing middle between them.

"I can't tell you how special you've made this day for me," he told her quietly.

Hannah felt her face flush. "Oh, it was nothing, Mr. Francis," she told him. "Why, that saddle of your has been re-sewn so many times, and I just thought that with that fine-looking horse, you might as well have a saddle to match—one that won't come apart on you come spring. I know you—"

"No," he interrupted, shaking his head. "I meant the family—the kids and all. I've never had such a—" His voice faltered, and he held her a bit further from him so that their eyes met.

"Not that the saddle isn't fine," he said, his gaze narrowing, "but when I think of all those 'discussions' I had to listen to on the frugality of gift buy—"

Hannah suddenly broke from his grasp. Giving a sob, she ran from the living room to their bedroom, where she slammed the door behind her.

Frank was stunned. He turned to Rebecca, who'd been standing near them. "What'd I say?"

Rebecca only shrugged.

Fifteen

*H*annah! Hannah!" Frank hurried down the hall to their bedroom and pushed open the door. He found her lying on the bed in the darkness, weeping.

Quickly she sat up on the edge of the bed and wiped her eyes. "I am sorry, Mr. Francis," she told him. "I didn't mean to run off like that—such a display—"

Tears fell anew, and he reached into his back pocket and handed her his handkerchief.

"What's wrong?" he asked her softly.

Hannah turned her head and blew her nose. What was wrong? How could she tell him . . . tell him that the money spent on that saddle she had been saving for three years. She had sold eggs and carded wool, decorated wedding cakes and baby-sat other people's children, scrimped and saved in a hundred little ways, all for the goal of buying Eli a new team of Belgians this very Christmas.

But there was no Eli now. There was no need of gentle drafters when Captain and the gray were barely used to do more than delight a sleighful of children or pull an occasional tree stump. Frank didn't like the drafters for field work, so there was no use for more.

But how could she tell him any of that? She couldn't say that the arms she longed to hold her were big and rough and burly, or that she missed the sound of her own native tongue, of songs from their familiar hymnal. She missed the talk of the home place and the stern and quiet control Eli had with his children as he directed them on the pathway to God.

There was no order in her life without him, not the order she had known and felt secure in.

She looked now at this man whom she had married and saw the gentle concern he held for her. He was so kind to them all—how could she ever hurt him? "It's the baby," she told him, evading his eyes. "The baby—moves a lot," she told him truthfully.

Quickly, Frank folded down the covers of their bed. "You'd better get off your feet," he instructed, as though amazed that he hadn't seen her fatigue before. "Of course, you've had a busy day. Why don't you take a rest?"

He went to the dresser and lit the oil lamp that sat there, turning its light down low. "You get changed for bed, and I'll send Becca to heat some milk for you."

"Mr. Francis," she objected, "I'll be just fine. I've had a few babies before, you know."

Frank brushed aside her words with a wave of his hand. "I'll take care of everything. You just get some rest and take care of that little one in there," he said, patting her swollen belly. "Lord knows being the youngest in this family isn't going to be easy, so he might as well enjoy the ride while he can!"

Seeing no way to dissuade him, Hannah resigned herself to bed rest and reached toward the headboard for her nightgown.

Frank instructed Rebecca to fix a mug of hot milk for her mother while Sam helped Isaac dress for bed.

Stephen and Henry quickly straightened the living room while the others changed into their nightclothes.

Once they were dressed, Frank gathered them together again in the living room, poured them small glasses of eggnog, and gave them two sugar cookies each. While they ate their snack, he got out the Bible and read. "And it came to pass in those days, that there went out a decree from Caesar Augustus, that all the world should be taxed. . . . And all went to be taxed, every one into his own city. And Joseph also went up from Galilee, out of the city of Nazareth, into Judaea, unto the city of David, which is called Bethlehem . . . To be taxed with Mary his espoused wife, being great with child. . . ."

Though they had heard the story many times before, they sat mesmerized by his words. They finished their evening with a chorus of "Silent Night" and went off to bed—except for Benjamin, whom Frank had called aside.

Once the others were upstairs, Frank and Ben slipped on their coats and hats and boots and walked to the barn through freshly fallen snow.

Ben assumed that his stepfather needed help with some last-minute chores, but when they got to the building, Frank led him to the grain room. He opened an empty bin where oats were normally stored.

"I'm sorry I couldn't give you these earlier," he told the boy, "but I didn't know how to wrap 'em." He reached down and lifted out a three-month-old bluetick coonhound pup by the scruff of its neck, and plunked it into Ben's arms.

The pup licked Ben's face while a second dog, twin to the first, whined at the disturbance. Frank picked up the other one and held it to him, carelessly scratching its ear.

"Are they really mine?" Ben asked him, hardly daring to believe such good fortune.

"So long as you take care of them," Frank said. "They aren't papered or anything, but they're supposed to be full-blooded. They were guaranteed to hunt." He imitated the accent of the man who'd sold them to him.

"Will you teach me to hunt 'em?" Ben asked eagerly, as he hugged the dog closer.

"You get your grades up and I will," Frank promised. "A boy who has no time for study won't have time for hunting, either."

Ben frowned, knowing full well his grades were not what Mr. Francis expected. As much as he liked his stepfather, he found his attitude toward school to be quite different from that of his father. Report cards had been sent home at the onset of Christmas vacation just two days before. After looking them over, Mr. Francis had told them point-blank that there was no way the ranch was going to be big enough to support more than him and their mother and a single hired hand. If they were going to make it in this world, he'd said, they would need an education, and he was nowhere near wealthy enough to put them through more than a trade school once they'd graduated high school. That left scholarships and grants, he concluded, and no D-average student was going to qualify for that.

Ben held the squirming coonhound to himself and sniffed its unique puppy odor. He made up his mind then and there that his grades were going to improve.

"Can I keep them in my bed?" he asked.

Frank ran his hand thoughtfully across the side of his face. "Well," he admitted, "I haven't exactly told your ma about them, yet."

"Oh, she'll like them," Ben assured him. "She likes dogs."

"She does?" Then how come, he thought, the minute Eli ever mentioned the words "cattle dog," Hannah used to break out in a tirade of lower German until the boss would put the thought far from him—until the next year's roundup.

As though reading his thoughts, Ben added, "All except heelers. She once saw a six-year-old boy get his face torn into by one of them, and she swore she'd never have one on the place. They aren't all bad dogs, but she never could quite get that out of her mind enough to trust one. She said she was raised with English shepherds on the farm back East, but we never found none around here, so we just did without."

"English shepherds," Frank mumbled, taking note of the breed. "Ben," he said finally, "I think we'd better leave these pups in the barn just one more night. Your mother doesn't feel well, and I'd hate to go in and wake everybody up. You just keep this to yourself a while longer, and first thing after church tomorrow, I'll tell her. It doesn't mean you can bring them in—it just means that you can keep 'em." He smiled. "You think you'll bust before then?"

Benjamin laughed. "I guess not," he decided, and reluctantly returned the puppies to their hiding place.

Sixteen

he cold of winter settled in, and the memory of the
Christmas holiday seemed far behind them.

Every day, warm water had to be carried to the
chickens and pigs and two dairy cows. It gave the animals a
warm drink to fill their bellies, ensuring their health over the
long haul of winter.

The heaters had to be checked on the large watering
tanks that were used for the rest of the stock. Now and then
the water pipes inside the house would freeze as well.

The tractor and vehicles were kept in constant repair so
that nothing would freeze up at a moment when they were
most needed. Chimneys were kept clear and a constant supply of dry wood brought in.

Inevitably, this time of year, the children began to show
the effects of their constant confinement.

"Mama!" Malinda hollered from the upstairs hallway.

Hannah poured the last of the morning's leftover coffee
into her husband's cup and glanced in the direction of the
desperate cry. She knew the cry of an injured child; this was

the whiny pitch that punctuated an argument.

"Just a minute," she called back and sat at the table, her attention focused on the conversation at hand.

"I just don't see any point in putting more money into a used battery," Frank argued. He sat at the table in his coat and hat, still cold and tired after hours of working on the family vehicles.

"Do we really need the truck this winter?" Hannah asked.

Frank sighed. Hadn't he just told her he didn't want to leave the family with only one car among them?

"Mama, Miriam took my glove!"

"I did not!" Miriam's voice came in defense. "Those were my gloves first!"

"Were not!"

"Yours had a hole in the thumb."

"Ma!"

Hannah sighed and rose from the table.

As she stepped to the hallway, Amos and Gideon looked up from the kitchen floor, which they'd been scrubbing, and grinned at each other.

"Bet they have to scrub the floor next," Amos speculated in a loud whisper.

Frank had forgotten that the boys were even in the room. He glanced at the puddle of mud his boots were leaving. "Oh! Sorry about that, boys," he apologized.

Amos chuckled. "That's all right, Mr. Francis," he said. "The twins'll get it when it's their turn."

Frank frowned in puzzlement. "Didn't I see you two here yesterday?" he asked. It was usually the older girls who mopped the floor.

"Yes sir," Gideon answered proudly.

"Didn't you do a good job the first time?" Frank questioned.

Gideon shrugged his shoulders. It didn't seem to matter whether the floor was actually clean or not. He just kept dipping the rag in the bucket and sloshing it on the floor until his mother told him he was finished and could go off and play.

"We weren't washin' it to get it clean," Amos explained happily. "We was just arguing."

Frank took the hat from his head and set it on the table. He hadn't meant to stay inside so long, but the coffee was warm and the battle against the worn battery futile. Upstairs a twin began to cry.

"Well," Frank said, "if you kids take turns scrubbing the floor every time there's an argument, come spring we'll have the cleanest hardwood this side of the Rockies!"

Scrubbing floors seemed to have little impact on the children's endless winter bickering. They argued over who used the shampoo last and who left the cap off the toothpaste. They blamed each other for lost combs and mismatched socks and leaving an empty toilet paper tube for the next person.

To break this monotony, now and then someone would contrive to throw a handful of popcorn into the cookstove— a very clever stunt, considering the number of people who walked in and out of the kitchen all day.

Hannah didn't seem concerned with their squabbling. With satisfaction she'd go to the root cellar and look over the rows of squash and potatoes and apples. Carrying up a few cans of peaches or applesauce from her well-stocked pantry, somehow the wind and cold outside and the noise level inside didn't seem to touch her. Gathering the little ones around her, she would read from *Treasures of the Snow* or *The Tanglewoods' Secret* or the big illustrated Bible storybook, and time passed contentedly by the glow of the oil lamp.

Frank was not so domestically inclined. The noise of the children aggravated him. He opened the door to find a pathway of flat, thick slabs of wood surrounding the kitchen, used as a train track or the wall of an imaginary fort. In the corner sat a clothes rack filled with hanging noodles that Hannah had apparently made. Above the stove, the warm air was drying a string of apple slices, brought up from the cellar to be preserved before turning soft.

As he passed Hannah and the children in the dining room late one afternoon, she glanced up and took in at once the filthiness of his clothes and the hardened look on his face.

Suddenly she realized that he was headed for the bathroom, and she heaved herself from her seat. Leaving the reading to Emma, she quickly waddled after him. "Francis! Mr. Francis!"

He was already in the bathroom, his shirt off and his left boot removed when Hannah banged on the door.

"What is it?" he asked in alarm, but Hannah pushed past him to the tub.

"Oh, Mr. Francis, you can't!"

"Can't what?" he demanded. "Can't shower?" He was covered with mud and manure, and the stench in the tightly confined space of the bathroom was almost overpowering.

"Well—it's just—that I have these—" She glanced from the tub to where her husband sat with his boot in his hand.

Frank stood then and pulled back the shower curtain. The tub was filled with bananas!

"Hannah, where in tarnation did you get all these? And what are they doing in the bathtub?"

Hannah blinked at him timidly and ventured a giggle. "Well, a truck broke down off the highway, and they were selling them really cheap. Sara Conners brought us ten dollars' worth."

"All right," Frank conceded. "But why on earth are they in the bathtub?"

"It was the only place I could think to store them on short notice where they wouldn't freeze."

"And what," he asked with rapidly waning patience, "do you plan to *do* with all these bananas?"

Hannah picked one up and offered it to him. "Eat them?" she ventured hopefully.

Frank snatched the banana from her hand and peeled it in a sort of madness. He took a huge bite from it. "Even *this* house full of monkeys can't eat that many bananas," he told her, his cheeks bulging as he shoved the remainder of the banana into his mouth.

Hannah burst into laughter. The scene was ridiculous: a tub full of bananas, Frank towering above her, his chest bare and his jeans and boots reeking with manure.

"The girls and I are going to freeze banana-nut bread. We thought we'd try frozen chocolate-covered bananas on a stick, too." She surveyed the excess fruit. "I'd better have the boys pack these in some empty boxes and put them in the pantry. It's cool enough there, don't you think?"

Frank nodded in agreement.

She turned as she reached the door. Holding her fingers on her nose, she added, "I'll have them hurry."

In mock outrage, Frank picked up his boot and threw it at the closing door. "Bananas in the bathtub!" he mumbled as she scurried, laughing, down the hallway.

When Frank was once again presentable, Hannah greeted him with a cup of steaming mint tea. He sat at the table across from her, then leaned closer. "How's that?" he questioned. "Any better?"

Hannah sniffed the air. "Oh, much."

He grinned and put a dollop of honey in his tea.

"What happened, anyway?" she asked.

"The windbreak," Frank said. "It's falling apart. I had to move the cattle out of there and close it off. I guess they'll have to use the barn for a windbreak for now."

Hannah gazed into her tea. He was forever complaining about the condition of the ranch. The criticism hurt her. Though he didn't actually say it in words, his meaning was all too clear. Eli had, after all, been a farmer. Raised on rich, black earth with simple equipment and a body of family and friends to help attend the work, the West had seemed harsh to him. Neighbors did not take to strangers, religious oddities at that, and their pathway to learning had been littered with obstacles and loneliness.

Frank shifted in his chair and spoke more gently.

"Maybe when we rebuild," he said, "we'll try putting up an eight-foot windbreak at right angles to the prevailing winds. And we'll try to get up some more sheds with a southern exposure for the younger cattle, so they can be separated for individualized feeding over the winter."

Hannah rose from the table and took her cup to the sink. "That would be nice," she said quietly. She didn't ask where the money for such a venture would come from, nor did he offer an explanation. The quiet moment of teatime quickly passed.

Passing out the good-night hugs and kisses, Hannah realized that Gideon was running a fever. She had him sit on the chair beside her while bidding the others goodnight, then rose to get the thermometer from the medicine cabinet.

"What's the matter?" Frank asked from the open bathroom doorway. He'd come up from the basement where he'd checked the heating tapes for the water pipes.

"Gideon's not well," Hannah said. "He had the sniffles earlier, and he seems awfully hot to me."

Frank followed her to the dining room, where a flushed and sleepy-eyed Gideon sat obediently. Hannah placed the thermometer in his mouth, and he quietly waited for it to do its work. Frank, too, placed his hand on Gideon's forehead and found it unusually warm.

"One hundred and two," Hannah read the instrument

aloud. She glanced at Frank. "I hear a respiratory virus is going around."

He nodded. He'd heard the same rumor himself at Hanson's Feed Mill earlier that day. And he'd worked long enough at the Petersheims' to know that a virus in a household that large meant weeks of illness as the germ traveled from one victim to the next.

"I'll set the vaporizer up," he said. He winked at Gideon and rumpled the boy's hair with his hand before turning to leave.

Working together, Frank and Hannah got the small boy changed into his pajamas, dosed with children's aspirin and smeared with Vicks', and tucked into bed with the vaporizer on his nightstand.

"I'll just go fetch a teaspoon," Hannah said.

Frank knew what was coming. Each spring, Hannah made a batch of "cold medicine" concocted from lemons and oranges, sugar, and dandelion flowers. She used it liberally throughout the long winter.

He leaned confidentially toward Gideon. "So tell me," he whispered, "how does that cough syrup really taste?"

Gideon smiled. "It's not too bad," he admitted. "But the tea is just awful." He grimaced.

Frank made a face as well. The minute anyone in the place so much as sneezed, Hannah put peppermint oil in the steamer on the cookstove. She ladled herbal tea with a drop of cod-liver oil in it down the throat of every occupant in the house, trying to thwart the germs that spread like wildfire through the family.

"Your ma's been tryin' to get me to drink that stuff every

year since I moved here," he told the boy with a grin and a wink. "And she ain't had no success at all."

Gideon giggled despite the ache inside his head. "Well, you're gonna have to drink it now," he warned him.

"And why is that?" Frank asked, checking the steam that flowed freely from the vaporizer. He stepped over to the crib where Isaac lay sleeping and gently covered him with a blanket.'

" 'Cause you've got to be a good example to us kids now," Gideon told him. "All dads got to be a good example."

Frank shook his head. "Not when it comes to drinking tea," he said. "Everything except that tea."

"Uh-huh," Gideon argued.

Sure enough, Hannah entered the room with a spoon and the bottle of cough syrup in one hand and two mugs of hot tea in the other. She handed one to Frank and set the other on the nightstand beside the vaporizer. "You drink that, Mr. Francis," she said. "It'll do you good."

Frank waited until her attention was on the liquid she was carefully pouring into the teaspoon. Then he grabbed his throat, crossed his eyes, and let his tongue hang out, bringing a roar of laughter from Gideon.

"Gideon Petersheim," Hannah scolded, "don't you make me spill this."

"That's right," Frank said. "You mind your mother."

He turned to Hannah. "Did you put peppermint oil in the steamer?"

She glanced over her shoulder in surprise. "How did you know?"

Frank just nodded in approval. "I think I'll finish this

downstairs," he said, and turned to go.

"Ma!" Gideon objected, his eyes wide with merriment.

Frank pointed at him from the doorway. "Boy, you're gonna catch a whole lot more than a cold if you don't keep your mouth shut and get under those covers."

"But Mr. Francis," Hannah reasoned, "he hasn't had his tea yet."

Frank came back to the bed and pulled Hannah up by the hand. "You've fussed over that boy long enough. What he really needs is a good night's sleep."

Hannah looked at Gideon once more as he snuggled securely beneath the blankets, closing his eyes as though grateful for the sudden sternness of his stepfather. "Well," she said thoughtfully, reluctant to leave, "I suppose so."

"Good-night, Mr. Francis," Gideon murmured wearily.

By the next morning, Gideon and Amos both were coughing and running fevers, while Leah had the stomach flu.

Frank drove into town after chores and stocked up on tissues and vitamins and a few bargain cartoon videos.

Each day, it seemed, a new wave of flu victims remained at home while the recovering patients returned to school. A temporary hospice was set up in the living room to make it easier for Hannah to care for them.

The siege lasted two weeks, though to Frank it felt like two months; then the virus departed, apparently bored with the Petersheim gene pool and eager to conquer some other hapless household.

Seventeen

hough winter was far from over by Valentine's Day, Frank determined to leave the children in Rebecca's care and take Hannah into Saratoga for supper. He stopped at the grocery store while doing errands in town and bought five small carnations for the girls, and some red-and-white balloons and heart-shaped candies to solace the boys.

When he arrived home, however, only Amos was in the kitchen. A strange, rather unpleasant odor was circulating the room, centering at two bread pans on the table and the sliced loaf that sat beside it.

"What is that?" Frank questioned in distaste, setting the bags he carried onto the counter.

"Bread, I think," the boy answered. "I don't think it turned out so good—nobody would eat it."

Frank sniffed at the offending loaves; it sure didn't smell like anything Hannah had ever baked before. "Well—here," he said, not wanting anything to disrupt his plans. He handed Amos the two loaves. "Take this and give it to the pigs."

Gladly the six-year-old complied.

Soon the children were trickling into the kitchen. Frank handed each of his stepdaughters a pink-tinted carnation and gave Henry the balloons to begin decorating the dining room. He poured the candy into a glass bowl and set it in the center of the table.

"What's this?" Hannah asked as she entered the room, carrying Isaac on her hip. She set him on the floor and he tottered gleefully toward Frank, who threw him into the air.

"Hello, Bud," he greeted him. Setting him down again, he looked at Hannah. "Why, it's Valentine's Day," he offered in explanation.

Hannah waved her hands at him to brush aside the notion. "That's a pagan holiday," she said.

"Maybe once," he justified, "but now it's just a day set aside to tell the ones you love you appreciate them." He grinned. "So get your coat on; you and I are going out for supper."

Several of the children moaned, disgruntled at being left behind and in their sister's care.

"Becca, see to it that they get some decent food in their bellies before they eat all that candy," he instructed as he awaited his wife.

Hannah bustled back into the kitchen, her coat half-buttoned, and grabbed her purse from the counter.

"Oh, wait!" she said. "Emma, there's a cake in the oven. There's pink frosting and sugar roses in the side cupboard." She glanced at the candy on the table. "Maybe you'd better leave it until tomorrow," she said. "Yes, frost it and just set it in the refrigerator."

Frank crossed his arms and studied the heart-shaped cake

through the glass door of the oven. He drummed his fingers on his arms as he stared at Hannah. "Pagan holiday, eh?"

She blushed and pulled on her mittens. "Well, we have to appease you heathens now and then," she admitted, and then quickly, before he changed his mind, hurried toward the car.

Soon they were seated by candlelight at the Wolfe Hotel Restaurant in Saratoga. Remembering the Mexican fiasco before Christmas, Frank ordered steak and potatoes.

Hannah smiled. There were no dishes to wash here, no squabbling children to separate, no homework to review or diapers to change. She leaned across the table toward her husband. "So," she inquired, "do you come here often?"

Frank buttered a dinner roll and glanced at Hannah. "Oh, yes. I bring all my women here."

She kicked him beneath the table. "What women?" she demanded.

"Doggone it, woman!" Frank rubbed his afflicted ankle.

Her eyes widening, she covered her mouth with her hand in a pretense of shock. "Mr. Francis," she whispered.

Their salads and sodas were set before them by their eager young waiter, bringing a pause to their conversation.

"Well?" she insisted the minute the young man disappeared.

"Well, what?"

"What women do you bring here?"

Frank studied a cherry tomato and poked it into his

mouth, chewing thoroughly and swallowing before returning her gaze. "Did," he corrected. "What women did I bring here?"

Hannah waited. She had often wondered about his private life while he had worked for them, but he was so closed and secretive.

Frank let her wait a moment longer, then smiled. "None, actually," he admitted. "You folks worked me too hard and paid me too little; I couldn't afford to eat in a place like this." He laughed. "I can't afford it now, either. Hope you were planning on washing dishes."

Hannah straightened and took her fork, delicately biting into the salad before her. She'd had enough of his teasing.

He smoothed a wayward strand of hair from his forehead and took a drink from the water glass.

"Truthfully," he said, "I haven't dated since my early twenties."

Hannah looked at him, a question in her eyes. She thought him attractive and charming in his own sort of way.

"Too painful," he confided.

"Then why . . ." she could almost not say it, ". . . why did you agree to marry me?" She looked down at her plate. Why had she asked him that? Hooking up with a woman with twelve children and another on the way, with a failing ranch to boot . . . he had to have been motivated by pity. And pity was the last thing she wanted on this day or any other.

"I admired you."

His words surprised her, and he hurried onward lest she think he'd had affections out of place.

"No, really. I was amazed at your strength when Eli died.

You didn't fall apart, you didn't dump your responsibilities on some relative or indulge in self-pity by letting your older children take over. I was impressed with your commitment—to the land, to the children, to your faith—and to me."

Hannah blushed beneath his compliments.

Their steaks arrived and for a moment, they savored the flavor in silence.

"So what about you?" he asked her finally. "Why did you ask me to marry you, instead of some other man from church? Why not Len or Rick?" He smiled mischievously. "Or did I just happen to be the handiest one around at 2 A.M.?"

"Mr. Francis," Hannah scolded.

She looked at him then, her blue eyes soft and gentle. "I trusted you," she told him. "I knew that the children and I would be safe with you—that if there was any hope for the ranch, that you would save it for us. And I—" She hesitated, then forced herself to continue. "I trusted you with my friendship. I didn't want to get to know anyone new."

It was all she could do, she thought, to get to know him, to trust him to come near the great, gaping pain that had entered her life. The truth was that she hadn't wanted another man after Eli. She hadn't even wanted Frank.

But somehow life had gone on. Despite her raging pain and emptiness, the sun had continued to rise and set. Bills came in the mail, school continued, bread burned in the toaster, and babies cried in the night. If she had to go on with the rest of the world, she would choose to go on with Francis Allison.

Her eyes blurred with tears that she fought to hide, and Frank reached across the table to hold her hand in his. He wanted to tell her that he loved her, that she was the best thing that had ever happened in his life, that he had no idea how really lonely life had been until she and the children had flooded into his pathway of living.

But he knew that she was not ready to hear those words . . . might not ever be ready, in fact. So he kept them to himself and simply waited silently, as he had since they had married, until her grief had passed and she was able to smile again.

They stretched out their time of freedom and quiet as long as they possibly could, finishing dinner with a cup of coffee and chocolate mousse.

They returned home to a dark and silent house, the children all asleep.

Hannah looked about the kitchen one more time as Frank waited to turn out the light.

"You lose something?" he whispered.

"My bread," she told him. "I baked two loaves of sourdough bread today."

Frank's eyes widened with enlightenment. "Sourdough," he said. "So that's what that smell was."

"I always set some starter aside in the winter," she explained, "in case we run out of yeast and can't get back into town."

He nodded at her foresight, though he couldn't actually remember a time when the roads had been blocked for more than a few days.

Hannah opened the warming shelf of the oven and peered inside.

"I took care of the bread earlier," he said, as though the

matter had simply slipped his mind.

"Oh." She set her purse in its usual spot and turned to the hallway, satisfied.

Frank offered no further explanation. He turned out the light and took his wife by the arm, happy to end the day on such a pleasant note.

Eighteen

$\mathcal{M}$arch arrived, and Frank put the bulls on additional feed to help ready them for breeding season. Though it still snowed from time to time, the land began to thaw and the unpaved roads turned into a slippery, rutted maze.

To pass the time, Hannah and the children made long drip candles and funny-looking ice candles. Though wax managed to splatter across the stove, table, counter, and floor, the resulting products were beautiful to look at and functional as well.

Frank was glad that Hannah was able to pass this knowledge on to the children, but like the sourdough bread, it was a precaution that he did not exactly agree with. To him, trust in the Lord meant a willingness to live in the present without clinging to the past.

If danger were to beset them, the Lord, he was certain, would allow grace for the moment. What skills they did not have, they would learn as the need arose. Her ways seemed to him like trying to prepare for a world holocaust; there was just no way of knowing what was needed until the moment came.

Still, he knew, it was her heritage that she was sharing with the children. It was no different from teaching them to understand the mountains they lived in or the weather around them. No, that wasn't what bothered him. It was that relying on one's own knowledge for safety and security was false. He hoped, somehow, that he would be able to convey that to them even as they learned the old skills.

March gave way to April. The ground was part mud, part snow, part ice.

Frank lay on the ground near the barn, realigning the chain beneath the manure spreader. Suddenly he heard Hannah's voice, and looking out he could see her feet near his head.

"Mr. Francis?" she questioned. "Are you finished?"

"Not yet," he answered. "You and the children start lunch without me. I'll be inside in a few minutes."

The feet didn't go away; they just rocked back and forth, heel to toe. "Are you almost finished?" she asked.

Frank stopped a moment. Hadn't he just answered that? "In a few minutes," he tried.

Hannah didn't leave. "Mr. Francis," she said, a small panic rising in her tone. "I need you to be done."

Somewhat annoyed, he slid out from beneath the manure spreader and looked at her. He might be totally lacking in experience, but he knew at once that she was in labor. "Do I have time to shower?"

Hannah shook her head. "Something isn't right," she said. "The contractions are very strong but nothing is happening."

"Did you phone the doctor?"

She nodded quickly. "He said to come right in. I called Sara Conners. She's coming to stay with the children until Rebecca gets home from school. Some of the ladies from church will bring supper over, so you needn't worry about that."

"Well, get your bag, and I'll at least wash my hands and put on a different coat."

"Mr. Francis," Hannah said in a worried tone, "what if we don't make it?"

Frank glanced at her in panic. Why hadn't she told him earlier? It was a seventy-mile trek to the hospital. If things were happening this fast, they could have stopped at the clinic in Saratoga. The idea of actually having the baby in the car sent a cold sweat across his brow. How could she do this to him?

"Oh, I wouldn't worry about the upholstery," he said, in an attempt at humor. "You can't do any worse than this cow manure I dragged in on my pants and boots."

Hannah's smile quickly turned to a grimace as another contraction seized her.

Frank caught himself watching her—and speeding.

Quickly, he redirected his attention to the road.

Her breathing returned to normal. "What if—the baby's wrong somehow?" she said. "What if—this is not right."

"Hannah—" he began to scold.

"I have not had labor like this, Mr. Francis," she snapped. "This is not my first child, you know."

Frank waited until she had calmed and the next wave of pain had passed. "The baby can't be 'wrong,'" he said. "Whatever God has chosen to give us can never be wrong."

Their eyes met briefly as he spoke. "The child belongs to God, Hannah," he said. "We just get to take care of it for Him for a season—no matter how healthy or sick it may be."

Touched by his open acceptance of this babe she would soon give birth to, Hannah turned away from him to stare at the rapidly passing countryside.

But all the while Frank was calmly encouraging his wife, on the inside he was rapidly sending prayers upward. *Please, please don't let her have this baby in the car without the help of a doctor. And please, oh please, keep Hannah and the child in Your hands. And please give us the strength for the hours ahead.*

Nineteen

*H*annah opened her eyes in the dimly lighted room. She could hear the quiet hiss of the radiator by the window and the hushed voices of nurses in the hallway. The bed where she lay was neat and clean, and the blankets tucked in around her were warm.

She glanced across the room to a large reclining chair where Frank nodded his head, his arms crossed before him as he slept.

He had showered and changed clothes, she noted with a smile. And then she frowned just a little. He shouldn't be there with her, he should be at home with the children. Rebecca was only fifteen, after all. She couldn't run the household indefinitely.

The labor they had worried about on their way to Rawlins had lasted ten hours. The muscles of her womb, stretched from so many births, simply hadn't the elasticity to push one more baby through the birth canal. In the end, a vacuum was employed, and her tiny daughter of only four pounds entered the world in a weak and delicate state.

There would be no more babies.

As though sensing her silent study, Frank woke up. He stretched and stood beside the bed. "How are you feeling?"

Hannah looked at the IV attached to her left hand and tried to scoot herself into a sitting position. "Sore," she answered.

Frank held her other hand in his and patted it gently. "You just take it easy. The doctor says you did a lot of hemorrhaging. I'm—sorry I wasn't here when you finally delivered her." He sounded disappointed.

Hannah brushed his worry aside. "You had to go home sometime; the children must have been worried." She looked at him, her concern showing in her drawn and tired face. "You shouldn't even be here now."

"Josh got home early from work, so Sara stayed with our children," he told her. "She's been there the whole time."

Relief swept over Hannah, and she smiled. "Have you seen her yet? Isn't she beautiful?"

"Yes, I've seen her. She has the prettiest face, so round and little—and the tiniest mouth." He didn't mention the isolette she lay in or the tubes that ran from her neck and feet. The hospital was ready to Med-flight her to a larger children's facility if her condition did not improve. Frank had signed the papers himself, and was prepared to go with her if the moment arose.

Josh was going to help with the chores and work with the boys until he returned. And Roxie was on her way now, to stay with the children.

He looked at Hannah and saw her troubled expression. "It's going to be all right."

"Mr. Francis," she said quietly, her eyes misting, "I cannot give you a child of your own now. I—"

"Don't you worry about that," he interrupted. "You've done enough for one lifetime." *And then some,* he thought.

"What are we going to name her?" he asked then. He had somehow assumed that the baby would be a boy, and hadn't given any thought to names for girls.

"Well, we can't name her Jack," Hannah taunted, and Francis laughed. "I have a sister with dark hair and eyes like hers, named Rachael."

"Rachael," he repeated. It suited her. "Rachael it is."

Little Rachael did manage to improve in health as the hours passed, but she was not allowed to leave the hospital. Hannah went home alone.

Because of the distance between the ranch and Rawlins, and the weak condition of the baby, Hannah decided not to breast-feed. Still, she made the effort to drive to the hospital every other day to see her baby and speak with the doctor about her progress.

Hannah didn't recover from the delivery as quickly as she had with the others. Eager for rest between trips, she assigned the bulk of the household chores to the older children, leaving Rebecca as baby-sitter while her husband tended the ranch.

Still, it seemed to Hannah that there was never an end to the tasks at hand, and checking to see that chores had been done properly often took longer than doing the job herself.

One evening she found time before supper to rest on the couch. She had just closed her eyes when a loud crash sounded from the kitchen. She recognized the cries of three-year-old Leah and hurried into the room.

In a pile on the floor, unharmed amid a scattering of colorful vegetable egg noodles that Hannah kept for decoration in a clear glass container, sat Leah.

Hannah snatched her from the shards of broken glass and noodles. "Bad Leah," she scolded. "Naughty!"

Leah cried all the louder, and Hannah shouted for Emma and Rebecca to come from their rooms.

"Emma," Hannah said as she entered the kitchen, "please clean up this mess; be careful of the glass. Rebecca, you should have been watching her."

"I thought she was playing with Gideon," Rebecca protested.

"It doesn't matter what you thought," Hannah said, her voice rising. "She could have been badly hurt. What if I hadn't been down here? You were responsible for her."

Rebecca's eyes brimmed with tears. "I'm *always* responsible for her," she cried. "Why aren't *you* responsible for her? You're the one who had her—not me!"

Hannah glared at her daughter. "You know I've had to be with the baby."

Rebecca let her tears flow. "I don't know why you had to have this baby!" she shouted. "I don't know why you had to have so many children!"

"And which one would you have had me leave out? Leah?" she asked. "Or perhaps you?" Hannah bit back further angry words, knowing that they would only increase the fury that sparked between them. She took a deep breath. "The fact remains that you were told to watch your sister, and your failure to do so put her in danger.

"And as for our reason for wanting to share our lives with so many of you . . ." she continued in a gentler tone, "your father and I wanted to share our love and God's blessings with a family."

"Then where is he now?" Rebecca asked. "Why isn't *he* here to take care of Leah and you and Rachael?"

The pain in her daughter's voice wrenched Hannah's heart. She longed to reach for Rebecca and hold her, to take this terrible ache from her, but the front door opened and the moment was lost.

Tears streaking her face, Rebecca turned and ran toward the hallway as Frank entered the kitchen with an armload of groceries.

"I got shampoo, formula, toilet paper—" He snapped his fingers. "Doggone, I forgot the powdered sugar." He looked at Hannah, oblivious to the storm that had just passed before him. "Did you need that today?"

Hannah answered him distractedly as she automatically began putting away the groceries he'd bought. "I needed it for the cinnamon rolls," she said, gesturing toward the pans that sat atop the stove.

Frank's shoulders slumped in regret. "I'm sorry, Hannah. I rushed through the store and just forgot."

"It's all right," she assured him. "I'll pick some up on my way from Rawlins tomorrow."

Frank sighed; there was nothing he could do about it

now. "I'd better join Steve and Henry at chores. Some of those bales toward the north wall are moldy in the center. We'll have horses down if we're not careful."

Hannah nodded, eager to end the trivial conversation and get back to her daughter. She hurried to Rebecca's room. *I understand,* she wanted to tell her. *It's all right to miss him, to feel cheated that he isn't here to share in the responsibility of raising the children he sired.*

But Rebecca would not be comforted. She would not be held in her mother's arms, nor would she answer to the calm words of reason Hannah offered. A wall of private grief separated them, and they left each other cold and distant.

Hannah knew she had to allow her daughter privacy and the right to keep to herself the feelings she had always shared. It was a part of growing up, and though Hannah ached for the closeness she'd always had with Rebecca, she comforted herself in the knowledge that it would return when Rebecca was ready.

But all through the evening, Rebecca's words played through her mind. Why wasn't Eli there? How could he leave them when they needed him so much? Was it all a lie, this trust she'd put in him?

After hours of tossing and turning, Hannah slipped out of bed and stepped quietly to the kitchen. There, by the dim light of the lantern, she thought through her problems while scrubbing the floor.

Rebecca was right, she concluded. She'd been a fool to give birth to so many children, always trusting that somehow she and Eli would be able to provide for them. It had never occurred to her that he wouldn't be there for them, that he would never even see the tiny smile of their youngest child.

"You lied to me, Eli Petersheim," she whispered aloud, venting her anger on her scrub brush. "You said you would be here. You said you'd take care of me.

"I kept my word," she cried. "I bore your children, I cleaned your house, I milked your cows. There wasn't a day I didn't—"

"Are we having an argument?" a voice interrupted.

Hannah turned to find Frank standing in the doorway, barefoot and clad in the baggy set of long johns he slept in. His hair was mussed, and he rubbed the back of his neck as he studied her.

Hannah ventured a chilly smile. "No, Mr. Francis." She was embarrassed that he had found her there and annoyed that her moment of self-pity had been broken. Impatiently, she pushed the bucket forward, sloshing the water before her.

Frank watched in some amusement. Her hair, still braided, hung across her shoulder to the floor. It was past 2 A.M. and dressed in her nightgown, she worked as though the sun could not possibly rise before the kitchen had been thoroughly cleaned.

"Odd time for washin' the floors, ain't it?" he asked. "Somethin' botherin' you?"

Of course something is bothering me, she thought. *Are you blind? Haven't you noticed the mess this house is in? Can't you see that I'm exhausted from driving back and forth to Rawlins? Can't you see the strain I'm under, or doesn't it matter to you? It's because the child isn't yours that you don't care or understand. . . .*

Silently she rinsed out her rag and continued scrubbing.

Frank shook his head. He thought she'd be grateful that she was no longer carrying a baby, that Rachael was not "wrong" as she'd worried, that spring was nearly upon them. The cattle had survived well and the feed, though stretched to the limit, would last until summer pasture was ready. They'd gotten a good deal on government land that year and the truck, for the moment, was running. Yet there she was, her hands raw from hot water, apparently mad about something he had or hadn't said.

"Hannah Allison," he demanded suddenly, "are you havin' another temper tantrum?"

"Temper tantrum!" Temper tantrum—when her heart ached from the burden of loneliness, when she mourned for the father her child would never know. "No, sir," she said distinctly, dipping the brush into the water and slopping it onto the floor. "I am not." She scrubbed viciously in circles on a spot that wouldn't dare, at the moment, show dirt.

Frank rubbed his hand across the stubble of his beard. "I didn't think so," he murmured in disbelief. If this wasn't a fit, it was something mighty close to it. Still, he wasn't exactly sure what the problem was, and she didn't seem willing to shed any light on the matter.

Finally it occurred to him that the entire business had come up just about the time he'd arrived home from town that day. Must have been the missing powdered sugar that triggered it all. She'd been fine before he'd left. Women were like that, he'd been told, all flighty and weepy after babies were born—some kind of chemical imbalance or other. More gently then, he asked her, "You mad about that sugar I forgot?"

Hannah tossed the scrub brush into the bucket with a splash and sat back with her hands on her knees. "Yes," she said in a voice dripping with sarcasm. "Yes, that must be it. Why don't you run down to the store and get some; we'll have cinnamon rolls for breakfast."

Rising from the floor, she snatched the bucket and walked to the back door where she flung the soapy water, brush, and rag into the yard.

From the corner of her eye she saw Frank turn from the room. Tears of anger and shame intermingled on her face as she stood at the sink and rinsed her bucket. She was angry that he had confronted her ill feelings in the middle of the night and angry that he was walking away. How could she have thought to marry such an insensitive, unthinking blockhead! But she knew it was not his fault that Rachael was underweight or that the trip to Rawlins took so long. It was not his fault that Rebecca resented the responsibility that had been flung upon her young shoulders. Frank was doing his best to support them, to be patient with a family whose grief was still fresh in their hearts.

Hannah stopped suddenly, her eyes widening as she shut off the faucet and listened. Was that the front door? A truck door slammed, then the familiar rattle of the truck's engine sounded in the yard. Hannah ran barefoot down the hallway and outside. Breathless, she opened the passenger's door and scrambled onto the cold vinyl seat beside her husband.

Frank jerked the vehicle into park and turned to her, small puffs of smoke rising in the chill night air as he spoke. "Woman!" he said. "Don't you know better than to run out here in your bare feet, and it not a hair above freezing yet!

And you just a week from having a child!"

Hannah reached across the seat and quickly flipped the switch to the fan, turning the levers to the heating system on as far as they would go. She drew her cold feet beneath her. "Mr. Francis . . . I didn't mean for you to actually go buy the sugar. I was . . . I was . . ." Her eyes met his. ". . . having a tantrum," she concluded.

Frank chuckled. He took off his jacket and wrapped it around her, despite her protests, then he patted the seat beside him with his hand. Hannah scooted closer, and he drew her to him, his arm wrapped around her shoulder. "The baby worryin' you?" he asked her softly.

Hannah shrugged. It was not easy to talk to him, to listen to all the "right" answers that he would tell her. She knew that constantly looking behind them did not help the family move forward. The future was always an uphill path, she thought, and right now she was tired of climbing.

"The kids are having trouble adjusting to the baby, aren't they? I mean, to her not coming home and all the extra running it takes to be with her.

"Leah's been a real handful while you're gone," he continued. "I had to paddle her twice for biting Becca. I've never seen her act that way."

Hannah stared at him. She hadn't heard about this. She didn't think that he even noticed the children's presence throughout the day.

"And Gideon hasn't been making it to the bathroom lately," he went on. "Every time I look at him he's wet. Do I ignore it? Make him change? Take him in to Doc Richards and see if he's got some kind of kidney disorder?"

Hannah shook her head, uncertain herself. "There doesn't seem to be enough of me to go around," she said. "Rebecca is angry that I leave her with my work, the children seem to be arguing every time I walk in the door. And I—"

Tears welled up in her eyes and the words choked in her throat. "I just want my baby," she said painfully, holding out her empty hands. "I just want to hold her. I want to bring her home."

Frank held her close in his arms and patted her back with his hand till her sobbing subsided. There were no words, he knew, to make the child they waited for grow stronger. There was only trust and hope that the Lord would see them through it.

"Hannah," he said then, raising her chin with his hand to meet his eyes. "Pray with me?"

Awkwardly she placed her hands in his and closed her eyes as he began.

"Dear Lord, please help this family," he prayed into the darkness. "Help little Rachael to gain weight so that she can come home. And help the other children to understand how important they still are to us—that we haven't replaced them or pushed them aside with our new baby. Help us to be patient with one another and to be the guiding light You've asked us to be. In Jesus' name we pray."

And Hannah said, "Amen."

They were quiet for a moment, thoughtful of the trust they'd now placed in the Lord.

Frank turned again to his wife. "You are going straight into that house to bed," he announced. "And you're going to sleep late or I'm going to know the reason why." He held his hand up to stay her objections. "Rebecca and I will get the children off to school, and then the two of you go on to Rawlins to visit Rachael.

"I know she'll miss school," he argued gently, "but I really think she should go with you. Maybe if she sees the baby, she'll understand."

Hannah nodded at the wisdom of his suggestion.

"I guess Sam will have to watch the others after school. I'll take Leah and Gideon out to the barn with me."

Hannah looked at him, surprised.

"I'll watch them," he tried to assure her. "I can handle a three- and four-year-old."

She opened the truck door, trying not to chuckle. "Yes, Mr. Francis," she told him condescendingly. "Oh! And Mr. Francis," she said suddenly, turning again toward him.

He hesitated, and she reached across the seat and kissed him. "Thank you for—your kindness. And—for being willing to get the sugar."

"Sugar!" he mumbled disgustedly. "Doggone women, anyhow." He got out of the truck and slammed the door behind him. "Scrubbing floors at all hours of the night. Throwin' water all over the yard . . . rags . . . buckets."

Hannah laughed and hurried on ahead, her feet aching from the cold.

"Mama, I don't want to go," Rebecca argued as she put on her coat.

Hannah said nothing. She leaned down to kiss Isaac

good-bye before reaching for her purse. "Make sure he takes a nap," she reminded her husband.

"Yes, yes," Frank assured her, escorting them to the door impatiently. They'd been through these instructions a dozen times.

"But I have a test in math today," Rebecca continued.

Hannah took her keys from the counter and opened the back door. "You can take a makeup test later this week," she told her, waving one last time to the children who remained behind.

"But I don't even want to see the baby." Rebecca seated herself on the passenger's side of the pickup and looked pleadingly at her mother. "Couldn't you just drop me off at school?"

Hannah started the engine and allowed it to warm. "Mr. Francis felt it would be a good idea if you came."

Rebecca crossed her arms before her and slumped sulkily into the seat. What her mother really meant was that if her stepfather said it was to be, neither one of them was going to argue with it. "Well, I still don't see why I should have to go," she told her mother anyway. "I've seen plenty of newborn babies—more than most girls."

Hannah smiled as they pulled onto the highway. It was true; Rebecca had more knowledge of childbirth and child rearing than a good number of girls her own age. Born in a time when large families were rare, even frowned upon, Rebecca was looked at by her peers with both pity and awe. And yet, for all her complaining, Hannah knew there was a trace of pride in her daughter's claim to being the eldest of such a large group.

They rode together in silence a while before Hannah decided to speak.

"I remember when you were born," she told Rebecca. "I was so young, and I'd never been away from home before I married your father. We'd just moved to a rented farm in Indiana. We didn't know anyone."

She smiled at her daughter. "Eli was in the fields from sunup to sundown. He had no one to help him—no family or friends—and we were strange people to modern farmers.

"You were my constant companion," she said affectionately. "I shared my experiences with you, all my adventures."

Rebecca looked at her mother thoughtfully. "Didn't you miss your mother? Your sisters?"

"Oh, yes," Hannah answered without hesitation. "I missed them terribly. I had no one to go to when you were sick, and I didn't know what to do. I missed sharing new recipes and spending the afternoon sewing with your Aunt Beth and Eli's sister, Twila. I was very lonely," she admitted.

"Then why did you and Daddy leave?" Rebecca asked.

Hannah was thoughtful. There were times, back then, when she had wondered the same thing. "Your father felt it was the right thing to do," she said. "He wasn't comfortable with some of the beliefs our families held. He felt that once a person believed in the Lord as his Savior, nothing could take that from him—certainly nothing as trivial as the clothes he wore or the music he listened to.

"Of course, these things influence one's growth in his Christian walk. They express a humble heart or a rebellious nature. But they don't cut off one's relationship with the Father."

"And did you believe that, too?" Rebecca asked. "Did you want to leave?"

Hannah wrestled with her answer, recalling the long hours of tears she had cried, knowing that her newfound truth would keep her from her family forever. "Sometimes," she said, "I was afraid that the only reason I said that I believed those things was because I'd fallen in love with your father.

"He was a handsome man, full of life and laughter." Hannah's blue eyes reflected the memory of the joy she'd felt. "What he dreamed seemed like such an adventure—like pioneers striking out into the wilderness alone, never turning back. And maybe," she confessed, "there was a touch of defiance in my decision to leave.

"But later, as I became the outcast instead of the world around me, I saw how off-center the importance placed on tradition had become, compared to the heart of the Gospel. I am glad," she said softly, "not to judge others that way anymore."

Contented with each other's company, their conversation turned to lighter matters, like the restaurant they would stop at before reaching the hospital. They discussed whether they'd have enough time to stop at the fabric store before Mr. Francis would lose patience with the little ones and come all the way to Rawlins looking for them himself.

Twenty

*R*ebecca's resentment toward baby Rachael had vanished. Seeing the small, fragile child lying alone in an isolette, without family and chatter and the warm inviting smells of home, made her realize how important her mother's visits to the hospital were.

In earnest then, she helped around the house and watched over the younger children, even helping with their homework assignments0 so that Hannah could rest in the evenings. She was no longer just the "eldest daughter," the one to whom the more complicated chores fell while her mother went driving off to Rawlins. Rebecca felt like part of the team, a very special link in the caring for Rachael, in the task of bringing her home.

By the end of two weeks, Rachael had gained another pound and was allowed to leave the hospital. The children cooed over her, amazed by her tiny fingers and toes. Their amazement turned to dismay as Rachael tightened up her muscles and screamed for hours on end each day, refusing to be comforted.

Hannah wondered if the formula she was feeding her was causing an allergic reaction, but the doctor said no. The special formula, which was costing them dearly, was imperative to maintaining the baby's weight and health. So Hannah and the children took turns pacing with her, rubbing her back and feeding her a mild mint tea to help the colic.

Frank seemed oblivious to the problems that stirred within the household. He was up before the sun rose, doing chores, in for a quick bite to eat, then back out again at daybreak to begin irrigation of the fields. When evening came, he was cold and wet and tired. More often than not, Hannah found him asleep in his chair in the living room or nodding at the kitchen table, unable to complete his meal.

His actions troubled Hannah. She wanted him to dote on the baby, to treat her as his own. And she wanted him to pamper her a little as well. She had, after all, come through a very difficult labor with a weak child who was both colicky and in need of feeding every two hours. Frank had always been so thoughtful and patient, yet just when she needed that kind of treatment most, he completely ignored her, and the children as well.

Friday morning, when the other children left for school, Sam remained at the table. Hannah looked at him in surprise. "Samuel, aren't you feeling well?"

Sam gulped the last of his milk and set the glass back on the table. "Yes, ma'am," he answered, wiping his mouth on his sleeve.

"Well, aren't you going to school today?" she asked, not at all pleased by his audacity.

"No, ma'am," he said quietly, his face beginning to redden beneath her glare.

Hannah's hands flew to her hips. "And just why not, if I might ask?"

"I'm going to help Mr. Francis in the fields today, Mom," he told her, and then looked at her with pleading eyes. "He's out there all by himself doing the work he and Dad used to do together. He'll kill himself if he falls asleep on that equipment."

Hannah studied him a moment. Of course, the boy was right. It had not occurred to her that Frank was now doing the work of two men. This, no doubt, was his way of getting the money to build the new shelters and windbreak he had spoken of earlier. "Does Mr. Francis know that you are staying home to help him?" she asked in a more gentle tone.

Sam evaded her eyes. "No, ma'am," he mumbled, and then added more bravely, "but I caught up on all my assignments and—I was hoping I could tell him that—you sent me out."

He looked at his mother hopefully, and finally she relented.

"All right," she said, "you may tell him."

Samuel bounded from the table and happily put on his work suit.

"Here," she called as he headed toward the back door, "take this."

She handed him a thermos filled with hot coffee and watched him leave. Ashamed of her selfishness, she prayed a request for forgiveness and vowed to put an extra effort into keeping Frank warm and well fed and undisturbed until the irrigating was complete.

Twenty-one

*M*ay second marked the end of school and the beginning of the cattle drives. Every spring the ranchers moved their cattle into the mountain pastures that they rented from the Bureau of Land Management. It was a happy time for the most part, with the boys and men traveling by horseback up the trails, eating by campfire and sleeping beneath the stars—some for the very first time.

In the past, Sam and Ben had ridden with the feed wagon. This year, for the first time, they would help drive the herd up into the mountains.

Unfortunately, Eli had never been particular about when his bulls were put with the cows. Nor did he keep accurate breeding records, beyond recording the birth of a calf and who the sire was. Consequently, Frank had no way of knowing exactly when each cow was due. Some had delivered in late February, some in March and April. Some looked due right smack on their way into the mountains, making for slow and tedious travel.

Frank preferred a more uniform program and was determined to instigate it. He knew no other way of turning the ranch into a profitable venture. But it meant a lot more trips into the mountains, a prospect he knew would not please Hannah.

Together he and the boys worked the herd higher, until at long last they were in their designated parcel. They checked the watering holes and searched the fields for signs of poisonous plants. They watched four calves come into the world. Ben made certain that they weren't in breech position, that they all took their first breath and first gulp of warm milk, and that each navel was disinfected. Frank knew that they wouldn't always be there to assure this practice, but it was good hands-on husbandry for Benjamin, and he was proud of the boy's progress.

Once the herd was settled, Frank was eager to return home. They had used their old, dilapidated cattle squeeze for the last time that year. The cattle squeeze, a hinged metal chute designed to keep the cattle still while they administered medication, branding, or dehorning, was rusted and bent and rewelded more times than Frank cared to remember. It had barely held while, to prevent snow burn, they'd stamped a one-inch-wide strip of nyanzol dye under the eyes of the calves before leaving the ranch. It was with no small pleasure that Frank anticipated tearing down the antiquated structure that he had struggled to maintain for so many years.

Hannah was not without her own anticipation. Eagerly,

she drew up a picture of her garden, and she and Rebecca and Emma carefully nurtured the seedlings they had sprouted toward a June first planting. Earlier that spring they'd filled wooden boxes with dirt and planted seeds of tomatoes, green peppers, zucchini, eggplant, and cucumbers. Cauliflower and broccoli added to their group, and with careful watering they set them on the wide sills of the living room windows where the morning sun encouraged their growth. By the time the threat of snowfall was over, their plants would be strong and tall and able to withstand the harshness of weather that the country had to offer them.

Gardening, however, was not all that Hannah had on her mind. A good deal of planning preceded her preparations for her husband's return.

It was dusk when Frank and the boys returned. Their muscles ached, and they were covered with dust. Ben had stepped into a hive of bees, and he was swollen and itchy where they'd stung him.

"What a fine bunch of desperadoes." Hannah surveyed them from the doorway. "Well, come in."

"Hi, Ma," Sam greeted her in a tired voice. He kissed her cheek as he passed her.

Ben followed. "I'll bring my bedroll in tomorrow," he promised.

"Put some antiseptic on those stings when you get done showering," she instructed, as he shuffled slowly down the hallway.

She smiled as she stood squarely before her husband. "And you, Mr. Francis," she asked softly, "are you well?"

Frank took his hat from his head and put his arms around

her waist, pulling her closer to him. "Oh, as well as might be expected," he answered, in a tired but contented tone.

"You mean for an old cowhand like you who just rolled in off the Chisholm Trail," she teased.

Frank grinned and swatted her lightly with his hat. "I'm not that tired," he assured her.

Hannah giggled and lowered her eyes. The feel of his arms around her was good.

"I'm glad you're home. I have so much to show you. But first," she said, leading him toward the kitchen, "a cup of real coffee and some hot cinnamon rolls."

"What d'ya mean, 'real coffee'?" he countered. "Are you implying that my coffee is not 'real'?"

Hannah chuckled and scooted ahead of him. *"Dei koffee taste vie drecht!"*

Frank merely lengthened his stride to keep up as she hurried down the narrow hallway. "Hey, I heard that!" he scolded, trying to grab hold of her. "Isn't that Dutch for mud? You can't talk about my coffee like that! Why, my coffee is known all over these parts," he bragged, puffing up like a strutting rooster as they reached the kitchen. "My coffee," he exalted, "is guar-an-teed to hold a spoon on its own and to put hair on your chest within thirty days!"

Hannah laughed aloud. "Somehow I've never seen a need for either of those things."

Unable to impress his wife with his culinary talents, Frank turned to the raised Port-a-crib where Rachael lay chewing the knuckle of her right index finger.

"Well, hello, sweetie pie," he greeted her.

Rachael's big brown eyes grew even larger and she kicked

wildly in her sleeper, her little jaw taking on a determined set as she moved.

Frank reached into the crib and gently lifted her up. Still her body was stiff and straight as she worked her legs to kick the air.

"This one's going to be a real corker," Frank told the infant's mother.

Hannah wasn't quite sure just what he meant by that, but if it had to do with strong will and determination, she could only agree. And in any case, she couldn't argue with the obvious pleasure Mr. Francis took in fussing over their daughter.

While he sat down to enjoy the freshly-baked cinnamon rolls and hot coffee, Hannah brought him the mail and set his boots and hat aside. Though the children and hounds were eager to be with him, Hannah kept their greetings brief and sent them on their way.

Once Sam and Ben were cleaned up, she sent Frank to the shower with a fresh set of clothing. In the bathroom he found clean towels, a new blade in his razor, and his favorite aftershave awaiting him. There was a new soap-on-a-rope at the shower head, a full bottle of shampoo on the edge of the tub, and a clean rug awaiting his feet. And this time, unlike many others, there were no knocks on the door, no urgent telephone calls, no sudden changes in water temperature or pressure as someone, either thoughtless or cruel, played at the kitchen sink.

As he showered and shaved, Frank wondered at the point of such adulation. Just what exactly had Hannah been up to in his absence that warranted such cajoling on his return?

Surely she hadn't overdrawn the checking account, he

mused thoughtfully. Had she decided to learn to drive the tractor . . . again? Last time her attempt had cost them the far right corner of the calf-pasture fencing, post and all, to say nothing of the damage to the tractor itself. No, he decided, she was too cheerful to have news of that magnitude waiting.

Clad in pajama bottoms and T-shirt, he settled into a comfortable chair in the living room and opened the newspaper. Hannah sat down right across from him with an expectant look on her face.

"Hannah," he said with exaggerated patience. "Was there something you wanted to talk about?"

Her eyes brightened. "As a matter of fact, yes." She withdrew a newspaper clipping from her pocket and unfolded it. "Look," she said, pointing to an ad for spring poultry.

Frank was unimpressed. "Aren't those layers doing the job anymore?" She and Eli, if he remembered correctly, would keep laying hens for two years and then butcher the lot of them, replacing them with a new set of pullets.

"Oh, they're doing just fine," she told him happily.

"Well . . . good," he said, baffled. He folded the ad and handed it back to her, then lifted his newspaper again.

"You see, Mr. Francis," Hannah continued, "if we were to buy 150 assorted meat chickens and buy the starter feed, then mix in our own corn and weeds and vegetable tops, we could save nearly three dollars on every chicken."

"One hundred and fifty!" he exclaimed. "Where are you going to raise 150 chickens?"

Hannah looked disappointed. "In the old toolshed?" she ventured quietly.

"The toolshed! Hannah, that thing is falling apart!"

"But you could fix it," she said confidently.

Yeah, in my spare time, he thought. But Hannah's blue eyes were watching him so hopefully. *Doggone woman. Why in the world does she have to surround herself with every type of critter known to mankind? Doesn't she have enough children to satisfy her nurturing instincts without adding 150 chickens to her workload?*

She waited with such anticipation, such hope in her clear blue eyes. How could he disappoint her?

He opened the paper and placed it directly before his face. "All right," he relented. "If you think we must have them."

"And some geese," she added quickly.

The muscles in Frank's neck were beginning to strain. "And turkeys!" he shouted. "You might as well get some turkeys so that Jolly doesn't feel left out!"

Hannah wasn't intimidated. "And turkeys," she added, crumpling the paper down in front of him and kissing him on the lips. She turned and sauntered merrily from the room.

"Hannah! Hannah Allison!"

As her name echoed across the barnyard, Hannah looked up from the pancakes she was frying on the griddle. The hair at the back of her neck prickled just a little; he was even more angry than she had anticipated.

Frank burst through the doorway and slammed the milk bucket onto the kitchen table. "Just what," he demanded,

"are those blasted creatures doing in my barn?"

"Mr. Francis!" Hannah said.

Frank stepped before her and glowered. "Don't you 'Mr. Francis' me," he warned her. "Not after you go and put those stinking things in the barn while I'm away."

Hannah busied herself flipping pancakes. "Oh," she said, as though suddenly realizing what he was referring to. "You must mean the lambs. The children and I rode to the sale barn last week."

"Mmm. And I'll bet you got them dirt cheap."

Hannah looked startled. She'd bought them for just over ten dollars a lot, but how did he know that? Silently she placed the flapjacks on a platter and scooped another cupful of batter from the bowl.

"They've probably got every disease known to ani-malkind," Frank continued. "You don't know the kind of places those sheep come from. You've got at least five different breeds there that I can see."

Hannah glanced his way. "But Frank," she pleaded, "they're so cute."

"Cute! You aren't going to think they're so cute when every beast on this range comes down with soremouth or some such plague. If you wanted sheep, you should have bought them from a reputable breeder."

Sure, Hannah thought, *for 135 dollars apiece.* All she had wanted were a few lambs for the children to bottle-feed and run and play with. Her father had always kept sheep on their farm. Her memories were full of images of chicks and lambs, sunflowers as round as barrel tops, and field pumpkins the size of boulders. She only wanted to share a little of that with her children. But Frank wouldn't understand. . . .

"I don't want those sheep near the cattle sheds," he was admonishing her. "And I don't want them in the stalls or climbing around on the hay."

Hannah closed the damper on the stove and stood quietly before him. "Yes, Mr. Francis."

He couldn't argue with her quiet compliance. With an angry grunt, he snatched a pancake from the top of the platter and stuffed it into his mouth. "I'm not hungry," he growled. Then he turned and stomped out the door, letting it slam behind him.

From the corner of her eye, Hannah could see Rebecca, who'd been sitting quietly holding Rachael all through the discussion.

"What?" Hannah demanded, in response to her daughter's knowing smirk.

"I told you he'd be steaming," she said smugly.

Hannah frowned. She had taken on bigger obstacles in her life. "We still have the sheep, don't we?" she said.

Twenty-two

*E*arly the next morning the boys and Frank put the young Angus bull with the heifers, which had been kept back from the herd to graze on the home pastures.

Later they took the posts that the lumber company had delivered and set them in the barrels of preservative, which would keep them from rotting in the ground.

As he and the boys began tearing down the old loading chute, Frank glanced from time to time at the garden plot, where Hannah was plowing with Captain. Though he had offered to run it through quickly with the tractor and plow, she would hear none of it. A tractor, she said, would only compact the ground and tear up the corners where the fencing was.

Captain was used to the garden and was gentle in her hands. And it was one of the few times, she insisted, that she could teach the younger children a little of the ways in which she and Eli had grown up.

To Frank, gardening was a nuisance. If he spent as much time with a field of alfalfa as most people did with their gardens, nothing would ever get done. Plagued by insects, hail, drought, weeds, a short growing season, and every four-legged critter known to the Western range, gardening in Wyoming simply did not add up.

But Hannah was persistent. She had two big garden patches, which she guarded faithfully each summer. Her face and arms grew tanned and freckled, but she could be found amid the mosquitoes and slugs, humming happily, doing her best to coax some poor, limp tomato plant into a life it clearly had no place in.

He smiled as he thought of it. How lucky he was to have a woman who felt so concerned about her family and the land around her. Most women he knew hadn't a clue of how to cook a meal that hadn't come frozen from a cardboard box.

Hannah, on the other hand, was a professional housewife, with over 200 years of ancestry to back up her convictions and training. She had no intentions of letting her children lose grasp of that, no matter how much modern technology they were surrounded by.

For a moment, while they dragged the wood away from the barnyard lot to a pile they would burn next winter, he was almost downright proud of her past—enough to overlook 150 chickens, but not quite enough to forget those troublesome sheep—not yet, at any rate.

Somehow he found time to repair the toolshed. Into it he and Sam hauled a couple old cracked and leaky troughs, no longer useful for watering stock, to serve as a home for the tiny chicks. He set heat lamps above, and screens across the top of the troughs to keep the chicks in and the cats out.

He made sure there was no risk of fire. Every year, it seemed, somebody lost an entire barn by putting a heat lamp over a pile of dry straw or a sheet of cardboard, all for the goal of raising a measly handful of chickens.

Hannah's poultry could come anytime now . . . their living quarters awaited them.

While the males of the family worked to put up aluminum stock gates and cattle guards, Hannah taught the older girls to make soaps—laundry detergent and hand soaps, perfumed bath soaps and practical shampoos. They were not always successful. Often the grease and lye separated, or the fat had not been rendered clean enough, or the hot grease spilled on the floor in spite of their efforts to be extra careful.

Running her "dairy" also kept Hannah busy. Caramel, their jersey cow, freshened just as Candy, her sister, was ready to be dried, a unique system that did not always turn out so cooperatively. With the coming of fresh milk, Hannah made butter and cottage cheese and farmer's cheese. She made soft cheese spreads that they used with baked slices of home-grown potatoes, and a thicker cheese for cheesecake or biscuits.

Twice the thickening pan of milk disappeared before Hannah realized that Frank was tossing out what he thought to be soured milk. It was only with much explaining that she could convince him that the milk, though it was indeed "sour," was not at all spoiled.

Ice cream was a regular after-service treat on Sundays. All the canned fruit that had not been used up during the winter was dumped into a sort of yogurt-base dessert that was too runny to be called yogurt and too sweet to be considered a sour cream concoction.

One evening Frank was in the barn doing his best to repair the elevator that sent the bales of hay into the loft. They used mostly huge round bales for the cattle, but the horses and cows and now Hannah's sheep would all feed from the square bales they stored in the loft each summer.

He'd repaired the wiring and oiled the track, and now he was struggling to loosen the rusted bolts in order to replace the old V-belt. He glanced up as Sam entered the barn, his hands in the pockets of his jeans, his look timid.

It was well past the children's usual bedtime. The house was quiet and dark, the only sound the occasional flutter of a moth as it banged against the light bulb above them.

"You're up late, aren't you?"

"Yes, sir," Samuel said. He brushed his long sand-colored hair from his eyes and stood to watch as Frank worked.

The wrench slipped from the stubborn bolt, and in frustration, Frank paused and turned to the boy. "Something on your mind?"

Sam hesitated. His timing could probably be better. But he had argued with himself for half the day before finally summoning the courage to say something. No, if he were going to tell him, it had better be now before the others were around to hear Mr. Francis yell.

"Mr. Francis," he began, "I told Chester Holland I would work for him Saturdays."

Frank turned back to the motor thoughtfully. Chester Holland was a rancher who lived on the ridge just beyond them. He owned a huge spread and a half-dozen businesses scattered across the south-central end of the state. His wife had died almost twenty years ago, and the two sons she'd left him had taken off the first chance they'd got. He was said to be a hard man to work for, even though the wages he offered were a little better than most.

But what worried Frank even more than all this was the fact that Sam hadn't asked about it first.

He looked directly into Samuel's blue eyes. "When did you do all that?" he questioned.

Sam stepped forward, relieved that he hadn't been rebuked . . . yet, anyway. He held the motor bracket while Frank continued working. "At the camp when we moved the cattle."

Frank's brow rose in surprise. "That long ago." They had crossed paths, briefly, the two ranchers, on their way toward mountain grazing. Chester had shared coffee at their fire, talked about Midwestern corn prices before moving on with his herd. Frank vaguely recalled his pausing to speak with Ben and Sam before mounting his horse.

"What made you decide to do that?" Frank asked. "You don't think there's enough work to do around here?"

There was an angry edge to his stepfather's tone, as

though Sam were shirking his responsibilities or neglecting his chores. "I'll get my work done before I go," he promised quietly.

"But you won't be here when I need you," Frank said.

Silence fell over the scene in the barn.

Frank wanted to give the boy his freedom. He knew Sam put in a lot of hours on the ranch, hours when boys should be exploring, should be cuttin' up with boys their own age.

But he'd come to rely on Sam, too. Ben was good with livestock, but he didn't have the skill and coordination his brother showed with his hands. And there was the matter of money. With thirteen children, there just wasn't a whole lot of spending money left at the end of the bills.

"How much is he paying you?" Frank finally asked.

"Nothing," Sam answered. "He's not paying me any-thing—just giving me lunch, and he's picking me up and dropping me off."

Now Frank was more than puzzled. "Why would you want to go to Holland's on a Saturday to work for nothin'—he got a good-looking granddaughter or somethin'?"

Sam chuckled, relieved. "No sir," he assured him sheep-ishly. "But he's going to teach me steer wrestling and calf roping." He looked at Frank intently. "I want to join high school rodeo, Mr. Francis," he told him. "And Mr. Holland's going to teach me. I'm going to be good at it."

Frank looked at the fourteen-year-old, so determined, so certain of what his goals were. Sam, he knew, was a hard worker, and if high school rodeo was what he set his hat toward, then there was little doubt that he would indeed give it all he had.

"I want to win a scholarship," Sam continued. "Mr. Holland says I've got a good chance at it—says I'm built for it."

Reality edged its way into the pride Frank was feeling. "I don't know, Sam," he said in a worried tone. "Rodeo takes money. It's not just the entry fees, it's the traveling from show to show and the time away from work. It's all the equipment and clothes. And most of all," he told him, "you've got to have a good horse. Your little bay just isn't going to do the trick. He's sure-footed on the trail, but he doesn't have the kind of speed or training you'll need for competition. Those horses cost money—lots of money!"

"But Mr. Holland's going to lease one of his horses to me," Samuel explained. "That's why I'm working for him."

Frank thought of all the stories he had heard about Chester Holland and the pro rodeo circuit. His basement wall, it was said, was covered with gold belt buckles and plaques, glossy black-and-white photos of himself with famous country singers and governors and mayors.

And yet it was the same hard drive that brought him stamina and courage to face those twisting, raging bulls that led his sons to flee their home and heritage. Chester Holland lived alone now—bitter, broken, and with little to show by way of companionship and friends. The land he'd inherited may have made him wealthy, Frank thought, but it lay empty and barren in the shadow of his success.

"I don't know, Sam," Frank finally said. "Chester Holland's not an easy man to get along with. Do you really think you're doing the right thing?"

Samuel smiled broadly, taking the warning as approval.

"Yes, sir," he answered. "And I know all those stories about how nobody can take all that—bull off of him for very long," he worded carefully, "but I've got to try, Mr. Francis. I've really got to try."

Frank sprayed the immovable bolts with WD-40, determined to let them sit for the night. He reached for a rag to wipe his hands. "Well, if you think you can finish what you start," he told him, "you've got my blessing."

Sam nearly leaped from the floor. "Thanks, Mr. Francis," he said happily. He stepped forward, wanting to wrap his arms around him and tell him how grateful he was for being there for him. Instead, awkward, grinning, he shoved his fingertips into his side pockets and backed toward the door. "I really appreciate it," he said.

Frank nodded, tossing aside the rag he'd used. That was enough for tonight. He reached for the light switch, then hesitated as Samuel paused in the doorway.

"Mr. Francis," the boy said suddenly, his tone serious.

Frank looked at him. "What is it?"

"Mama isn't going to like it," Sam said quietly. Turning, he left the barn.

Frank listened to the sound of Sam's boots crunching against the graveled path as the boy headed for the house. Then he shut off the light and gave a deep sigh. "No, she certainly isn't," he agreed aloud.

Twenty-three

$\mathcal{M}$r. Francis, how could you!" Hannah exclaimed. Frank rubbed his hand across the back of his neck and frowned. She was slamming dishes again and turning from the stove to the table to the sink so rapidly that he could not avoid bumping into her. Finally he leaned against the counter and waited for her to meet his eyes.

"Will you be still, please," he asked, "so we can talk about this calmly?"

Hannah set a stack of breakfast dishes firmly into the sink, sending water up over the sides to drip down the cabinet to the floor. "I will not be still!" she insisted, ignoring the mess and grabbing a plate, rubbing it vigorously with the dishrag. "I don't see how you could just send him off with that man without ever discussing it with me—without ever even mentioning it until he was sitting in the driveway—you and Samuel both!"

Frank shifted his weight uncomfortably. "Well . . ." he stammered, "I just forgot."

Hannah glared at him. "You didn't forget," she contradicted him. "And you knew exactly how I'd feel about it."

She returned to rinsing dishes, stacking them haphazard-ly in the drainer. "His work here will be neglected. Now the burden falls double on Benjamin," she argued. "And I don't believe a boy that age should have so much spending money."

Her husband brightened. "But he isn't going there to earn money."

Hannah looked at him in surprise.

"He's going to learn rodeo."

Her mouth dropped open in disbelief, and Frank slammed the palm of his hand against his forehead and winced. How could he be so stupid? He'd meant to broach the subject slowly, working into that fact only after pointing out the long history of ranching Chester had to his credit, and that the skills he had learned in rodeo had only been a reflection of the tools he later needed to become a successful rancher. But now his chance for careful explanations had passed.

"Rodeo!" Hannah exclaimed. "Rodeo! What does Samuel have to do with learning rodeo?"

Frank stepped up beside her. "He wants to learn, Hannah," he said. "He wants to learn well enough to win a scholarship toward college. It isn't as though—"

"No," Hannah interrupted firmly. She shook the dishwa-ter from her hands and wiped them on the front of her skirt, and began pacing. He'd seen that determined set of her jaw before. "I will not allow my children to participate in public sports—particularly one that is so unnecessarily dangerous."

"Dangerous!" Frank argued. "It's no more dangerous than runnin' cattle up to mountain pasture. He's not bull-riding," he tried to reason. "And he's not bustin' broncs."

Hannah paused. Perhaps she had misunderstood. "Is he—working at the rodeos?" she questioned.

"Well, he'll have to help out with the other kids," he told her, "but mostly he'll be in roping and steer wrestling. Shoot," he said lightly, "he might not even take to it at all. Old Chester's no easy man to work for."

"No!" Hannah insisted again, resuming her pacing. "I've seen steer wrestling before," she told him. "Jumping on those horns and twisting an animal to the ground is certainly not a part of everyday ranching routine, Mr. Francis. And I won't have Samuel strutting around with those other boys, flaunting himself like some puffed-up rooster. They'll be out all night, traipsing around the state."

"The camp-overs are well chaperoned," Frank argued in a tired voice.

"Chaperoned by whom?" she hollered, stopping before him. "By men like Chester Holland? Is that the kind of person you want Samuel to imitate?"

"Of course not, Hannah. There'll be other men there, other families. The companionship will be good for him."

Hannah's eyes reflected her fury. "I will not allow him to abandon his responsibilities to go running off for some—some egotistical contest!"

Frank stood taller, facing her now, his jaw set as firmly as her own. "And I won't work these kids every waking moment of their lives on this ranch! He's got to try and find his own way in this world, and if rodeo is how he wants to get there, then he deserves the chance to at least try!"

Still Hannah stood her ground. "No. I will not allow a son of mine in the rodeo!"

He leaned close to her, equally determined. "And I'm not tellin' that boy no," he said, his voice steely. "You understand me?"

Hannah glared at him, holding back the hot and angry tears that threatened to surface, her chest rising and falling as she fought the urge to scream in his face. It was *her* son, after all. Not his! Why had she ever trusted him with her children's care? Why had she ever thought that he would understand the slightest reasoning behind the traditions they had followed?

And yet in actuality she realized that he understood her traditions all too well; it was this very understanding that he was using against her now. He knew full well she would not challenge a decision that her husband had declared final. He knew that she believed it was his place to lead her and the children in the pathway of their lives. He would be accountable to God for this leadership, just as she was accountable for her ability to support and influence his choices.

Silently she turned from him and stepped back to the sink, her cheeks flushed and her eyes misty. "Yes, Mr. Francis," she answered resentfully, but she would not meet his eyes. "I understand."

He reached for his hat beside the door and placed it on his head. "The boys and I are going out to fix the north gate. Gideon's to stay here and pick up that wood he scattered."

He waited for her to speak, but she nodded in silence instead. "We'll be back by noon," he told her. Forgoing the usual kiss he received when leaving, he left the house, letting the screen slam firmly behind him.

Twenty-four

ithin three weeks every Petersheim child was throwing about terms like "pigging string," "pulling leather," and "tight legging." They spent each spare moment roping bales of hay, fence posts, and even Hannah's lambs when they thought their mother wasn't looking. And though Frank did his best to steer the supper conversation away from that summer's most popular bull rider, somehow it always seemed to work its way back into the mouths of the children.

Frank reexamined his decision as he worked to re-stretch the barbed wire he and Samuel had strung that winter when one of the bulls had torn through a weak section. Hannah had certainly made her position on the subject clear—a little too clear, as far as he was concerned.

He'd expected a long stretch of cold silence . . . no more snuggling on the couch on movie nights or those special lit-tle bakery treats she brought to him first before the kids got their hands on them. He'd observed all that with her and Eli years before. At times the tension at the supper table was as thick as the morning fog that settled in the surrounding valley.

But it was never long before the argument was settled, and the two of them were on speaking terms again. Only rarely, he recalled, had he heard them shout at one another, and then in quick, short spurts of lower German, with Eli ending the matter—at least whenever he or the children were present. And if Hannah had been unhappy with that situation, he'd never known of it, for she seemed contented and peaceful in their mountain home.

"Ben," he called. The boy had accompanied him to the pasture not far from the barn. "Check that post." He set the wire stretcher across the section they'd replaced, awaiting his answer.

"It's solid, Mr. Francis," Ben answered.

Frank nodded. "Step back," he said, using the tool to tighten the metal the heat of summer had expanded.

But peaceful, he continued in thought as he worked, was no longer a word he would use in connection with Hannah. Not only was she now sullen and quiet, limiting their conversations to what was absolutely necessary to keep the household running, she was downright vindictive in her actions toward him.

His coffee cup in the morning was set half-filled before him, or the coffee left cold and muddled with grounds. If he mentioned it at all, Hannah would set a new cup in front of him so soundly that it spilled into his eggs or oatmeal. These things, along with the silent and icy glares he was receiving, were expressions of her ongoing displeasure. He didn't know what else to do but to ignore them.

"Mr. Francis!" Benjamin hollered. "It's too tight!"

Frank focused his attention on his work, readjusting the tension. Clamping the metal stretcher onto the next row of barbed wire, he waved his gloved hand in thanks to Ben.

Just yesterday Hannah had dumped his laundry fresh from the dryer into a heap in the corner of the bedroom. When he asked where his dress shirts were, she'd gestured in the general direction of the pile.

Just how, he wondered, was he supposed to respond to such nonsense? Patience, it was clear, had done little to dissipate her unruly mood, and compromise was out of the question. They were equally unmovable in their points of view.

He tugged now at the wire to test for tautness and called to Ben. "That'll do it!" Carrying the wire stretcher, they started back toward the house.

It was nearly four o'clock, a busy time full of the clamor of afternoon chores and supper preparations. And yet Frank and Ben approached the backyard to find all the children gathered by the tire swing on the large crabapple.

Henry was swinging upside down, his shaggy blond hair hanging straight from his head, his T-shirt sagging to reveal his belly.

"What are you kids doing out here?" Frank questioned, looking toward Rebecca, who sat in the grass with Rachael in her arms.

"Mama said we had to stay outside until the yellin' was over," Amos volunteered. He had picked a handful of grass and was slowly moving a plastic cow toward it for feeding.

Frank listened, his ear inclined toward the back door. "I

don't hear anything," he said.

Amos cocked his head and squinted his eyes against the sun to look at his stepfather. "That's 'cause you ain't started yet," he said, explaining what appeared to him to be obvious.

"Oh," Frank said. He turned to the group with a stern scrutiny, searching their faces for any telltale signs of guilt. "And just who is it I'm supposed to be yelling at?"

For a moment, the children did not answer.

Then, "Mama," Emma told him quietly.

Frank's brow rose. "Oh?"

"Mr. Francis," Sam suggested, "maybe the boys and I should do chores."

"Yeah," Ben agreed quickly, and the younger children got to their feet. "That's a good idea."

"We'll go along," Rebecca said, motioning to the girls.

Frank glanced at the porch door, wishing he could join them rather than face whatever confrontation awaited him indoors. "Yes," he mumbled in hesitation, "a good idea."

"Call us when you're finished," Stephen hollered over his shoulder.

"Sure," he muttered. He set the wire stretcher on the ground beside the back door and wiped his hands across the front of his jeans. Given Hannah's present disposition, he wondered just exactly who it was that was going to be doing the yelling. "Doggone," he said quietly beneath his breath, "I shoulda brushed up on my German—never can tell if I'm bein' cussed out!"

Tentatively, he removed his hat and ran his hand across an unruly stack of hair. Then, taking a deep breath, he opened the screen door and stepped into the kitchen.

"Hannah," he greeted in as firm a tone as he could muster, "what's this the children tell me?"

"Good—afternoon, Mr. Francis," Hannah said hesitantly in a small voice as she turned from the kitchen counter to meet her husband. Her blue eyes were soft and moist and woeful.

Frank knew then that whatever it was she had done, he was going to overlook. She could have driven the tractor straight through the center of the house, and he'd have brushed it aside with the wave of his hand. For that tiny look had spoken a rush of words she hadn't said, had built a bridge that spanned the gaping chasm they'd put between them. What he wanted to do was to hold her, to draw her close beside him once again and smell the subtle sweetness of her skin.

"Mr. Francis," Hannah began quietly, "I've broken something—" She didn't finish, but turned instead to the pantry where their canning jars were kept, where pies and bread and cinnamon rolls sat wrapped on shelves out of reach of little hands.

The wooden door that separated this room from the kitchen now displayed a gaping hole where smoked, etched glass had been.

Frank glanced through the opening to the floor on the other side, half expecting to find the shattered pattern of leaves and wildflowers. He shook his head in dismay. "We're never going to find another one like it," he told her. "That glass must have been put here when the house was built. I don't think they even—"

He hesitated as he looked at his wife. Her face was flushed, her eyes downcast.

"Hannah," he tried more gently, "I'm sure we can find something just as nice as what you had here. It's the glass I was talking about," he clarified. "They don't make that kind anymore."

She looked up at him in remorse. "I broke it," she repeated.

Frank scratched his head. What was worrying her? Was it the cost of repairs? "This isn't going to take much to replace," he tried explaining. "Really, I can put it in myself. We'll just order it from the hardware next time we—"

"I broke it, Mr. Francis," Hannah interrupted, "when I slammed the door."

Frank studied her again. So that was what this was all about. She'd gone just a little further than she'd wanted in this expression of opposition and had come to him to find a way of calling a truce.

Leaning against the closed door, Frank grinned and held out his arms for her to come to him.

She drew in a small, jerky breath as relief mingled with joy spread through her. He wasn't angry. Though their disagreement over Samuel was far from resolved, it had somehow moved to a more communicable plane. She wanted to be touched by him again, to be held within his arms.

Frank wrapped his arms around her waist and pulled her to him. "Seems like a whole lot of tantrums been goin' on around here lately, haven't there?"

Hannah evaded his eyes, and Frank shook her ever so lightly. "Huh?" he continued, looking for some sign of admission. "And it ain't the kids doin' it, either."

"Yes, Mr. Francis," Hannah said. "I mean—no, Mr. Francis."

He smiled. "And just what do you think I ought to do about that, eh, Mrs. Francis?"

Hannah shrugged and struggled to back away from his hold.

"Oh, no," he promised, "you're not getting off that easy."

"The—the children," she tried to excuse herself, glancing across her shoulder at the back door, but laughing all the same. "I think—I hear the children."

"They'll be just fine," he told her, losing his grip but reaching out quickly enough to seize her wrist as she turned to flee. "Now about my shirts," he began, "and that cup of coffee I was wearin' the other day."

Frank shifted his weight forward off the pantry door and Hannah pulled hard, freeing herself and stumbling backward, but earning enough space to reach the back door before him.

Once in the yard, she turned to face him. "I'm not changing my mind," she insisted as she backed toward the barn. "I still don't approve of the rodeo."

Frank nodded from the porch and smiled. "Well, so long as you can keep your opinion from breaking up the furniture, we'll do just fine," he said. "And I'll talk to Samuel, Hannah—I'll see that he keeps this in perspective. I'll even go there next Saturday and watch over things a little—see how they're doing. All right?"

Hannah smiled gratefully. "That's fine," she told him

quietly. "At least it's a step in the right direction."

Frank folded his arms across his chest. "I'll step you in the right direction," he warned her, "if my eggs don't stop swimmin' in my coffee come mornin'!"

Twenty-five

*L*ater that week Frank rode up into the mountain pasture, taking Stephen and Henry with him and leaving the older boys in charge of chores on the home place. Late Friday night the threesome rode back carrying two whitefaced, bawling calves.

Frank brought the calves right into the kitchen and set them on the floor while Ben took care of the horses. "Miriam! Malinda!" he called. "Here, Leah," he said as he waited for the twins, "you and Gideon pet this one. Put your hand in its mouth."

The twins came running, and Frank set them to work on the other calf.

"Where did they come from?" Hannah asked as Frank began to mix a powdered colostrum and scours preventative with warm water.

"The little one there is a twin; the mother's young and the other calf is twice its size. I didn't think it would make it this far, but it's doing pretty good." He smiled. "That larger calf was standing next to its dead mother. I don't know if her heart gave out or what. There were no signs of blood, and the calf was licked clean. I'm sure it had been nursing."

Hannah didn't reply. She knew the costliness of the loss.

Stephen and Henry appeared in the doorway, carrying a couple calf bottles.

"There are some new nipples in that drawer on the back porch," Frank said. "Stephen, go grab a couple."

Before long, the bottles were fixed and the calves, though awkward at first, were nursing greedily.

Frank stood back and watched the children celebrate the new life. It was something that he, too, never grew tired of. Somehow, seeing a hillside dotted with calves running alongside their mothers made all the winter work worthwhile.

Hannah poured him a large glass of cold grape juice and he drank it eagerly.

"You and Henry feed those calves twice a day, get them on some clean straw, and give them a starter mix," he told Stephen. "If they're still alive October first, I'll give you twenty-five dollars apiece."

The boys' eyes widened; they had never had that much money to do with as they pleased. Quickly they set about getting the calves into a stall in the barn.

Hannah mopped up the mess the calves had made of the kitchen floor while Frank sought out the shower.

The children were all in bed, and Frank sat down at the computer to enter the birth of the calves. Rachael's whimper interrupted his thoughts, and he rose and went over to the crib.

The baby was, as usual, soggy. He changed her, locating a cloth diaper with the convenient Velcro strips Hannah had sewn into some of them to use instead of pins. She was probably due for a bottle, he decided, so he lifted the wiggly two-month-old in his arms and went in search of Hannah.

He found her on the front porch, pensively gazing at the stars. She looked lovely, her dark hair shimmering in the soft moonlight. There was a peacefulness about her as she studied the hilltops.

His conscience nudged at him a little. He had meant to spend more time with her. A woman left to simply nurture the land and children and home was soon drained of her ability to serve.

Even his father, in his selfish state of addiction, realized this, and from time to time, when he was halfway sober and could scrape the money together, would take his wife to the local tavern to hear the bands play and make an attempt at dancing. Frank remembered the small spark in his mother's eyes for days afterward, and the merry tunes she would hum as she worked.

Of course, he had no intention of taking Hannah to a tavern, but he knew how important it was for a man and a woman to have a relationship outside the home they worked in. For Hannah and him it was even more important, for they had no life beyond the children and ranch they nurtured. They had no common childhood friends or past memories or dreams that had come true or failed.

Rachael gurgled as she crammed her little fist in her

mouth, and Hannah turned from admiring the night. She smiled at the odd-sized couple behind her. "I didn't hear you come out."

"Rachael seems hungry," Frank replied. They went into the kitchen where Hannah heated a bottle of formula while Frank paced with the now frantic baby.

At last, with Rachael snug in her arms, Hannah settled in a chair at the kitchen table while her husband, his arms crossed and his feet propped on a chair across from him, watched the baby satisfy her hunger.

Finally he broke the silence. "You were awfully quiet this evening. Something bothering you?"

Hannah hadn't meant for it to show. She shifted the baby in her arms and chose her words carefully. "Do you really think it is wise to pay the children for chores they should be doing anyway?"

"You mean Stephen and Henry?"

"Yes."

Frank idly twirled an empty cup left on the table. "They need goals at times," he said.

Hannah set the bottle on the table and lifted the sleepy infant to her shoulder, gently urging a bubble from her. "Shouldn't the privilege of learning a trade be goal enough?" she asked quietly.

Frank's eyes narrowed thoughtfully. "Part of that business is the pay we earn when we do a good job."

"The children already receive the benefit of that in their clothes and food and the blankets on their beds," she argued, disturbing Rachael. She quickly returned the bottle to the baby.

"But kids never see that," Frank told her, leaning forward in his chair. "That's like us being grateful for the sun coming up each morning. We'd be in a lot of trouble if it didn't, but we don't think about that; we just expect it to be there.

"It's the really extra-special days—the beautiful sunset or the stars—that we stop to be grateful for." He hesitated. He'd been meaning to bring up a related subject, and now seemed as good a time as any. "I've been thinking of giving the children an allowance."

"Oh, Mr. Francis," Hannah moaned. "You'll have them expecting money every time you ask them to lift a finger."

Frank got up and paced around the room. "I don't think so," he argued. "I think they'll feel more responsible and a part of the team. I think they need their own money to break up the monotony of time and work."

Hannah's strong disagreement was evident in her expression.

Sensing his defeat on the bargaining table, he tried another tactic. "I was thinking of setting an amount aside for you, too," he told her. "Kitchen money, they call it."

She frowned. "My kitchen is just fine."

"Yes, but this way, if you want to buy some extra dessert or a cookbook or magazine subscription, you don't have to feel like you're taking it away from the budget. You can do what you like with it."

"That's ridiculous," she told him, yet her tone was thoughtful.

Frank could see that, though she still argued, her eyes had taken on a new sense of interest. After all, didn't she deserve a little spending money, too? What was so wrong with a woman wanting a few things of her own without having to ask someone's permission each time she spent a dime?

Perhaps this way, too, she could understand the children's need for a little money of their own—even if they did spend it foolishly or become greedy for more or think they should be paid each time they were asked to do a chore. Weren't those the very evils adults had to cope with every day? And wasn't it better to deal with those pitfalls now when they were young, instead of waiting until they were grown and overwhelmed by the responsibility of budgeting whatever bounty God gave them?

Smiling, he leaned down and kissed Hannah's cheek. "I promised Ben I'd work a little with those dogs of his," he told her. "I'll be along soon."

Twenty-six

*E*ach year the Double Bar H held a Fourth of July picnic for all the high school rodeo families in the area. The occasion marked Hannah's first visit to the ranch where her son now worked.

High on the ridge, Chester Holland's lodge home sat simple and plain in the midst of a neatly sculptured lawn. The split rails surrounding the front of the property were in good repair and brought to mind a more rustic era, contrasting with the vehicles that dotted the field at the side of the house.

Just beyond the barns were the freshly painted white metal poles that made up the modern arena where Chester and his prodigies practiced. Though he specialized in bull-riding courses for young men with the stamina to face a Brahma bull and his own short-fused temper, he also encouraged steer wrestling and roping events for those whose ambition leaned toward the all-around cowboy awards.

Samuel had entered steer wrestling, calf roping, and team roping events in the unsanctioned rodeo competition that day. And it was a silent and tense afternoon that Frank spent sitting beside his wife on the benches while Samuel awaited his turn.

"Mama!" Gideon interrupted her silence, breathless as he climbed past people in an effort to reach her. "Mama, they're having a mutton bustin' contest," he said excitedly. "Can I sign up for it? I'm old enough."

"Mutton—what?" she asked in annoyance.

Gideon could barely stand still. "Mutton bustin'!" he repeated earnestly.

"Mutton bustin'," Frank said, leaning toward her, "is a contest for youngsters who want to try and ride sheep instead of bulls." He chuckled. "They turn 'em right out of the chutes and let 'em run."

He glanced at Hannah's disapproving frown. "He won't get hurt," he tried to convince her. "No more than he would playing any other sport."

"All right," she agreed curtly, as a wide grin spread across Gideon's face. "But take Benjamin with you!" she shouted as he ran off into the crowd.

Frank smiled, pleased by her willingness to compromise, but her stare quickly returned to the arena where the older boys were team roping.

Shortly Amos was before them, wanting to join the ribbon race, hoping to be the first to pull a red ribbon off the tail of a young Angus steer released into the arena.

Stephen and Henry found them next. Chester Holland had a group of green broke Shetland ponies set up for bareback riding. And the twins were certain they could ride in the burro obstacle course if only their mother would allow them entry.

Hannah threw her hands up in frustration. "Ask your father!" she finally snapped at the small group.

The children's eyes widened, and even Frank blinked in surprise. She had never called him their father before, never even implied it.

Hannah looked at him squarely. "Well?" she demanded.

Frank waved his hand to dismiss them. "Go ahead, go ahead," he told them all. "Just be back by the tables when the barbecue is ready. Don't go running off alone."

"Yes, sir," Stephen and Henry answered in unison, and off they all went, happy to claim a part of their Western heritage.

Hannah watched them, clad in the T-shirts and blue jeans, cowboy boots and hats that Mr. Francis had bought for them. Where, she wondered sadly, had the shaggy locks and straw hats of the past gone? They'd once worn plain blue buttoned shirts and run barefoot the summer long, thinking only of fishing and draft horses and field crops. They played beside the kitchen door with wood and paper and toys they'd fashioned with wire and twigs. They dreamed of farming and Sunday singings and fast trotters in front of ebony buggies.

Suddenly, somehow, without her knowing exactly how or when, they had changed. Their life was cluttered with cattle and cowboys, saddles and shiny belt buckles. She didn't recognize the path that they were taking; she trusted blindly the choices the man beside her was making for them.

It frightened her, this lack of knowing. She fought it staunchly, giving measure only after much balking and fuss. Timidly then, she glanced at Mr. Francis. How easily he blended with the world around him. He understood its past and rushed to meet its future. He had taken her children and made them equal to the challenge that the West would soon demand of them.

Their faith, she realized, had not altered with the changing of their clothes. They were more approachable than she had ever been, easier to talk with in this community in which they lived. It was not their "style" that spoke a testimony to others now, but the effect their faith had made upon the way they lived and the choices they made.

Earlier that day, Chester Holland had come to talk to her while Frank was getting Sam registered in the draw.

"Mrs. Allison," he said bluntly, sitting down beside her, his gnarled hands fidgeting in his lap, "I've worked with a lot of boys in my day. But I sure can tell what a difference your beliefs have had on that one." He gestured toward Sam as he stood with the other boys. "Wish I'd taken the time to teach my own sons some of that."

He smiled at her, awkward, the blue of his eyes softening amid a weathered face. He touched the brim of his hat lightly with a gloved hand and rose from the bench beside her. "Ya done a fine job, ma'am," he said quietly, and then turned and left for the chutes where a group of young boys had gathered.

"You want some soda?" Frank asked.

Hannah shook off her pensive mood. "Yes," she answered, "I would, please."

He smiled briefly, stood and found his way to the tall, hard plastic water troughs Mr. Holland had filled with ice and every brand of soda pop a person could want.

Returning with a sweaty, icy can of Pepsi for himself and one for Hannah, he sat beside her again as the steer wrestling began.

Sam, he had to admit, had come a long way in his riding since the cattle were prodded up to the mountain pasture last spring and the idea of rodeo had first worked its way into his mind. He'd put a lot of hours into training, too, trying to build up his arm muscles and improve his agility.

Chester Holland had been right about him. Built like Eli, the boy had long arms and good coordination. He was big and strong for his age with the kind of wide shoulders that football coaches liked to see.

Of course, his time was not as good as the more seasoned high school rodeo contenders that day, but it was a decent showing and it held the promise of better scores to come.

More importantly, though, was the pride and confidence Frank saw in the young boy's eyes. For Sam, the timing hadn't mattered. He'd thrown the steer and done his best. He hadn't fallen off his horse or jumped and missed the steer altogether. He hadn't gotten caught up and dragged around the arena or been tap-danced on by a 500-pound steer in front of the entire county and all his family.

He was a part of the team now, one of the "boys" in a sport not many had the courage to try. He'd taken a step into manhood, Frank knew, for he'd accomplished something he'd made up his mind to do—and done it well. Eli, he thought, would be proud of him, even if his past would have kept him from approving of rodeo.

Sam stood and brushed at the dirt on the seat of his jeans with a swipe of his hat. He placed it back on his head as he reached for the reins of his horse and glanced over his shoulder toward his mother and Frank. Grinning, he touched the brim of his hat and nodded thanks.

And suddenly, for Frank, all the burdens he'd carried over raising so large a family lifted a little. All the times he'd worried over spending money or lectured about grades or wondered if he was being too strict or not strict enough, didn't seem so difficult now. For in that slight moment of gratitude, the struggle felt worthwhile, the obstacles less intimidating, the battle less unsure. Samuel was walking, living proof that it was going to be okay, that God would continue to guide them in their efforts to raise these children, and that whatever it took to get the job done would somehow be provided.

For the remainder of the day, the children scurried in and out before them with ribbons and prizes, awards that were given by Mr. Holland for simply having the courage to participate in the day's events.

They ate barbecued beef, potato salad, and homemade ice cream that their host provided. Later in the day when the sky grew dark, fireworks burst into the heavens, and all the children were given small American flags to honor the occasion.

The air grew damp and chill, the mosquitoes tormented people and beasts alike, and little by little the crowd thinned and the party ended.

Twenty-seven

*B*y the next weekend, the Hereford bulls had been hauled up to the mountain range to be with the main group of cattle.

The lambs Hannah had raised were now fat and sassy and able to squeeze through or jump over just about any enclosure that had kept the cows in. Her garden grew big and prosperous.

Frank and the boys poured concrete in the feedlot by the water tanks and placed a ten-foot strip on either side of the feed bunks. They replaced the old wood in the rail fencing in the home pasture and put board fencing around the barnyard and feedlot in place of the worn-out woven wire.

While they built the new windbreak and shelter, the lambs knocked over their water jugs and stood in the way of their hammering. Whenever Frank would come in from the hardware or feed store, the lambs would run out to meet him, pouncing off the pickup or his back like a pack of lonesome pups.

They pulled the laundry off the clothesline and chewed

the flowers in the front lawn down to the nub. They ate the coonhounds' food right out of their bowls and even went so far as to unhook the battery wires from the tractor.

"Hannah," Frank warned time and time again, "if you don't find a way to keep those ornery critters out from underfoot, one of these days we're gonna have lamb chops for supper."

Out she would go with wire and wood and nails and patch up another hole they'd gone through—and then the next morning they'd be loose again.

Then one Sunday afternoon the family returned home from church to find the lambs dead, their bloated bodies scattered across the front lawn all the way to the irrigation ditch.

Hannah and the children were aghast.

"What happened to them, Mama?" Gideon asked.

"I don't know," she mumbled as they walked past the carcasses. "What do you think, Mr. Francis?"

Frank was stumped. There were no signs of predators, no blood or bits of torn wool. There were no poisons in the area that he knew of.

Then he spotted it. The door to the toolshed that housed the chicks was gaping open. "Come on," he said darkly, motioning to Hannah, who came along behind the children.

Frank first assumed that the children, in their hurry to finish chores before leaving for church, had forgotten to lock the door. Upon closer examination he found that the latch had been knocked clean from the door itself. The chickens' feeder had been knocked to the ground, and very little feed remained beside it. Their troughs, too, were trampled and broken. The lambs had done the mischief themselves, and had paid the price for their gluttony.

For a long time, no one spoke.

"Henry, please clean this up for me," Hannah finally told her son in a quiet voice. "You twins see if you can catch the chicks and get them safely back in here."

She turned then, and the other children ran off ahead of her to change from their Sunday best.

"I'm sorry about your lambs," Frank told her gently as they walked toward the house.

Hannah shook her head and angrily wiped the tears from her face. "It's my own fault," she admitted. "My own stubborn fault."

Frank turned her to face him. "How is it your fault?"

Hannah's misty blue eyes evaded his. "I should have listened to you. I knew you didn't want those sheep here—not you or Eli. I asked for them three years ago, and you both insisted that a cattle ranch was no place for sheep."

Frank had forgotten. She was right, of course. She had tailed Eli for hours before she'd found the courage to ask him about the sheep. He had simply told her no, and the matter had been settled. Somehow Frank didn't feel he'd earned that type of authority over her . . . and somehow he didn't really want it, either.

"I—just thought it would be all right this time. Obviously, I was wrong," she said regretfully.

"It wasn't wrong," he told her, his hands on her shoulders. Then he changed his mind. "I mean, it was wrong to go at it so unprepared. We should have thought it through. We should have built a pen and a shelter."

"You wouldn't have had time for such things—and the money needs to go toward the cattle, anyway."

"Not if you feel that sheep are important," he argued.

Then he stopped and took the hat from his head and mussed his hair that had been combed so neatly for church. He studied her. "You're probably right," he surmised.

Hannah smiled. "What am I right about?"

"I probably would have said no, for all those reasons."

"You would have," she insisted.

"And I would have been right."

"Yes, Mr. Francis," Hannah agreed.

"But the ranch is yours, too—the land and the buildings and the money. You need to tell me when things are important—"

Her eyes were laughing in spite of his attempt to be serious.

"—before I say no," he finished dryly.

Hannah sputtered in laughter. "My point exactly." The importance of the sheep mattered little in the shadow of economic priorities. She grinned victoriously. "Whatever you say, Frank," she said, and turning, sauntered off toward the house with a lighthearted skip.

Frank widened his stride in pursuit. "It's 'Mr. Francis' to you, lady!" he called after her.

Often in the hot, still days in late July, Frank would send Hannah with one of the children into Saratoga for supplies at the hardware. It gave them a chance for time alone—something rare in a household their size. Usually they would treat themselves to an ice-cream soda at the Wolfe Hotel before heading back home.

It was on one of those days that Frank came off the roof of the toolshed, hot and sweaty, his face sunburned from his outdoor tasks. He'd run out of roofing nails. If he called the hardware quickly, he could leave a message asking Hannah to pick some up. But when he turned the corner of the house, he found Stephen and Henry rolling about in the dirt of the backyard, apparently determined to pound the stuffing out of each other.

Frank seized them by the scruff of their necks, one in each hand, and pulled them apart. "What's going on here?" he demanded.

"He started it," Stephen said angrily, spitting out the grass he'd somehow gotten in his mouth during the scuffle.

"Did not," Henry argued. "You pushed me!"

"Well, if you hadn't stepped in front of me, I wouldn't have pushed you!"

"You've got the whole doggone yard to walk in—how come you got to walk on my shoes?"

Stephen reached across his stepfather toward his brother, and Frank held tight to the two of them until they ceased their squabbling and stood still.

"Didn't I send you boys down to the cellar to clean out those old newspapers and empty canning jars?" he asked.

Henry and Stephen grew quiet, avoiding his gaze. They hadn't been in the cellar all day—had forgotten it, in fact, in their eagerness to practice roping on the steer head Ben had carved out of a piece of plywood and stuck into a bale of hay up in the mound.

"We were practicin' ropin', Mr. Francis," Henry finally answered him.

Frank scowled at them in disapproval. "Ropin'," he muttered, shaking his head. He escorted them to the back porch and seated them soundly on the steps beside one another. "I want the two of you to take turns saying something nice to each other until I get finished inside. And then I want you down in that cellar, cleaning it like you should have been doing in the first place!"

He stepped briskly into the kitchen, grabbed the phone book from the counter, and thumbed through the pages. "I can't hear you," he called after a moment, and then added, "and it'd better be in English!"

"Ropin'," he mumbled again as he found the number he'd been looking for. He stepped toward the telephone in the dining room, but then turned back suddenly toward where the boys were sitting.

"I like your bike," Stephen said resentfully.

"You color nice," Henry told him quietly, his chin propped in his hands, his elbows on his knees.

"You know a lot about—"

"And Stephen!" Frank cut in from the doorway, pointing at the boy through the screened door. "I just recalled. If I hear anymore about you roping that cat, we're gonna have to have us a serious talk."

Stephen glanced behind him, wondering why his stepfather called it a talk. They both knew full well the only talking going on would be his yelping and promising not to do whatever it was he knew better than to do in the first place!

"Yes, Mr. Francis," he responded dutifully. He sighed wearily. "It's your turn," he said to his brother.

"No, it's not," Henry argued. "It's yours."

"Yours."

Frank shook his head and turned toward the phone. Hannah would be home before he knew it if he didn't get moving fast. Quickly he dialed the number, only to find that his wife had indeed left the hardware store ten minutes before.

"Doggone kids," he grumbled. If he hadn't stopped to interrupt the boys' squabbling, he'd have saved himself a trip into town.

He pulled the keys to the truck from his jeans' pocket and then stopped to check the sweat beneath the armpit of his shirt. Not too bad, he decided, then ran his hand across his chin. He hadn't taken the time to shave that morning, and the stubble beneath his calloused hands sounded like sandpaper against a rough board.

"I ain't never gonna get finished today," he concluded, heading toward the bathroom. He opened the bathroom door and stopped still. Closing the door again with a slam, he turned to the staircase that led to the upper bedrooms.

"Which one of you kids put these geese in the bathtub?" he hollered, his face red, his features livid.

There was a hushed silence, then the quick scramble of little feet. Malinda came bounding down the stairway to stand before him.

"I did, Mr. Francis," she admitted. Her blonde hair was tied in pigtails, her blue eyes wide. She wore an oversized white hockey shirt with green stripes and the number five printed on the front and back.

Frank felt like a giant confronting a dwarf! How could such an open, innocent face have caused so much havoc? Without a word, he placed his hands on her shoulders and turned her in the direction of the bathroom, marching her down the hallway to the scene of the crime.

He opened the door, revealing a room splattered with water. Washcloths were draped across the floor, and Hannah's bottle of rose-scented bubble bath lay empty on the edge of the tub.

Malinda looked up at him. "They wanted to go swimmin'," she said quietly. "And they were dirty, too."

Frank looked back at the tub where four gray, down-covered goslings swam happily among the bubbles, dirt, and droppings. He placed his hands on his hips and looked Malinda in the eye. "Weren't you told not to bring any more creatures into this house?" he asked, recalling an incident involving a litter of baby bunnies that mysteriously found its way into the hall closet and had to be hand-fed with an eyedropper every few hours.

Malinda smiled weakly as she nodded her head.

He sighed, his eyes rolling toward the ceiling. "Where's your mother when I need her?" he mumbled.

Brushing aside the towels that were piled on the lid of the toilet, he seated himself and pulled Malinda along across his knee. He swatted her soundly before setting her back on her feet.

But instead of crying, as he'd expected, she turned to him with an angry scowl on her face, her lower lip protruding in a pout. She stomped her foot.

"Doggone it, Mr. Francis," she said, in perfect imitation of him. "Emma said you weren't gonna spank us 'cause we're girls. That stings!" She rubbed the seat of her pants to emphasize the point.

Frank stood up, mustering all his self-control to keep a firm expression on his face. "Well, you'd better have a talk with Emma," he told her, "and set her straight. And I'd better not find any more livestock in the house! Now you get this bathroom clean and those geese back out in the barnyard where they belong."

The sound of the van turning into the drive had never been such music to his ears. Unshaven, Frank greeted Hannah with a quick kiss and headed toward the truck.

"Where are you going?" Hannah questioned. Her arms were loaded with the bundles he had sent her for.

"To the hardware!" he hollered across his shoulder. "Where there aren't any kids!"

Blinking in bewilderment, Hannah turned to the house.

Twenty-eight

Over the next few weeks, while Hannah was busy sewing dresses and stocking up on notebooks and paper for school, Frank took the three oldest boys to the mountain pasture to bring down the first string of cows.

These were his best cows, and he began to creep feed the calves immediately by giving them extra grain coated in molasses and vitamins. They were fed through small openings in the panels through which only they could fit. They were branded and given shots, dehorned and castrated before being returned to their mothers in the nearby pasture.

Going to the theater was something most of the Petersheim children had never done. Though the expense was perhaps the most obvious reason why, it was not the only deterrent. There was the question of how many trips would be made to the bathroom, with children stepping in and out of the aisle in front of and on top of other paying customers. There was the chance that at least one of them would get lost on the way back and end up wandering about the theater, tearful and afraid. There was the probability that Rachael would get fussy ten minutes into the film. Or someone would throw up or decide to take his shoes off and forget to put them back on before leaving.

All these things occurred to Frank as he drove the family toward Rawlins where the "big" theaters were. But it was a treat that he as a boy had looked forward to, and he wanted these children to experience it as well. So, without discussion or debate, he ordered the family into the van as soon as the dinner dishes were done, for a Sunday afternoon drive.

Hannah, though she did not voice her objections to his sudden desire to view the countryside, frowned as she situated the baby in the car seat. She had letters to write, and Sunday afternoon was the only time, it seemed, to get them done.

Besides, she thought, adjusting her own seat belt, they had seen the countryside before—every day of their lives! What could possibly be out there today that they hadn't seen yesterday? Still, she traveled in silence, wondering at the occasional nervous grin Frank shot her way.

By the time they pulled up to the theater in Rawlins, a thousand destinations had crossed her mind . . . the movie theater not being one of them.

Hannah looked at the sheepish grin that covered her husband's face to the marquee outside her window.

"*Bambi*?" she questioned.

Frank shrugged and chuckled, a little embarrassed. "Why not?"

"Why not?" Hannah demanded. "Why not? Have you lost your mind?"

Wincing, Frank held his hands up for protection. "Oh, no!" he pleaded. "She's gonna hit me. Lord, don't let her hit me!" he pleaded as the children roared in laughter from the back of the van.

Hannah's lips were pursed in a determined set, her eyes voiced her criticism as she crossed her arms before her.

Tentatively, Frank reached across the seat and tested the muscle of her left arm. "Woman," he said determinedly, "you're gonna have to quit haulin' them sacks of grain around. You're gettin' too strong for me." He whistled and rolled his eyes as Henry fell out of his seat into the aisle in laughter.

Hannah refused to see the humor in his performance. Silently she opened the door of the van and removed Rachael from the car seat. "Come, children," she said quietly.

It was a phrase that held a quality of magic in it, Frank thought, used most often in public or in times of danger when swift obedience was needed. While others around them called repeatedly to their seemingly deaf children, Hannah and Eli had only to mention that one solemn command, spoken in a quiet voice.

He watched now in admiration as the children quickly and silently filed from the van and gathered on the sidewalk beside their mother. It was a training, he knew, that began when they were barely able to walk, reinforced by the example of the older children and of the parents themselves toward one another. It was not questioned nor argued. Like much of the Amish tradition, it was simply obeyed.

Joining them, he took Hannah's arm and escorted her down the sidewalk to the entrance of the theater. Proudly he paid the enormous fee and ushered them all inside, savoring the delight that filled their eyes as they viewed the inside of the theater—many of them for the first time.

He led them all to the concession stand, where they stood with their noses pressed against the glass. He told them to pick out one box of candy each, while he ordered a round of small sodas and a box of buttered popcorn to share with Hannah.

Hannah's mouth dropped at the overpriced items, but a stern look from Frank kept her from noting this fact aloud. His eyes softened as he looked at her.

"Please," he said quietly. "It's important to me."

Hannah lowered her eyes. He did, after all, work very hard for the money they had, and aside from the issue of owning sheep, he had never denied her request to purchase something. Still, she thought a little angrily, he should at least have discussed this with her first.

She gave a small, impatient sigh. "All right," she promised, a glint of defiance sparking in her eyes as she met his gaze. "But I want my own popcorn."

Frank chuckled. "Two popcorns," he amended to the clerk. "With lots of butter."

Rachael did indeed get fussy, and Hannah had to leave with her for a while, but they soon rejoined the family. There was a minimum of interruptions and all shoes were account-ed for as they headed back toward home.

Chore time was a rushed event that evening as dusk befell them. Frank hadn't changed all day from his church clothes, and for chores he simply slipped a lightweight work suit over top.

They had just finished milking when Amos came running from the back of the barn. "Mr. Francis!" he called, breathless. "Mr. Francis, one of the sows is hung up!"

"Hung up?" he questioned, quickly following the boy. "Hung up on what?"

Before Amos could answer, they'd reached the pens where the sows and their litters were kept.

The boar, it appeared, had jumped the metal panel that divided him from the females, who had given birth the month before.

The young sow had done her best to escape him and had tried to leap the panel opposite his, breaking her leg in the process. It was caught, mangled in the wire, and she stood there, patiently waiting for someone to free her.

Frank shook his head. "Why do these things always have to happen on a Sunday night?" he asked of no one in particular.

"Sam!" he called loudly. "Go in the house and get my rifle and some cartridges."

"Ben," he continued as the older children watched sadly, knowing the loss of the sow would cost the family a year of production while another piglet grew to replace her, "you go fetch that flashlight off the dresser and some butcher knives and the saw.

"Amos, get a bucket from Mama for the heart and liver; tell her what's happened."

Off the boys went, a sense of urgency hurrying their steps, while Frank secured the boar in his own pen, vowing to run a strand of electric fencing across the top of the panel come morning.

There was barely enough light to see. Frank took the Remington .22 Sam handed him, raised and aimed it, and fired.

Quickly, as the sow dropped, Sam held it on its back while Frank inserted a knife just in front of the breastbone and slit the artery. Since the family had no great desire to experiment with black pudding or scalding, the dead sow simply bled out onto a heap of hay which would later be tossed into the manure pile as fertilizer for the hay fields.

Time, Frank realized, was of the essence. It was dark with no lighting on that side of the barn. The mosquitoes were vicious, totally oblivious to the spray that Hannah had thoughtfully sent out with Amos and his bucket. By morning, flies would have swarmed the meat, laying their eggs inside it.

"Samuel and Ben," Frank told the boys, "you finish up the stock. Henry, bring the wheelbarrow around. Stephen," he ordered, "hold this flashlight still."

Carefully he sawed through the breastbone with the tools Sam had brought him from the house. He removed the head and cut around the anus, tying it with a piece of baling twine to prevent leaks.

He gutted the pig swiftly, wasting the intestines, which were used for casings for sausage. He tossed aside the stomach, as well, which used with intestines, made "chitterlings."

And he ignored the head and feet, knowing Hannah would have wanted them for the spicy lunch meat, headcheese, while the feet could be boiled or pickled.

But with the hot weather and the immediate problems of flies and spoilage, he couldn't dawdle or wait for the meat to "set" as he did in the winter months when butchering normally took place.

He was just about to saw straight down the backbone when an owl hooted and Stephen turned, taking the light with him in the direction of the sound.

"Stephen!" Frank snapped, bringing him back to the project at hand with a jolt. "Boy, if I cut my arm off next time you turn away, I'm gonna tan you good!"

Stephen stood motionless and silent in concentration, but from behind him, Frank heard the two youngest begin to giggle.

Annoyed, he glanced to where they stood. "Just what is so funny?" he demanded.

"Mr. Francis," Gideon said, "if you cut off your arm, how you gonna catch us?"

Released from the tension at hand, the others began to laugh aloud until even Frank could not help but join in.

"Well, I'll—I'll have to send your mother to do the catchin'," he said.

The boys guffawed. Their mother was, after all, a girl, and in their minds not capable of any real running.

"Hey," Frank reminded them, "she caught me, didn't she?"

Stephen snickered. "And you were runnin' like a fence post," he pointed out, "two feet under."

Henry joined him between hiccups. "Couldn't have moved you with a bulldozer, Mr. Francis."

"—just tryin' to get away so's Mama couldn't catch you," Stephen added.

"All right, all right," Frank conceded. "You'll see," he warned. "Your day'll come, and we'll find out just how fast the bunch of you run!

"Oh, Henry," he mimicked in a high-pitched tone. "Honey, can you come by and take a look at my car? It just doesn't sound right. There's this little pinging noise.

"But darlin'," he continued in a much deeper tone. "I been out there twelve times this week already, and I ain't heard a thing. You sure you ain't runnin' over the cat or somethin'?"

The boys roared with laughter, and Frank broke into sobs. "But Henry," he pleaded in a desperate voice, pulling his hands to his heart, "Henry, I've just got to see you again!"

"Oh, no," Henry objected with eight-year-old vehemence, "not me. I ain't lettin' no girl talk to me like that."

Frank winked at him as he turned back to the meat. "We'll see," he told him. "We'll see."

Soon the hog was quartered and carried in the wheelbarrow a section at a time to the house. There Hannah set it in cold brine water in the bathtub for the night.

Covered in blood and grime, the weary butchers washed as best they could in the kitchen sink and went to bed, knowing the remainder of the preserving would be left to the women come morning.

Canning began in a flurry, and the meat chickens were butchered. The remaining herd was brought in.

And one morning, along came Mr. Pickett of Pickett Brothers Packing. He was a heavyset man, somewhere in his fifties with a gray and balding pate, pale blue eyes, and the disgusting habit of cigar smoking.

His family had come with the first settlers out West. He and his brother now managed the family business and bought directly from the ranchers in the area.

Hannah fluttered over him as he stepped from his powder blue Lincoln Continental. "Why, Mr. Pickett," she greeted him, "do come in. How did you know I had just baked a fresh batch of apple turnovers?"

"I could smell them clear into Saratoga," he replied.

Hannah rushed to get him an empty can to serve as an ashtray before the tip of his cigar ended up on her clean floor.

"Won't you sit down and have a cup of coffee?" she offered. "Mr. Francis is busy working on the pickup.

"Leah," she told her daughter, "go and fetch him quickly. Tell him Mr. Pickett is here."

She smiled cordially at her guest. "Could I talk you into a turnover?"

Mr. Pickett seated himself in a chair at the kitchen table. "I don't see how I can refuse."

Within a few minutes Leah returned to her mother. "Mr. Francis says he'll be finished in a little while."

Hannah poured Mr. Pickett another cup of coffee. They talked about the weather and the high school basketball team, the abundance of potatoes and the likelihood of frost soon.

Eventually the conversation waned. Hannah wondered what her husband could be thinking, keeping Mr. Pickett waiting like that. Didn't he realize that their entire year's wages hinged on the goodwill of this man?

Finally she stood from her chair and removed her apron. "Perhaps Leah did not explain to Mr. Francis that you were here," she said uncomfortably. "Maybe we should just go and find him ourselves."

"A good idea," Mr. Pickett agreed. Though he still smiled, it was clear to Hannah that his patience was being taxed.

Sure enough, Frank was still tightening bolts on the pickup. He was covered with grease and barely glanced up from beneath the hood of the vehicle to greet them.

"Mr. Francis," Hannah interrupted him, "Mr. Pickett has come."

"Hello, George," Frank acknowledged without cheer. "What brings you to these parts?"

Hannah's eyes widened. He knew full well why George Pickett was there! Why on earth was he acting so peculiar?

"That's a fine string of calves you've got in the front pasture," Mr. Pickett complimented.

"Yep," Frank agreed. "Isaac, hand me that socket wrench—that one."

Isaac, Hannah noted with dismay, was nearly as greasy as his stepfather.

"Is that new stock?" Mr. Pickett inquired. "I thought I saw

the Petersheim brand on them."

Frank paused in his work, but there was a frown on his face as he spoke. "They're out of Eli's heifers—we fed them up last winter. And the Petersheim brand stays, even if I am half owner."

Mr. Pickett was alarmed by his tone of voice; he had no intention of insulting the man. He changed the subject. "Well, you've got a nice crop of calves out of the rest of them, it seems. I can give you a fair price for them if you throw in the front lot."

"They're not for sale," Frank said, returning to his work without another glance.

Hannah's breath caught in her throat. What did he mean, they weren't for sale? How did he expect them to survive the winter?

Mr. Pickett laughed aloud. "You can't mean to house the entire herd, Frank."

Frank stopped and stood uncomfortably close to the man. "If you'll excuse me, George," he said, leaving little doubt to his meaning, "I've got to finish this before noon."

Mr. Pickett's lower lip tightened. "Suit yourself, Frank," he told him. "But I think you're missing an excellent opportunity. You never know what the market will be like come winter."

Frank said nothing, but returned to his work beneath the hood, while Hannah apologetically walked Mr. Pickett to his car.

She then returned to the house to check on Leah and the baby and to quickly prepare some lunch. She said nothing of the conversation, but waited patiently while Isaac and Frank washed the grease from their hands and arms and faces.

She set a meal of meat loaf and fresh salad greens and canned peaches before them, but still she didn't say a word. Frank, on the other hand, was now cheerful and talkative, chattering the entire meal to Isaac and Leah.

Hannah fed the baby and washed the dishes, and Frank went out on the back porch to oil saddles. Finally she summoned the courage to ask the question that was tearing her up inside.

"Mr. Francis," she said quietly, interrupting him as he worked. His arms, tanned by the summer's sun, glistened with sweat as he strained to soften and clean the leather.

"Mr. Francis, I do not believe we can actually survive the winter without the sale of at least some of the calves. The older boys need boots again, and Gideon and Amos need shoes and mittens—I've looked at our checking account," she rushed on painfully as Frank stopped his work and listened.

"Perhaps," she suggested timidly, "if you apologized to Mr. Pickett, we—"

"No," Frank stated strongly. "No."

Hannah stepped to the other side, where he was rapidly buffing the saddle horn. "But we've done business with the Pickett Packing Company for five years," she encouraged. "I'm sure they would—"

"And for five years," he interrupted, pointing at her with the rag he had put saddle soap on, "the contracts have been loose, if not nonexistent."

"Are you accusing Mr. Pickett of being dishonest?"

"I'm accusing George Pickett," he clarified, "of doing

poor business. I'd rather take my chances with an electronic auction. And I'd like to ship those prime calves to a custom feedlot up north of here and try to fatten the rest myself. By June, those choice steers should weigh 600 pounds. If we keep this group on pasture next summer, they should finish easily at 900," he finished enthusiastically.

"But what will we live on between now and June?" Hannah asked.

Frank did not meet the intensity of her eyes. "Well, I was thinking of taking an outside job for awhile," he suggested hesitantly.

"Doing what?" she questioned.

Frank did not want to answer her. "The loggers need a—"

"No!" Hannah nearly shouted at him. How could he even think such a thing after what had happened to Eli?

Frank reached for her hand, but she jerked it away. "It's a trucking job, Hannah," he tried to explain.

"No!" she insisted. "Not there! How many husbands am I to lose to one company?"

"It's only for two months," he tried to tell her. "I won't be—"

Hannah covered her ears with her hands and ran tearfully into the house.

Twenty-nine

*I*t was a long and silent day that followed. Hannah refused to talk about it and went about her work busily avoiding her husband.

Frank, of course, understood her objections, unfounded though they were. To him, truck driving was no more dangerous than ranching. An unruly bull or an unreasonable horse could trample him just as easily. There were no guarantees in life.

Still, Hannah, he knew, had not forgiven the logging company for taking the life of the man she had grown up loving, and he wouldn't insist that she try.

He closed up the barns and checked the cattle gate to be sure that Henry had locked it after throwing down hay. The moon was big and full and silvery, and the air was crisp. He gazed out one last time at the cattle he had resolved to sell come winter—even if it had to be through the Pickett Plant.

A hand touched his shoulder, and he started.

"It is a lovely herd, isn't it?" Hannah said.

Frank leaned against the gate. "The best I've seen."

They were silent a moment, standing beside one another, content in each other's company.

"It will probably be even better next year, won't it?"

Frank was still staring across the fields to the mountain beyond them. "Probably," he answered.

Hannah moved closer to him and placed her arm around his. "I was thinking of all the risks you faced when you married me. The children could have turned against you. I may have—displeased you. The ranch could have taken all your savings and then gone under, leaving you with nothing but a lot of mouths to feed and no home to live in.

"But you took the risk," she said, turning to face him. "And now it's my turn. If you think that keeping the steers one more season will benefit this family, then I'm willing to go along with that—even if it means working off the ranch for a while. We'll manage."

Frank glanced at the warm blue eyes that had added so much meaning to his life. "We're gonna make it, Hannah," he told her. "I promise we will."

In silence, Hannah smiled, leaving her trust in his judgment and the loving care of the Lord.

It was not easy for Hannah to watch Frank pull away on a Monday morning late in August. He would be staying with the logging crew at a higher elevation for the next five days, and returning late Friday night.

He assured her time and again that his fate and their

future were in the hands of the Lord and no amount of worrying was going to change that. And though Hannah had nodded obligingly, she could not forget the day she had gone to identify Eli's body. Cold, still, his head tilted to one side where his neck had broken in the fall while topping trees. Death had made itself final without question or reason. In one swift moment her life and her children's had been changed forever, singed by loss.

How could she ever survive such a loss again?

School quickly became the catalyst that eased her distress. Gideon started kindergarten, and with mixed emotions she watched her little boy skip off to the bus stop with the others. With his lunch pail in hand, his brand-new backpack filled with crayons and pencils and glue, he waved good-bye without a second glance.

The harvest, too, demanded much of Hannah's attention, for there were beets to pickle and sauerkraut to make. In the high country, winter came swiftly. Hannah and the children hurried to finish their preparations: cleaning stalls, scattering manure and old bedding across the empty gardens, putting fresh straw in its place. Caulking windows. Putting away the summer clothes and taking inventory of boots and mittens and blankets.

And yet . . . despite the activities of each week, Hannah found herself counting the days till Frank's return. Each Friday she spent putting the house in order and preparing pastries, stews, and casseroles to please her husband.

But Frank hardly seemed to notice. After finishing his week in the timbers, he would attempt to cram into Saturday all of the work he had missed at the ranch. He and the boys cut and stacked wood weekend after weekend in a race against time.

One Saturday was spent separating the cattle. Though Sam and Ben did all of the chores necessary to maintain the herd, they couldn't separate them into their winter pens without the aid of their stepfather.

The work went smoothly and without incident. It was already dark by the time Frank and Sam and Benjamin entered the kitchen.

"Here's the milk, Ma," Samuel said, setting a bucket on the counter beside the sink.

They were dirty, their clothes ripe with the mixture of horse scent and leather and sage. Their faces were ruddy from the cold north wind that blew dirt and bits of hay into their eyes and from the adrenaline that flowed as they pitted their wits and their horses' instincts against the stubborn will of the cattle.

Hannah stood at the stove, stirring vegetables in a large kettle. "Becca," she told her daughter, "pour the milk through the separator. No, no, no!" she shouted at Benjamin as he stepped toward the hallway. "Get those boots off!"

Frank took his hat and whopped the young man across the shoulder, sending a mist of dust into the air. "You heard your ma," he taunted, "get your boots off."

Benjamin grinned sheepishly at his parents and bent to comply with their wishes.

Rebecca walked over to her stepfather and held out the sleeping Rachael.

"Sorry, I can't," he told her. "My hands are too cold." With a wink he crept up behind Hannah and placed his hands at the back of her neck.

Hannah shrieked and whirled to face him, her spoon flinging bits of tomato and onion to the floor.

"Now look what you've done!" she scolded as Rachael awoke with a lusty wail. "You should be ashamed of yourself!"

"Oops," he replied, backing toward the sink. "Guess I'll just wash up."

Emma comforted Rachael while Rebecca carried the milk pail to the back porch where the large separator was kept.

"You should have seen Roundy," Sam commented as he opened the refrigerator and poured himself a glass of juice. "Not one of those heifers got past him."

"There wasn't one cut," Benjamin added enthusiastically. "The steers didn't fall over one another or bottleneck between pens. Even the bull—"

Hannah gasped as she turned to Frank, who was pouring himself a mug of hot coffee. "Mr. Francis!" she exclaimed. "You let Benjamin with the bulls!"

"No," Ben objected.

"No, no," Frank echoed quickly. "I penned the bulls. Ben just latched the gates."

Hannah sighed in relief and continued to ladle the hot stew into bowls. "Set these on the table," she told her eldest son, "and call the others."

When the last bowl had been filled, Hannah set the ladle beside the kettle and turned, but Frank blocked her pathway and wrapped his arms around her so she couldn't leave.

"Admit it," he said quietly, his blue eyes tired but filled with a sort of peaceful victory.

"Mr. Francis!" Hannah chided, her cheeks coloring as she attempted to pull from his grasp.

Frank glanced toward the dining room where the children were settling.

"They've seen it before," he said lightly. "Now, admit it."

Hannah crossed her arms in irritation. "I don't know what you're talking about."

Frank chuckled. "You do, too. You know we wouldn't have gotten half that work done using Captain and the tractor." He looked down to meet her eyes. "Isn't that right?"

Hannah tapped her index finger impatiently against her arm. *If you had sold the herd when you were supposed to,* she thought, *there wouldn't have been any need to separate them.*

Frank shook her ever so slightly. "Isn't it?" he repeated.

"Yes, Mr. Francis," she relented dutifully.

Sighing, Frank straightened. There was no victory for him in her condescending tone.

"And you missed me," he added dryly, releasing her and putting his hands in his pockets.

"Yes, Mr. Francis," she answered quietly.

Suddenly Frank's hands flew to the air as he moaned, rolling his eyes to the ceiling. "Then say it like you mean it!"

Hannah, startling even him, threw her arms around his shoulders and pulled him to her in a kiss. Not a "the-children-are-watching" peck on the cheek, but a kiss that held such intensity that even he could not doubt the meaning behind it.

"Oh," he said, as she turned to carry the last bowl of stew to the dining room, "you did miss me."

Hannah only smiled. "Yes, Mr. Francis," she concurred.

Thirty

One Saturday early in October, Frank slid his foot into his boot and discovered, quite uncomfortably, a small bandy egg that had been tucked into the toe and held there by a wad of gum.

Quickly he removed his foot from the oozing yellow mess and glanced down the long kitchen table at the faces around him.

The children sat busily eating pancakes, gulping down their juice, totally oblivious to the slimy condition of their stepfather's right foot.

Puzzled, Frank glanced at Hannah, who was busy at the stove with another platter of pancakes.

As though sensing his gaze, she turned to him, curious that he had not begun to eat. "Do you feel well, Mr. Francis?" she asked.

A tittering of voices sounded from the table, and Frank turned quickly. "Aha!" he pronounced. "Which one of you laughed?" He searched the wide, startled eyes of the children. "Was that you, Stephen?"

"No, sir," Henry answered before his brother could speak. "It was me."

Frank narrowed his eyes at the boy. "And just what was so funny?"

Henry's face reddened as the room grew silent. Finally he spoke. "Amos dr-dropped his pancakes in his lap."

Amos, who had indeed dumped his entire plate down the front of his jeans, looked about the room tearfully. Then, as the others once again broke into a gale of giggles, he offered a tremulous smile.

"Amos, clean yourself up and get another plate," Frank said. Then he hobbled toward the bedroom, one boot on and one in his hand, in search of a clean pair of sock.

Later that day, when he put on his insulated work suit to change the oil in the van, he found the hankie in his inside pocket filled with shaving cream.

The next week Frank discovered globs of shoe polish on the underside of the tractor wheel. More than once he reached for the handle of the van door and found it lathered with Vaseline.

Never once was he capable of finding a culprit in all of this mischief. And no one, it seemed, was ever there to witness his blunders as he stepped into the assortment of preconceived traps.

He returned one Friday long after the children had gone to bed, only to find his and Hannah's bedroom empty, the covers crumpled and tossed. He set down the large navy blue gym bag that held his laundry and took out his shaving bag for use the next morning.

The door behind him opened, and Hannah appeared, her finger to her lips. "Rachael," she whispered in explanation0.

"Is she sick?"

Hannah shook her head. "Just fussy. I think it's her teeth."

He nodded. Teething, he'd come to realize, was a traumatic experience that every infant must endure, accompanied by much slobbering, gnawing, and tears. Why, he wondered, as he set his boots in the corner beside the dresser, did God intend for it to be so difficult to transfer from milk to meat? His mind wandered to the apostle Paul's words about meat and milk. There was a parallel; it was difficult for some folks to leave the "milk" of new faith behind them and go on to more "meaty" levels of understanding.

In his state of weary meditation, he did not notice that Hannah had opened the gym bag and was holding his shirt, sniffing the collar.

"Mr. Francis!" she exclaimed suddenly, forgetting her injunction to silence.

Frank glanced at her in the mirror. The shocked expression in her eyes told him instantly what she was thinking. He took the shirt from her and tossed it back into the bag with the rest of his laundry.

"Come here," he told her, and stepped to the dresser, where he unzipped the travel bag that held his shaving equipment. "Smell this."

Hannah leaned forward and sniffed what was supposed to be a bottle of aftershave. Suddenly she made an awful face and rubbed her nose, backing away.

Frank returned the cap, chuckling. "Those kids put perfume in my aftershave! I put that on Tuesday morning at 5 A.M. The guys are still calling me Franny!"

Hannah sputtered in laughter. "They certainly have been up to no good these past few weeks."

Frank sat on the edge of the bed. "Are they pulling these pranks with you?" he questioned.

Hannah shook her head and slid beneath the covers of their bed.

"I can't figure it out," he said, bewildered. He had dealt with outright disobedience before, but this didn't exactly fall into that category.

"They miss you," Hannah told him, propping her pillows behind her.

Frank removed his socks and tossed them in the direction of his boots. "They've got a funny way of showing it."

Hannah shrugged. "They're used to you being here, working with them, answering their questions. Even Samuel," she pointed out, "is just a boy. He doesn't really want the responsibility of a ranch without you here to guide him."

Frank reached for the lamp beside their bed but hesitated, looking at her. "He told you that?"

"He doesn't have to," she answered. "It shows in his eyes when he knows the pump is jammed or the barn was left open. He looks so defeated.

"And Mr. Francis," she added, "the tractor stalled out again. Samuel left it in the hay field and moved the heifers near the loft by the barn where he could throw loose hay from the bales we'd put in for the sheep. But he's afraid you'll be angry with him for giving up and leaving it there."

Frank studied the matter thoughtfully. "I'll talk to him," he promised, then leaned over and shut out the light.

Thirty-one

The next morning, Frank did not rush to fix the tractor as Hannah had expected. Instead, he lingered after breakfast with a cup of coffee, wandering from room to room as though memorizing every sight and sound, as though he'd missed the house itself in the week that had passed.

He settled momentarily in the living room and watched as Rachael, who lay in the center of the oval rag rug, finished her bottle. Determined then, and unaware of her audience, she tossed the bottle from her and flipped over to her stomach. Her eyes widened, her cheeks puffed, and her tiny lips formed a thin and somber line. Stealthily she propped her hands beneath her and rose up on her knees. Like an engine prepping for take-off, she began rocking to and fro, uncertain of how to actually leave the ground, but willing to make the effort nonetheless.

Frank set his coffee aside and knelt opposite her on the rug. Rachael didn't see him at first, but when she stopped her rocking for a moment, she recognized the figure who towered above her in imitation. With a piercing shriek, she laughed and flattened to her belly, arms outstretched, feet kicking wildly behind her.

Frank crawled toward her and snarled like a grizzly bear. Isaac, who'd been playing nearby, answered his roar and ran at him from across the room. He jumped onto Frank's back eagerly.

"Hannah! Hannah, save me!" Frank called out as he snatched Rachael from beneath him and turned to his back, holding her above his head as Isaac tumbled to his side.

Hannah hurried at his call and smiled at the scene before her. She lifted Rachael from his arms as Leah came to join in her brother's fun.

And Frank suddenly realized the answer to his dilemma.

From then on, it was he who dashed out of corners with a roar to startle the unsuspecting traveler. It was he who knotted shoelaces together in the middle of the night or put gelled oil in the thumb of an older boy's work glove.

By the end of October, he was not only exhausted from the cold, demanding work in the high country, but he had run out of ideas for pranks.

So it was a mixed blessing when he awoke one Sunday morning to the sound of the telephone to learn that snow had hit the mountains, the roads were closed, and his job was over. As the routine of their days replaced the gnawing loneliness they'd experienced, the need for roughhousing and special attention waned.

Frank began repairing equipment that would be stored for winter, and taught Stephen and Henry how to clean the tack properly for the horses.

Hannah watched the snowfall from her kitchen window as it hit the lower hillsides. The land, once brown and barren, now sparkled in the glitter of fresh snow. Inside her kitchen, the stove emitted a glowing warmth and the tantalizing aroma of fresh-baked cinnamon rolls.

Rachael sat on the floor beside her, trying to unlock the secrets of a set of old measuring spoons that Hannah had tied together with a piece of bright red yarn.

Leah and Isaac were busy in the living room, making towns and railroad tracks out of pieces of scrap wood that Frank had brought in from the workshop for kindling.

Hannah glanced at her husband, who sat in the dining room, his glasses balanced on the top of his head as he studied grain bills and ledgers.

"Mr. Francis," she said, shaking the dishwater from her hands and drying them on her apron. "May I speak with you?"

Frank looked up from his papers. "Sure," he answered, curious about her timid expression.

She brought him a mug of coffee, though he hadn't asked her to, and his brow raised in question as he took it.

"Mr. Francis," she began, taking the chair to the left of his and resting her arm on the table. "There is a dance at the high school. Becca would like to go."

The high school dances were well chaperoned and, within the confines of the school yard, free of alcohol and drugs. Hannah and Frank had met most of the group that Rebecca considered to be her friends. She was sixteen now, a responsible girl, and her grades reflected her desire to go on to a two-year business school.

Why, Frank wondered, was Hannah asking his opinion about such a routine decision. "Does she need a ride?" he questioned.

"No," Hannah said. "There will be someone to take her and bring her home. And I believe Samuel is going, also—he and some of the boys from his class."

"Well, if Sam is going—" Frank turned back to the winter's projected grain consumption, but Hannah didn't get up.

"Do they need something?" he wondered aloud.

"Sam is all right," Hannah said. "But Rebecca would like a new dress—something more—" she gestured with her hands—"fanciful," she concluded. "But not immodest."

Frank nodded. "That's fine," he assured her. Still Hannah remained.

"What is it? Don't we have enough in the checking account to cover it? What kind of a dress is it!"

Hannah chuckled and attempted to calm him. "I should have what I need here. If I run short of something I can pick it up reasonably in Saratoga."

"Oh," he said, relieved. But still he saw the worry in her eyes. "What is it that's bothering you, Hannah?" he asked her quietly.

"Richard Buckley," she said. "He asked her to the dance."

"Richard Buckley," Frank repeated. "Do we know him?"

Hannah shrugged. "We know his family. Pete Buckley's boy—off the ridge."

Frank nodded. Their family ran an appliance store near Elk Mountain. "Isn't he that little redheaded boy who used to come around to the socials with a pocketful of firecrackers?"

Hannah nodded. "Only he's not so little anymore." She smiled. "And he seems to have settled down. His parents plan to send him to a repair shop to apprentice this summer after graduation. I think he plans on working out of his father's shop."

"Well," Frank surmised, "that sounds levelheaded. What do you think?"

Hannah stood then and paced before the table, pausing at the cabinet in the corner to touch a small, faceless doll that had once been hers.

"When I was a girl," she said, "our parents did not interfere or question the choices we made about whom we would go to gatherings with. There were always plenty of young people around, and accepting a ride in the buggy of a neighbor boy was no indication of a commitment to a more serious relationship.

"The decision to marry, within the faith, of course, was always a private matter, shared only between the two who were getting married. Perhaps they would go to the bishop for counsel, but announcements and open speculation among the family only came after a wedding date was decided."

Frank watched her intently as she fingered the little doll on the shelf. Then she turned and joined him at the table again.

"When Eli and I left the community, we joined a group less conservative in many ways. But they didn't allow their sons and daughters to date until they were eighteen. The boy would go to his parents first and ask if he could begin to court a particular girl. If, for whatever reason, they felt she wasn't suitable, the subject would be dropped and go no further."

"And if they approved?" Frank asked.

"If they approved," she continued, "he would ask the girl if he could approach her father. If she agreed, he would go to her father and ask if he might begin dating his daughter."

Frank rolled his eyes. "It's a wonder anyone ever got married!"

Hannah laughed. "Once the parents had consented, the young people would draw up a written dating contract, setting guidelines and expectations. They didn't date others during this time period, nor did they give their consent to date unless they felt a strong inclination toward marriage in the first place."

"But it sounds more like an engagement period than a time for going out together," Frank argued. He took the reading glasses from the top of his head and set them on the papers scattered before him.

"In a way it was," Hannah agreed. "The actual engagement might last as little as six months—two weeks in some cases!"

Frank shook his head. "How can you tell if you want to get serious about someone if you've never gone out with them?"

Hannah traced the corner of the paper before her thoughtfully. "I suppose," she finally said, "it's because they had grown up together in the same community, gone to school together and church. Many of them were baptized on the same day. They went to youth gatherings and knew each other's families. And if an outsider came from another area, his relatives would put him up and give him work and answer for his reputation. By the time anyone actually dated, they knew just about everything they could about the other person's past."

Frank toyed with the rim of his coffee cup. "Is that how it was with you and Eli?" he asked, and Hannah nodded.

He drew a deep breath. "Well, I'm afraid we don't have such close communities here," he told her. "And so long as Rebecca stays in a group, and shows good judgment in selecting someone of sound character and strong faith, I see no reason to object to her accepting Richard Buckley's invitation."

It was clear from the look on her face that Hannah did not feel the same certainty. But she rose and smiled nonetheless. "Rebecca will be happy with your decision." She turned to leave, but Frank grabbed her hand.

"And will Rebecca's mother be happy with my decision?" he asked her.

Slowly Hannah pulled her hand away. "I know that young people will find a way to sin if that is what is in their hearts," she said. "I just don't want to put Becca in a situation she may not be ready to handle yet."

"But if we don't give her any leeway, how will she ever be ready when it comes time to make a commitment that should last a lifetime? We don't want her to decide to marry just to gain a little freedom from us. Tight reins," he added, "make for a stiff-necked horse."

"And no reins," Hannah pointed out before returning to the kitchen, "make for a wild one."

Thirty-two

*T*he late October snows that closed the mountain roads did not end in their usual pattern that year. Instead of the graceful interlude of cold but sunny days, the valley beneath the mountains filled with an unseasonable amount of snow.

Snow, of course, meant a guarantee of moisture for the fields the following year and less irrigating over spring and summer. But it also meant higher grain bills to maintain cattle weights over the winter. Frank realized, painfully, that the money he had earned to last them until spring was dwindling rapidly.

Unaware of their predicament, Hannah spoke about ideas she had for Christmas. She still vividly recalled the arguments they'd had the previous holiday season, and she'd prepared herself for compromise. By Thanksgiving, however, she recognized the frown that creased Frank's brow each time she mentioned the word "Christmas." It occurred to her that he'd requested no food lists for Rawlins, no inventory of boots or jackets or mittens. There'd been no mention of presents or ornaments or candy. She knew that it wasn't a preoccupation with the sudden change of weather that was causing Frank to lapse into moments of brooding silence.

Hannah had been taught all her life that her husband's task was to protect her from the badgering of the outside world, freeing her physically, financially, and mentally. The purpose of this freedom, she believed, was to put her gifts and abilities into nurturing the place he called home and the children they would bring forth. A woman was to extend that care to the church, the community around them, and the needs of the poor within the greater world.

Her responsibility to him then, was equally as large. Through her counsel and skill, she was to provide an environment that would build and maintain the confidence a man needed to confront the world, to do battle against the evil around him and the conflicts within him.

It was not her place to judge the motives of his failures; these things, she felt, were between him and his Maker. Nor was it her position to mumble and moan, or to bring them to the charity of others unless all other courses had failed. For charity, she knew, brought a man to shame before the eyes of his children, no matter how justifiable the need may be.

So Hannah changed her mind about Christmas. Because of the snow that year, several of the men decided to take snowmobiles into their own fields to hunt coyote, and Frank had gone with them. As soon as he left, Hannah headed for the attic to begin a search for provisions. She enlisted Samuel and Ben to carry boxes down to her bedroom.

Then she called Rebecca to her. "You're old enough to understand this," she told her eldest daughter. "The harshness of winter has caused an additional burden on the ranchers of the area."

Rebecca nodded. Their family was not the only one concerned about the increased consumption of feed. Friends at school talked of canceled plans to visit relatives over Christmas. And rumor had it that truckloads of hay were being brought in before the snows blocked off access to the more isolated ranchers.

"Rick says a lot of families are selling their cattle because they'll run out of hay before spring."

Hannah nodded. "Yes, and the market is so flooded with beef right now that the price has dropped lower than it's been in over twenty years."

Rebecca's eyes widened. "Are we in trouble, Mama?"

"Not yet," Hannah assured her. "But we must watch our pennies closely." She stepped to the box of material on her bed. "I've been thinking that you might be able to make Miriam and Malinda some nice doll clothes for Christmas. What do you think?"

Rebecca searched the material, lifting a swatch of calico here, a soft muslin there. She grabbed at an old collar of fuzzy white fur. "I could make a snowsuit for each of their dolls," she decided.

Grateful for her daughter's understanding and cooperation, Hannah put her arm around her and gave a little squeeze. "You can put your supplies in here," she said, handing Rebecca a plastic sack.

They looked at each other and smiled. With her finger to her lips to seal their secret, Rebecca giggled and tiptoed from her mother's room.

It was not difficult to convince Samuel and Ben to make toy rifles out of wood for Stephen and Henry. Nor did Emma object to sewing a rag doll for Leah. Stephen promised to make a slingshot for Amos, and Henry would make a bow and arrow set for Gideon.

To Hannah, the best gift of all was seeing the delight her children had in secretly being the bringer of Christmas to another child.

Frank returned from the coyote hunting dirty and exhausted. Hannah gave him a day to rest and shower and fed him a good meal—then she joined him in the barn for the evening milking.

He had come to recognize the presence of his wife during milking as a sign that a private conference was in order. The only place inside the house for them to really be alone to talk was the bedroom, but somehow, by the end of the day, they were both too tired to begin any lengthy conversations. So the barn had become a sort of mutual meeting place, where the sheer threat of extra chores kept the children from venturing within hearing range.

"Mrs. Francis," Frank scolded as he glanced up from beside the jersey cow, "will you never learn to cover yourself with more than just a shawl? This is Wyoming, woman, not the Pacific Islands! It's *cold* out here!"

Hannah hugged the black shawl closer to her and held a sheet of notebook paper more tightly in her hand.

"I won't be but a moment," she assured him. Her tone was brisk, and she summoned an attitude she generally reserved for young children and unreasonable teenagers.

"Mr. Francis," she said, "since you must admit that in the course of our marriage I have been more than generous in compromising with what you deem to be 'Christian' traditions, I think it only fair that *this* holiday season you honor me the same way by experiencing one of our holiday traditions."

Frank looked up from the flank of the cow. What in the world was she talking about? After all, they were both Christians, and Christmas was—well, Christmas!

Hannah could see that she was not winning his enthusiasm. "When I was a little girl," she told him more gently, "my mother and older sisters, well—spoiled me. Every Christmas," she continued, her eyes warming with the memory, "they would sew a new dress and pinafore and bonnet for my dolly."

Frank smiled at the vision of her past: a barefoot little girl in braided hair, freckles scattered on her nose. He could imagine the child she used to be.

"I know," she said, misconstruing his humor, "you would think a woman with eleven children couldn't possibly spoil them, but she did—each and every one of us, whenever the opportunity arose.

"Not that she undermined my father's discipline," she continued. "But she always—well, pampered us. She'd cook our favorite food or remember the color we liked best, or would put fresh flowers in a canning jar on the dresser on the morning of our birthday, or tie a balloon to the foot of the bed if it was in the winter.

"And I—" She hesitated, avoiding the pale blue of his eyes as he stood and set the milking pail aside. "I wish to do those things for my children this Christmas—if you will help me."

Frank leaned against Caramel, the placid jersey, and gently stroked her thick coat. "What did you have in mind?"

Hannah handed him the list of supplies she had written on a piece of paper—reasonable items for sewing and crafts and woodworking.

He studied it for a moment. "Is this all?" he finally asked.

"Well, I had some things in the attic already," she told him. "And—I was hoping you could make Emma a bookshelf for her room. With hearts cut out of the sides."

Frank folded the paper and tucked it neatly into his pocket, thinking about the construction of a bookshelf as he returned Caramel to her stall.

"And for Isaac," she went on, as he lifted the bucket of milk and started toward the door, "I wondered if you couldn't sand down some of those chunks of wood in the scrap pile—or cut some in odd sizes, and stain them—a good number of them."

He looked puzzled, so she explained. "You know how he loves to build castles and forts and such with pieces of wood. Well, these wouldn't be just chunks of wood anymore. They'd be special—they'd be his."

They stepped from the barn together into the clear, cold night. Hannah shivered as the wind passed through the thin material of her shawl and quickened her pace.

Frank did not answer her right away, and they walked to the house in silence.

"When do you need these things by?" he asked, patting the list he'd tucked into his pocket.

"As soon as possible," Hannah told him. She smiled and raised her finger to her lips. "But don't say a word to the children!"

Thirty-three

*B*efore long, the house was buzzing with the sounds and sights of Christmas. Carols played on the radio. Each evening Amos and Gideon and Leah filled the kitchen table with construction paper and old Christmas cards. There, in a sort of assembly line fashion, Amos cut the edges of the colored paper and a scene from a card they'd saved from previous years. Gideon would glue it to the center of the construction paper, fold it in half and print in his neatest handwriting, "Merry Christmas." Then Leah would decorate it with red or green rickrack and sprinkle it with glitter.

Later, Hannah would write a note and seal it in an envelope made from a roll of white shelving paper she had brought with her to Wyoming years ago.

This same paper was also used to wrap their presents. Then they'd take blocks of wood on which Eli had carved different shapes: a bell, an angel, a tree. They would dip the blocks into green or red or blue acrylic paint and print the figure, or a combination of figures, on their paper.

Hannah had also taught them to use a sponge to dab on

a colorful design, or to run their finger across an old toothbrush to splatter the paint. The rule was that they take their artwork to the shed where their creative "mistakes" would not matter quite so much.

Malinda and Miriam, eager to add to the festivities, dabbed bits of glitter onto the edges of pinecones and hung them on strings. For the tree, a feature their stepfather insisted they could not do without, the girls sewed small stuffed cows and donkeys, bells and snowmen from patches of material Hannah had saved for quilts.

Hannah was busy sewing. All day long she worked on shirts for the older boys, a dress for Rebecca, a soft stuffed teddy for Rachael. And for her husband, she made a burgundy corduroy bathrobe with his initials sewn on the pocket.

Frank was occupied in the workshop, not only with the shelf for Emma and the blocks for Isaac, but with his own idea of a gift for Hannah.

As Christmas drew nearer, Hannah and the girls shifted their focus to the kitchen and produced sugar cookies and gingerbread men, thumbprint cookies, chocolate chip cookies. They made candies and pies, kuchen and ham.

Roxanne came from Medicine Bow, this time delivering in person the basket filled with puzzles and crayons, mittens and earmuffs, socks and candy canes. She organized a taffy pull for the children and talked Frank into a sleigh ride with Captain.

Frank and Hannah watched from the sofa of the living room as Roxie and the children crowded beneath the tree Christmas Eve and sorted through the labels on the packages.

One by one they opened their gifts. When Roxanne unwrapped the wreath of vines and dried flowers that Hannah had made for her, her eyes filled with tears. She stepped to the couch where they were seated and hugged Frank and Hannah both. "Thanks," she said, "for making me a part of your family."

"The blessing is ours," Hannah told her, reaching for her hand. Indeed, Roxanne exuded a sparkle of youthful energy that drew the children to her. No longer was she a sullen creature in the corner, adding to the workload. Hannah looked forward to her visits.

She was nudged out of her reverie by Frank tugging gently on her arm. "It's your turn." He handed her a package.

Inside Hannah found a lovely box, which her husband had made and varnished. On the lid was a detailed carving of an oak leaf. "It's beautiful!" she exclaimed.

"Aren't you going to open it?" Frank asked.

She looked more closely at the box, then carefully raised the clasp and opened the lid.

Lying inside was a thin gold necklace.

"Mr. Francis . . ." Hannah said softly as she lifted it out.

Frank smiled, pleased by her reaction. It was, he imagined, the first piece of jewelry she'd ever owned besides her wedding ring.

"It's so lovely . . . but you shouldn't have."

Frank shrugged. "Well, I couldn't just give you an empty box, could I? Your mother wouldn't have approved."

Hannah smiled, thinking about her mother's conservative attitude toward jewelry. Frank didn't know how accurate his statement was. "No, Mr. Francis," she agreed, "my mother would not have approved."

By January, winter had taken on the attitude of a grizzly. Blizzards, which were not uncommon in that part of the country, became a source of bragging as veterans of those hills told their tales. Snowstorms that covered whole herds of sheep in a matter of hours . . . cattle who literally suffocated from their own breath as it formed ice across their nostrils and mouth. And more tragically, children who had never made it home from school, but stood lost and frozen in the bitter white whirlwinds just yards from the warmth and safety of their own homes.

The schools closed periodically, and frozen water pipes became a way of life. Hannah made a special effort to keep the fires hot, the meals warm, and the children busy. They cut long strips of paper dolls and snowmen and hung them from the curtain rods of the windows. Hannah mixed batches of homemade clay from flour and salt, oil and water, adding a drop or two of food coloring into small containers for variety.

For weeks, it seemed to him, each time Frank closed his eyes on the couch to sleep or picked up the paper to read, some little person would amble over with an aluminum pie pan filled with clay-dough peas and carrots, mashed potatoes and beef. Frank would, of course, chortle with gratitude as he pretended to gobble his meal. He'd wipe his mouth with his hankie, which he then used to cover the plate. Summoning a loud belch, much to the delight of the giggling chef, he would return the plate and concentrate once again on his paper or midmorning nap.

In between snowstorms, when the sun shone brightly on the icy plain, Rebecca asked if she could invite the girls from the church youth group for pizza one Saturday afternoon. Of course, Samuel and Benjamin greeted the plan with enthusiasm; the rest of the children grumbled mildly at the additional housework and preparation required. But before long they all grew excited about the proposed break in their winter routine.

Hannah had been raised in an environment that encouraged creative fellowship. In an area where radio and television, bowling alleys and theaters were forbidden, the young people had to rely entirely on their wits to find decent entertainment. Thus, an assortment of games had been handed down from generation to generation, from community to community.

Rebecca begged her mother to search her memory for such a game, one she had not already taught them, and while the girls washed and dried the supper dishes, Hannah took pen and paper and wrote one down.

Preparing pizza for a half-dozen girls was the easy part of giving the party, Hannah decided. The harder part was keeping the little ones—and the bigger boys—out of the dining room where the girls were gathered. Sam and Ben were quickly subdued with the threat of the loss of their allowance. And Frank finally succumbed to pressure and, pulling the

VCR out of the hall closet, let Mickey Mouse entertain the little ones until bedtime.

The six girls were all in the same grade and class. They had all been born in Wyoming except for Rebecca and Haley Thompson, whose father worked for the government as an engineer and traveled from assignment to assignment every few years.

Their parents were ranchers, for the most part, though some also worked at the refinery in Sinclair or took odd jobs in the winter months to supplement their income. Regardless of their economic background, they all attended the same school and most of them had played together since early childhood.

"Let's play Dutch Blitz," said Amie Carmichael, whose parents owned the ranch at the end of the lane not far from the Petersheims.

"No, we can play that later," Haley objected. "Teach us something new, Becca."

Rebecca smiled. Her home was well noted for its good food and variety of entertainment. "All right," she told her friends. "Help me move the table."

Once the large wooden table and bench had been moved to the side, five chairs were set in a circle.

"I'll be in the middle first," she said, then called, "Mama, come and give everyone the name of a city."

But it was Frank who answered the summons. "Your mother's busy with Rachael," he announced. "What can I do for you?"

Rebecca's eyes widened, and she replied, "You have to give everyone the name of a city. And it has to be a big one—

no Gopher Creek, New Mexico, or something."

Frank nodded and stepped to the girl seated nearest him. "You're New York."

"No, Father," Rebecca objected. "You're supposed to whisper it. Now you'll have to pick another one."

Frank turned to her, startled. Did she realize what she'd said? Had she done it because her friends were present and she didn't want to explain "Mr. Francis"? He had noted in the past that the moment their friends appeared, the children often dropped the Amish dialect that normally slipped in and out of their conversations at home. Gone, too, were the scarves the girls sometimes wore, and put temporarily out of sight the faceless dolls that lined their beds, sewn by their mother or passed down from the grandmother they never knew.

Were they ashamed, he wondered, of the traditions they followed that no longer held meaning for them? Or was it perhaps that the familiar of everyday was saved for family use, like the common everyday plates or a comfortable pair of slippers?

Suddenly aware that the girls were waiting, he leaned down and whispered the name of a city to each girl in the circle.

"Very well," Rebecca said primly when his job was complete, "you may go." She dismissed him with a wave of her hand, bringing giggles from the other girls and a teasing look of warning from Frank as he turned to leave.

"Now," she instructed her friends, "I'll be the operator. I say, 'Long-distance call from Philadelphia to Chicago,' and if that's the name of your city, you have to jump up and change seats before I can get in your chair. If you don't, you have to be in the center next. And if I call out 'All lines are busy,' everyone has to switch chairs."

The girls played noisily for some time before switching to a more quiet game of cards.

Frank sat in the living room with his stocking feet propped up on the coffee table, engrossed in a magazine. Hannah had just come from tucking Rachael into her crib upstairs when Rebecca, wide-eyed, entered the room.

"Mr. Francis," she said, "it's snowing."

Frank looked at her, puzzled by the concern in her tone. "It's just flurries," he assured her. "The weatherman predicted no accumulation—not till late Sunday."

Rebecca shook her head. "I mean, it's snowing!"

"All right! A snowstorm!" Benjamin shouted, then cowered quickly at Frank's glare.

Getting to his feet and tossing the magazine aside, Frank stepped to the front window and pulled the curtain aside.

Sure enough, the wind had picked up again and obliterated any semblance of visibility the darkness may have allowed.

"You'd better call their parents," he told Hannah. "Tell them if it keeps up for more than an hour, we'll just have them stay here for the night."

Sam had meant to leap into the air as his sister turned to go tell the other girls, but one look from Frank cut him short.

"And if there's any nonsense out of you two," he said to Sam and Ben, who stood side by side grinning from ear to ear, "I'll find that woodshed, blizzard or no! You understand?"

"Yes sir," Ben answered somberly.

"Yes—sir," Sam choked out, smothering an overpowering urge to laugh.

The weatherman's "flurries" lasted all that night and into the next morning. The girls, much to Rebecca's joy, stayed not only for the night but until the following afternoon.

And though Sam and Ben managed to control their basic tendency toward competitive showing off, Frank sighed in relief when the last of their guests was headed down the highway to her own home.

Thirty-four

*B*y February first the blizzards had stopped and a warm spell melted the thinner sections of snow. Pipes thawed, vehicles started, and one no longer needed a sledgehammer to chip the ice off the animals' water buckets every morning. School resumed its usual schedule, and in a flurry of happiness, Hannah's hens began to lay eggs. Frank actually whistled as he left for the barn each morning, and Hannah's thoughts turned to the seed catalogs that came in every mail.

By Valentine's Day, however, a bitter cold had embraced the West. Forty and fifty degrees below zero were not uncommon, and Hannah watched the woodpile and larder anxiously. Seed catalogs or no, spring was still a good two and a half months away.

The wind sent a winter chill through the smallest crack around the window frames, wooden slats of the floors, even the walls of the kitchen cabinets. Hannah used small pieces of wood to keep the stoves going, saving the larger chunks until bedtime, hoping to keep the house warm for as long as possible before the nighttime temperatures brought the inside of the house down to a chilling fifty degrees.

Once again water pipes froze, school was canceled, and vehicles refused to start. A portable heater had to be put into the bathroom before Emma was able to wash it, otherwise a wet rag would stick to the sides of the commode and tub. Ice formed in the bathtub and sink, where they ran the faucet continuously in an effort to keep the pipes open.

The kitchen floor was so cold that it was impossible to wash the dirt from it, for everything froze the moment it hit the ground. Laundry piled up mercilessly as the drain to the washer clogged with ice. And food froze on their dishes before they were able to wash them, making grease a near impossibility to remove.

Tired and cold, the family huddled around the stoves in chairs, wrapped in shawls and blankets. While Rebecca held Isaac and Emma rocked Rachael, Hannah read stories to the younger children to pass the long, bitter hours before sleep allowed a temporary respite from aching fingers and toes.

Knowing of their lack of wood, Frank managed to get the tractor running long enough to pull some dead wood from the fields. But the oil for the chain saw was so thick that it wouldn't run the machine properly.

The cattle had long since ceased to maintain their scheduled weight, and it was all he could do to keep them sheltered and fed and watered.

The van no longer ran with any predictability, despite the fact that he'd had a new battery put in the year before and the heater block was plugged in.

Frank was cold and tired from thawing pipes in the basement . . . especially since he'd gone through all the trouble that fall to insulate them and wrap them with electrical tape. Still, somewhere along the curves and twists, the pipes had frozen. Exhausted from his efforts, he joined the family for lunch. With all the children at home, Hannah had switched her main meal to early afternoon, saving dessert or a light snack for later in the evening.

As they gathered at the dining room table, Frank asked the blessing. He had just taken a spoonful of peas for his plate and was scooping a helping for Gideon beside him when a loud crash sounded from his left. There on the floor next to Emma, mingled with the glass of the broken dish, lay their chicken-and-noodle casserole dinner.

"Emma!" Hannah scolded harshly, rising from her chair. "How could you be so careless? How could you waste the little food we have?"

Emma blinked at her mother. She hadn't meant to drop the bowl; it had simply slipped from her fingers before she could stop it.

"You are old enough to behave more responsibly," Hannah continued. "I expect more from you than the younger children. What are we supposed to—"

"Hannah!" Frank interrupted, also rising from his chair. "That's enough. It was an accident."

Frank could feel the eyes of the children staring at him. He had never shouted at Hannah before, never corrected her in front of them.

Gaping at him, her eyes misting with tears, Hannah fled from the room, her chair tipping to the floor as she left it for the solace of the bathroom.

Rachael began to scream her objections at the tense emotional outbreak, and Isaac, confused by their angry voices, sat sobbing in his chair.

"Emma," Frank said more quietly, "clean up the mess. Henry, give her a hand. Sam, you take the baby." He pushed his chair aside. "Ben, talk to Isaac. And Rebecca, see what you can do about getting some food on the table." He strode quickly down the hallway.

"Hannah," Frank said, rapping lightly on the bathroom door. "Open up. Please." He heard her rise and blow her nose. Then the latch was unfastened.

Hannah opened the door, and Frank stepped inside. It was uncomfortably cold in there, but he leaned against the wall beside her and propped his boot up on the edge of the tub.

Hannah toyed with the Kleenex in her lap, turning it over in her hands while Frank breathed out the cold air in a huff before him.

"It's cold in here," he commented.

Hannah nodded timidly.

He took a bath towel and draped it across her shoulders. "I—shouldn't have yelled in front of the kids," he apologized. "It wasn't necessary. I'm sorry."

Hannah began to weep again. "I shouldn't have scolded her. I embarrassed her in front of all the others, and she's always so helpful to me, always willing to work hard."

Frank could only nod. Emma, it seemed, was always willing to help with the younger children or to work in the kitchen with Hannah. She had her moments of giggly silliness when her friends were around, and she sometimes seemed to argue with him just for the sake of disagreeing. But she always took her work at school and home seriously, even beyond what they expected of her.

"It was an accident," Frank said. "She didn't mean it."

"I know that," Hannah said, angry with herself. "It's just that there's so little food left, and I've been so careful—" Realizing she had said more then she'd intended, Hannah turned back to her Kleenex, evading her husband's eyes.

Frank rose slowly from the wall he'd been leaning against. "What do you mean?" His mouth was a thin, firm line as he gazed at her intently.

Hannah hadn't told him that the shelves in the pantry were filling rapidly with empty jars, nor had she bothered to explain that she was butchering her hens, having finished the year's supply of venison earlier that month.

"Mr. Francis," she tried lightly, "it's not like we're on the verge of starvation. Why, when I was little, we went one winter with only—"

"Hannah," Frank insisted, placing his hands on her shoulders and meeting her eyes, "are we running out of food?"

Hannah stood and looked at him, the worry she'd hidden so long rising to the surface. "We must be careful, Mr. Francis," she told him honestly. "We must be very careful."

Frank stepped from her, thoughtful.

Hannah regretted not having dealt more stringently with her groceries. Perhaps she should have refused Rebecca her pizza party. Or maybe she should have omitted desserts and saved her flour and sugar and oil for more important basic foods. She should have made a greater effort to tend the potato patch to gain higher yields when the bounty was possible. Next year, she vowed to herself, she would put aside more carrots and beans and winter squash. She would raise more chickens for broilers and rabbits for meat, she would increase the amount of cheese she made over the summer when the abundance of milk warranted it.

But all these things she *would* do, did not fill the empty pantry today.

"You should talk to Emma," Frank said quietly. "You should tell her why you—overreacted. She's old enough to understand."

Hannah nodded in agreement. She would talk to her right away. He opened the bathroom door, allowing the meager warmth from the hallway to enter.

Hannah could smell the scent of pancakes frying on the griddle.

"I told Becca to fix something," Frank answered her curious expression.

"Emma," Hannah called as they stepped into the hallway. "I'd like to speak with you."

"I'm going to run into town for awhile," Frank told her as Emma joined her mother in the hallway.

Hannah held her daughter and apologized for speaking so sharply, and praised her for the helpful spirit she always showed. Once again Emma broke into tears as she told her mother how the hot bowl had slipped from her hands.

Hannah didn't notice that Frank had gone to the bedroom, nor did she hear the gun case open. It was not until she recognized the sound of the bolt sliding back as he checked the chamber of the 30.06 that she realized where he was going.

"Emma, go and eat now," she said and turned quickly toward the stairway.

"Mr. Francis!" she called as she mounted the stairs two at a time. "Mr. Francis, please don't!"

Thirty-five

*F*rank glanced at his wife before sliding the rifle back into its case and putting a box of cartridges into the pocket of his winter coat.

"Mr. Francis," Hannah pleaded as he started toward the doorway she was blocking. Please, don't sin because of my anger."

Frank hesitated, studying the deep blue of her eyes. Then, "Stand aside, Hannah," he told her quietly.

Hannah placed her hand on his arm. "Frank, don't. We're not hungry yet."

His face took on an ugly determination. "Yes, but a lot of families are," he told her. "People in the valley—a lot of them with big families like ours—and nothing to eat."

"But it's against the law."

Frank jerked his arm free. "Whose law, Hannah?" he asked. "Does God's law let the antelope starve to death from overpopulation while people are trying to keep their children full of potatoes and cornmeal? Whose law is that?

"You think some animal activist in Washington knows a

hang about what goes on in this country?" He gave her no time to reply. "Of course not! And even if he did, how many kids would be sick from strep throat and influenza or whatever other virus comes around to prey on the weak before statistics would force them into letting us have food—food that's right in front of us and dying because there are too many antelope to feed on the little bit of grass this rocky land will give up to grow!"

"But it is God's law," Hannah insisted. "It's His law that we obey our country's law, and He'll provide another way within the realm of what's legal. Mr. Francis," she pleaded, "God cannot bless this family if you lead us only to an easy path. We must be faithful to Him, even if it means killing our own stock to feed ourselves and those around us."

They said nothing then, but searched each other's eyes, weighing the depth of the arguments, the truth of intent.

Finally Frank sighed, and the tension went out of his shoulders. "All right," he agreed. "I'll talk to them. I'll see if the game warden has heard anything from the Bureau of Land Management. And I'll stop at the church and see if anyone's been over to check on those people in the valley."

He meant to walk past her, but once again, her hand delayed his departure.

"Then leave the rifle," she insisted quietly.

Frank's jaw took a determined set. "I'll see what I can do; I won't promise more than that." He brushed past her to the hallway, the rifle case firmly in the grasp of his left hand.

It was late when the pickup pulled into the ranch again. Hannah could see from the floodlight in the lot that Donald Wheeler was with him in his own rig.

The coonhounds bayed wildly from the far corner of the barn where they were secured, as Don and Frank hoisted two freshly gutted antelope to the beam of the machine shed. They pulled them out of "critter range" and secured the rope to the large log that framed the building.

Hannah watched as Don returned to his pickup and headed home. Then she quickly climbed back into bed and pretended to be asleep when Frank entered their bedroom.

His clothes smelled of gunpowder and blood and the frosty night air. He made no effort at being quiet, and took his time in lighting the lantern on the dresser beside their bed. He emptied the change from his pockets onto the dresser before seating himself on the edge of the bed. First one boot and then the other thudded to the floor. Then, wearily, Frank glanced over his shoulder at his wife.

"There were about thirteen of us," he said. "Two of the men from the sheriff's department led us out to a kind of gully where a herd was penned in. They stood there and turned their backs—said they couldn't see who was firing if they were asked, then waited until we'd hauled out all the antelope we could carry.

"Don and I took five of them on down to the valley. We're going to see about getting those folks some wood tomorrow. I thought we were bad off this winter—"

He shook his head almost in disbelief. How could he have been so blind to the needs of the people around him? Even to the needs of his own family? He had gotten up each day, grumbling about the work added to his usual routine, grumbling about the cold he'd had to work in.

Yet all the while he thawed his pipes, it did not occur to him that others, less prepared than he, may have no water at all. As he grumbled about running low on firewood after trying so hard to put in an ample supply that fall, he did not see that the people who were his neighbors lived in such a shabby home that no amount of firewood could have kept them warm during that subzero period.

"Maybe you and the girls could make some quilts for the Brownings this summer," he said as, exhausted, he lay on the bed beside her. "And I'll help Tyler get some insulation in there after irrigation this spring. Let them trade us a couple young piglets for it so they won't take it as charity."

Then he turned onto his side and pulled the blankets to his shoulder. "I want some carpeting in here, Hannah," he told her, "after the steers sell. I know you and Eli had this idea of a 'plain' home, but it's too doggone cold in here, if you ask me, and I don't want the kids getting sick."

He glanced into the darkness, trying to gauge the meaning in her silence.

"I don't want to argue over it," he said in a tired voice.

Still, she said nothing. Was she asleep after all, he wondered?

"You pick out what you want, and I'll make arrangements in Saratoga to get someone out here first thing after the auction."

Silence echoed in answer.

"Hannah," he whispered hoarsely, "are you asleep?"

She smiled into the darkness and suppressed her laughter. "Yes, Mr. Francis," she replied.

At long last the cold weather gave way. The Chinook winds that swept the mountainside softened the earth and the hearts of the people around it.

Hannah planned her garden for spring, checking over the seed she would need and gathering information on a new breed of fast-growing meat chickens that she was thinking of raising.

Frank used the time to replenish their wood supply and the Brownings', to drive to Rawlins for staples he could buy in bulk: flour, sugar, pancake syrup, canned fruit.

He bought Sam a new pair of blue jeans and Ben some leather work gloves. He bought the coonhounds a hundred pounds of kibble and took Amos to the dentist to have a tooth pulled.

He felt satisfied then, that they would make it, that they had come through the worst of it and spring was just around the corner.

And then it snowed. A huge, heavy wet snow that threatened to weigh the rooftops down began just shortly after Saint Patrick's Day and continued on into the following week.

That Tuesday, not long after the children had left for school and Frank had gone out to move a stack of bales closer to the bull pens, Hannah heard a strange sound.

She had just stepped into the kitchen when Frank entered, holding his left arm in his right hand, blood oozing out of the sleeve of his insulated work suit as he hurried to the sink.

"Get the coat off! Get the coat off!" he said, tugging at the zipper and stopping then to press against the area that was bleeding.

Hannah pulled and jerked until the one-piece suit was at his waist. Nimbly she rolled his sleeve up over the deep puncture on his left forearm.

He paled and stumbled backward.

Quickly Hannah pushed him to the nearest chair. "Put your head down!" she told him. "Take a deep breath."

Frank did as she said, and within moments the color had returned to his face.

She took a clean towel and wrapped it tightly around the wound. "Hold this," she instructed him, placing his right hand firmly on the end of the towel. As he did so, she reached into her apron pocket and produced a diaper pin, securing the towel as best she could.

"Isaac," she called into the hallway as she grabbed for her coat, "come!"

"What are you doing?" Frank asked as she rushed to put Rachael into her snowsuit.

"I'm taking you to the clinic for stitches," she replied, and then hollered again, this time in the dialect of her ancestors, for her two-year-old son to come quickly with his coat.

She pounded a boot onto Rachael's foot and stood just as Frank was struggling from his chair.

"I'm not going to any clinic. We can't afford it."

"Sit down!" Hannah shouted at him, and Frank, startled by her tone of voice, complied.

When she was satisfied that he would be still, she dialed the number of the clinic in Saratoga and said that they were coming. She put Isaac and Rachael into the van, then carefully helped her husband into the passenger's seat.

He didn't argue any further, nor did he speak until, seventeen stitches later, they were on their way home again.

"I don't know why I didn't see that irrigation ditch," he said.

"It was covered with snow," she tried to justify for him. "You couldn't have seen it."

"I've lived here as long as you have!" he argued, angry with himself. "You'd think I'd have known it was there, wouldn't you? The front wheel went in, and the whole thing just flipped. I must have ended up on that old tree stump at the edge of it. I never even knew that jagged point had punctured me until I saw the blood on the snow and realized it was mine!"

Frank shook his head in dismay. "I'll have to get Josh over to help get the tractor off its side and out of there. I just hope the rear axle didn't break."

Hannah turned her eyes to the road. She didn't give a hoot about any rear axle! All she cared was that her husband was all right, that he hadn't been killed beneath the metal of that huge machine or buried beneath the snow inside the irrigation ditch.

Would she have ever had the sense to look outside in time if he'd been trapped there? And what could she have done, anyway, with just Isaac and Rachael at home? So many times she had heard of such accidents, knew of ranchers being maimed and crippled for life.

She thanked God then, as they traveled in silence, that Mr. Francis was not now among that number, that she and the children were not left to face the reality of life without him. She had not realized until that moment how much she had come to rely upon him, how comforted she was by his presence.

The need they'd had to pull together, to make the ranch successful and to build a home for the children, had fused a closeness in their lives that a more casual courtship may never have seen.

She turned the van into their driveway and parked it. Suddenly she started at the hand touching her shoulder.

"What's the matter?" Frank asked quietly, noting the tears that had fallen on her face in the silence of their return.

She wiped them quickly with her hand and smiled. "Nothing. I'm just—glad you're all right."

Thirty-six

*W*ith a screwdriver, Hannah carefully pried the plank away from the attic wall and set it on the floor. Frank would be outside with the milking and feeding for at least an hour, and Rebecca had promised to watch the children downstairs until she returned.

The velvet-lined box that Hannah withdrew flooded her memory with the old home place where Eli's grandmother had lived. Hannah remembered the huge family gardens, the gentle eyes of the dairy cows Eli helped to milk, the soft voice of Grandma Zimmer as she called the family to meals.

Eli had been her favorite. He had taken so after his grandfather, following him everywhere, learning all he could about faith and farming and family, that she had doted on him from the time he was little.

Yet he was independent and strong-willed like his grandfather as well, so it didn't surprise Grandma Zimmer to learn that Eli was leaving the community, going west with a new sense of faith and order to start his family. Unlike many others who had criticized and shunned them, Grandma Zimmer had given him her blessing—and an inheritance of the bells.

Hannah opened the wooden box Eli's grandfather had made. Inside were seven silver bells that had belonged to the Zimmer family long before the first of them had left Europe for the freedom of the new America. They had belonged to the family before the Zimmers had left the state church, and were passed along at the christening of the eldest male within each family.

They had been used as collateral for the down payment on the purchase of land back East. And Edna Zimmer had passed them on to Eli, knowing he would never own a part of the homestead of his father to pass along to his son.

The bells were held now for Samuel, though he didn't know of them, to secure a purchase of a homestead and a ranch if they could not provide a down payment for him. And as the eldest in the family, it would then be Samuel's responsibility to earn enough to help his younger brothers to establish their homes.

All but Isaac, the youngest boy, would one day leave the Petersheim ranch. It would be Isaac's job to build the grandparent cottage, which would attach to the main house. He would ease the burden from his stepfather's shoulders to his own, and the land there would become his, for him and his family. His wife would be the caretaker who aided Hannah as she aged, and their children would be the flowers along her and her husband's last pathway toward eternity.

Hannah shivered now as her hand touched the cold metal of the bells. Eli would be furious if he were alive and knew what she was thinking. He would never have allowed her to sell one of the precious bells. He'd have starved first.

But Mr. Francis was not Eli. He didn't know of the existence of the bells or of their value. He wouldn't have understood the significance of seeing that the boys were capable of continuing in agriculture so that they, too, might have the freedom to teach their sons the trade. He would never know that her gesture to help him would have been deemed an act of defiance by those who had raised her, for she certainly wouldn't tell him.

He would only know that the money for the hydraulic system would not take the last of what was left to live on, and they would be able to keep the heifers and bulls for breeding and the best of the steers for fattening.

"I don't know what else to do," Frank had told her late one night as they lay in the frosty silence of their room.

It was cold, and Hannah pulled the covers to her. She wanted to draw closer to him, to share in the warmth of his body, but he was tense, upset. She lay quiet and still instead.

"I've cut expenses everywhere I can," he said, his tone determined and angry. "But every time I seem to save a dollar, the grain price goes up two. Every time I say 'I can do without that' and sell something, another pipe bursts and takes that money! We can't seem to get ahead."

Hannah rolled onto her back and stared at the ceiling, as he did. She wanted to tell him that they had been through many winters of broken pipes, rising grain bills, and little heat. Yet somehow they had survived. God had always provided when the need was felt most; perhaps, she thought, so that they would remember that He was there to be relied upon. Hadn't Francis told her that himself, time and time again?

Then her eyes widened as she heard the jagged sound of

his breathing. His shoulders trembled, and his voice tightened. "I never meant to let you go hungry."

"Francis," she objected gently, trying to pull him to her.

"No," he told her, refusing even a little comfort. "I'm just a ranch hand. I should have sold the steers to Pickett when I had the chance—just like you said. I don't know whatever made me think I could lead this family or manage a ranch. I'll never do anything more than walk in the shadow of Eli Petersheim!"

He turned to his side then and pressed his face to the pillow and wept.

Hannah, who cried silently beside him, reached her hand to touch his back. "Please," she whispered into the darkness.

He didn't move.

"Please," Hannah begged him again.

At last he turned to her, slowly, putting his arm beneath her head as she moved to rest against his shoulder. Gently he stroked her hair, feeling the softness of it against his neck. He sighed wearily, and her fingers reached across his chest, comforting him.

"It's not true what you said," she told him quietly. "You are a good provider. You have been a fine father and husband. You've done the best you can." She paused. "I never asked you to be what Eli was, to be more than him—or less. I only wanted you to be yourself, to be Mr. Francis. I only—"

Frank drew her to him and silenced her words with his lips. The salty trace of her tears trickled from her cheek to his mouth. "Hush," he told her. His voice was quiet. "I know you never asked a thing of me. You never asked more than what I am."

She felt his chest rise and fall again as he wrestled with his thoughts.

"But I asked it of myself," he said in quiet disappointment. "I expected it of myself."

Thirty-seven

Frank opened the door that led to the back porch and slipped off his muddy boots. He'd spent all day at Tom Carlson's helping to fix the hydraulic system on the tractor. Tom had agreed to put the tab on hold until the spring sale, and the burden he'd felt since the accident seemed to lift right from his shoulders.

He stepped into the kitchen and closed his eyes as he inhaled the delicious aroma of roast and potatoes. Walking to the sink to wash, he noticed that the house was unusually quiet.

"Hello!" he called. "Where is everybody?"

He had just finished washing, and was dripping water on the floor as he searched for a towel, when Hannah entered.

"Oh, there you are," he greeted her cheerfully. "For a minute I thought I was the only one here—it's so quiet."

Hannah brushed her cheek lightly against his in a brief gesture of affection. "Well, you are almost alone," she informed him. "Roxanne took the children for pizza and to the theater in Rawlins."

"All of them?" he questioned in disbelief.

Hannah nodded.

"Is she crazy?" he exclaimed happily. "I didn't even know she was coming."

Hannah didn't tell him that she had called and asked Roxie to come for the weekend, or that the money to pay for such an outlandish treat had come from their savings account.

Instead, she went to the oven to remove their meal.

Frank, of course, credited the sudden blush in his wife's cheeks as a symbol of endearment. The fact that she had prepared such an elaborate meal and set the table so beautifully for two led him to believe her intentions extended toward the romantic.

Gallantly he held the chair for her as she approached the table, then hurried to light the lantern, adding to the intimacy of the setting.

Oh, Frank, Hannah thought, *don't start acting like a silly schoolboy. It's going to be hard enough to tell you the truth without having to disillusion you about why we're suddenly alone.*

"I don't know how to act," he said giddily. "Maybe I should knock over a glass of milk or something so it feels like home."

Hannah filled their plates in silence.

"I wonder what made Roxie decide to come up all of a sudden," he continued. "I thought she had some big date this weekend—or maybe it was next."

"Mr. Francis," Hannah said, changing the subject abruptly, "when I was a little girl we owned a very large farm—over 200 acres."

"So you've told me."

"But my father had a taste for fine trotters. Oh, it was against church policy, certainly, but my father was very good at disguising those horses—to make them look less valuable than they really were."

"I remember," he said. "You told me all about it when the kids put paint on old Captain for their circus."

She went on as though he hadn't spoken, rising from the table to the corner cabinet where she lifted a tiny doll and set it before him. "Those horses never did pay off the way my father had hoped they would."

Frank lifted the small, faceless doll and rubbed his thumb across the intricately sewn bonnet. Dressed in a plain brown jumper and muslin pinafore, the little doll had been made by Hannah's mother when Hannah was just a child. Silent now, he waited for her to come to the point.

"Pretty soon we were having difficulty paying bills after harvest and buying seed on credit. And so my mother 'stole' one of the horses."

Frank leaned back in his chair and crossed his arms before his chest. It was no coincidence, he realized, that he was alone at the supper table with his wife.

Hannah glanced at him. He knew. She hadn't even told him yet, but he knew! Feeling guilty about the look of disappointment in his eyes, she took a gulp of water and toyed with the edge of the tablecloth.

"She sold the horse secretly—without papers—at a terrible loss, and then she purchased beeswax and cloth, ribbon and yarn. She starting making dolls like that one."

"And what did your father say?"

"Nothing, at first," Hannah told him. "He was busy in the fields. Making dolls was a womanish thing. He didn't pay any attention at all until the harvest sale, when all of the women brought their handwork to the county square. And there was my mother with hundreds of little dolls.

"She sold them all and had orders from two gift shops. When we got home, she gave my father enough money to pay off their small debts—and to pay for the horse she had sold."

"I'll bet he had something to say about that!" Frank imagined, knowing her father to have been a stern, opinionated man.

Hannah chuckled at the understatement. "Yes, he did."

"Well, I can't really say as I blame him," Frank admitted, "though it was his own fault. He obviously had his priorities jumbled. Still," he added, "no one likes someone else to go behind their back—even when they are making a mistake."

"Yes," she agreed quietly, "that's exactly what my father said—only louder."

Frank laughed, then he leaned forward and placed his hand on hers. "Hannah," he asked her, "why are the children with my sister?"

Color rushed to her face as she withdrew her hand. "Because," she answered, "I thought you might want to yell."

"Oh, really? Yell about what? Hannah!"

She had jumped up to get something, and he followed her into the kitchen.

"Hannah," he protested, "what are you talking about? Did you sell some of the cattle?"

"Don't be ridiculous," she chided, cutting into a cake. "Who would I sell the cattle to?"

Frank sighed audibly. "Well, that's a relief. So what is it I'm supposed to get all shook up about?"

Hannah set down her knife and turned to him. Taking his hand in hers, she led him up the stairway to the attic. She pulled aside the loosened board and showed him the bells, still intact in their hidden casing.

"They're beautiful," he told her. "But I don't get it. What do they have to do with your mother selling a fancy trotter?"

Hannah did not meet his eyes. "I got all the way to Sinclair with one of the bells inside my purse," she confessed, "before I decided to turn around and come back."

"Oh," he said more quietly. Yes, he did feel a sense of disappointment that she hadn't talked about her decision with him first. "But the bells are yours," he said. "I'd have no right to get angry over something like that, especially if you were using the money to bail us out of a tight spot. I'd—be grateful, actually."

Hannah smiled and returned the precious treasure to its cubbyhole. "I told myself that very thing, Mr. Francis," she admitted. "But it didn't do any good. It was kind of like the sheep thing." She toyed with a loose thread on a button of his shirt, avoiding his eyes. "Sure, I had the right," she confirmed. "It's my ranch, my bells—it's even my son whose traditional heritage belongs to my past."

She hesitated. "But that's not what being partners is all about. And I did ask you here to be my partner—and to be yours."

Frank gently brushed a wisp of dark hair from her eyes. "So you figured I needed some time to yell about all of this," he speculated.

Timidly she looked at him. "—Or—something," she retorted.

His brow raised in surprise as Hannah took his hand in hers again and swept him through the house back to the dining room table. There she extinguished the atmosphere he'd so carefully created earlier and turned on the lamp above the table.

She cleared a spot for them to work, then went to the corner cabinet for some papers, which she set across the table before them.

"Since the van is paid for," she explained in a businesslike manner that in spite of Frank's best efforts brought a continual grin to his face, "why don't we get a short-term loan using the title as collateral?"

"You mean, to pay off the hydraulic system until we sell the heavier steers?" Long ago they had agreed that acquiring a loan to meet their monthly living expenses was not only self-indulgent but foolhardy in the long run, for the payment itself would then become an additional burden once the ease of the moment had passed.

Hannah crinkled her nose in a frown. "Well," she said, advancing her idea, "I'd rather pay off the loan and the work on the hydraulic system at the same time."

Frank was too enthralled by her enthusiasm to tell her that arrangements had already been made to pay for the tractor repairs later, free of interest and without liens and titles.

"I wanted to invest the money from the loan in materials," she said.

"You're going to make dolls?"

Hannah chuckled. "I'm afraid, Mr. Francis, that if you

waited for me to make enough dolls to pay our loan off, we'd be in the poorhouse for sure."

"Well, I didn't mean I thought you *should* make dolls, I just—" He stopped short, scanning the papers that were spread across the table. "No!" he said, pointing his finger at her. "No sheep!"

Hannah could not resist the chance to tease him. "But Frank," she pleaded, reaching for his hands.

"No!" he insisted, seizing her hands to hold her still. "I said no sheep!"

"But you said if it was important to me, I should—"

"No!" he interrupted distinctly. "Anything but sheep. I don't want those smelly, tick-infested critters roamin' around this place! You can't keep them out of the feed; you can't keep them in the pasture. You have to pert near have an island to keep the ram out, or you have lambs dropping in the dead of winter. You might as well give up every stitch of sanity you might have had!"

Hannah could contain herself no longer. "Well then," she ventured, "can I make confections?"

"Con—what?"

"Confections," Hannah told him. "You know, candy. Roxie and I have selected five basic types." Again she handed him the paper full of figures.

"Roxie's in on this?"

"Yes, she wants to help," Hannah told him. "Actually, she called all the stores to compare prices and bulk. And she coordinated the baskets and the colored cellophane and bows."

"My sister Roxie?" he exclaimed.

Hannah frowned. "Yes, your sister, Roxanne," she confirmed. "She's going to be in charge of sales and promotion from here to Casper."

"Why?" he asked her suspiciously, earning himself a sound thump on the arm.

Hannah glowered at him. "Because she loves us."

Frank rubbed his arm. "Well, the Roxie I know wouldn't have lifted a finger to help anyone a year ago. Must be something you've said."

But Hannah only shrugged her shoulders. "People change," she said gently. "Perhaps the Lord is working in her heart."

Thoughtfully, Frank nodded in agreement as Hannah began to clear the dishes that were still sitting on the table.

"Hey!" he objected suddenly. "Don't I get to yell? I thought we did all of this so I could yell."

"Must you?"

"Well," he said, somewhat disappointed, "we may never get the chance to be alone again."

Sighing, Hannah returned the plates to the table and folded her hands primly before her. "Very well," she conceded. "You may yell."

"Now?" Frank asked her.

"Yes, now."

"Ready?"

Hannah nodded.

Frank drew a deep breath and then, as his face reddened to a scarlet hue, he bellowed as loudly and as long as his lungs allowed. "How was that?" he questioned proudly.

"It was quite sufficient."

Frank clapped his hands together. "Good," he concluded, taking the newspaper and heading toward the living room couch, "consider yourself yelled at."

Thirty-eight

*F*rank had no idea what he was getting into as he handed his wife the checkbook and waved good-bye to her and his sister.

They returned home late, bubbling with conversation, and began unloading boxes and boxes until the back porch was overflowing with supplies.

Come Monday morning, Hannah was up bright and early, her counters lined with shiny tin pans, bowls, and measuring spoons.

The children were whisked out the door for school, and the madness began. Flour, oil, sugar, and pecans took up every available space, and circles of what Hannah called "bird's-nest" pie dough awaited their turn in the oven. Dolloped with a scoop of hot caramel-pecan mixture, these little nests lined muffin tins by the dozens. When thoroughly browned, they were topped with yellow-colored coconut for "straw" and toasted a few moments longer. Once cooled, they were sealed in freezer wrap and placed in pie-stacking pans inside the deepfreeze.

Now and then the phone would ring, and Hannah would open her three-ring notebook and scribble in another address or customized order.

For a time, things went smoothly. The house, though a little less tidy, was relatively neat, meals were still on time, and the children were clean and orderly.

The weather shouted promises of spring, and as the water flowed from the mountaintops, irrigation began in the fields.

Determined to help the Brownings with their poorly seeded pastures and inadequate equipment, Frank pulled Sam and Ben out of school several mornings to assist, much to the boys' delight.

As they grasped at the hours of daylight, they didn't notice the lovely pastel-colored divinity candy that dotted the tabletops throughout the house that week, nor did they note the rocky road candy Hannah and Rebecca mixed by the kettleful all weekend.

The moment the irrigating was finished, Frank and Tyler Johnson began installing insulation, which had been donated by the church, at the Browning home.

Tyler, a local carpenter and fellow member of their church, was also a young father. He found a ready listener in Frank, and told him in detail of his frustrations in dealing with a sixteen-month old. From what Frank could gather, the boy was a strong-willed little tyke who knew just how to get some excitement stirred up between good ol' mom and dad.

"Well, I'm not sure I'm the one to give advice," Frank told the younger man with a smile. "My situation is a little unusual. I guess I was pretty lucky to be friends with all the Petersheim kids before becoming their dad."

He thought of the time he had spent playing tea party and mud cakes with Emma when he had first worked at the ranch, and how he'd helped Stephen learn to ride a bike. He had listened to Henry play his harmonica and sat with the twins when they'd had the measles.

"Seems to me, though, that you might be doin' far more talkin' than is necessary for a child that age. A well-placed swat and a stern 'no' might get your point across better."

But he thought, too, of how easy it was to sum up the basics of child care with a swift gesture of discipline, when really, it was much, much more than that. It didn't necessarily take a lot of time or a good deal of wisdom to build a foundation between a parent and a child. It took fairness, he thought, as he stapled a roll of fiberglass into place, and an understanding of what was expected from one another.

He recalled being with Eli when he caught Benjamin smoking on the machine shed roof, and the day Samuel announced during milking that he'd accepted the Lord Jesus as his personal Savior. These times, he knew, unscheduled and unheralded, were the milestones in a child's growth, and the foundation in raising up a child. What a parent did at those moments made all the difference in how discipline was received when it was really needed.

He turned to the young father beside him as they paused to unroll and measure a new section of insulation.

"You know," he said, "I don't think there's any set, fast

rule for disciplining. Some kids just need a stern look and a firm reminder to get them back in line. Others seem to push that limit just as far as it will go to find restrictions they'll respect."

Tyler removed the tacking nails that extended from his mouth. "So, how do you know what each one needs? You've got thirteen of them!"

Frank shrugged as he stretched out the roll onto the floor and pulled the measuring tape from the clip on his belt. "You get to know them," he answered.

Tyler chuckled. "Me and Jason can't exactly hang out on the ball field yet. What do you talk about to a baby, anyway? How's your teddy today?"

"I think you just sort of *be* together," Frank answered. "Let him climb around while you're watching television—give him a bite of your pizza when your wife's not looking. Crawl around on the floor with him. Just let him know you enjoy being with him. That's what it's all about," he assured the young man. "You'll figure out what he needs as you go along. But if you stay strangers, just living in the same house sharing dishes and carpet and your wife until he's nine years old and you can hang out on the ball field, then what you choose about discipline won't matter, because it won't work, anyway."

Tyler smiled as he tugged on the next strip of insulation and headed toward the far end of the attic. "Thanks, Frank," he said. "I'll try that—" He paused to itch where the irritating fiberglass had gotten under the collar of his shirt. "Just as soon as I shower tonight!"

As he pulled into the drive, Frank made a mental note to ask Hannah to invite the Johnson family over for dinner some Sunday just as soon as the candy-making venture was over and things were back to normal.

He frowned as he thought of the absolute mess they had gotten into. If he'd had any sense at all, he thought, he'd have realized that a woman with one child, let alone thirteen, couldn't possibly keep up with a household and a candy factory at the same time.

He blamed himself for letting her talk him into agreeing to this. After all, if he had told her about the bill for the hydraulic system being taken care of, she wouldn't have felt the need. But she and Roxie had seemed so excited about it all that he couldn't throw water on their dream. He'd figured it would be a good experience for Roxanne to get involved with the family, and at the same time, would allow Hannah an opportunity to help significantly with their financial needs.

He sighed now as he braced himself to face the folly of that decision.

"Mom!" Samuel's voice hollered from the stairway. "I can't find any socks!"

"Look in the basket!" Hannah hollered back, rushing about madly with a decorating tube full of pastel pink icing.

All around the kitchen and dining room were trays of various flavored truffles. Icing tubes of pastel blue and green, yellow and pink sat in various stages of fullness, oozing trails of sticky sweetness wherever they lay.

"I looked there!" Sam called back. "There aren't any."

Hannah turned her cheek for Frank to kiss. "Then wash some in the sink!" she shouted back. "Hello, Mr. Francis," she said more quietly.

Frank dipped his finger into the icing and poked it into his mouth. "When's supper?" he questioned cheerfully.

"Oh—I'm—" she started to apologize. Then her voice hardened and she jerked two chocolate-covered candies from the tray before her and set them in his hand. "Here," she told him curtly.

Frank suppressed his rising anger as he set them on the counter. "No, thank you. I had some for breakfast, remember?"

He glanced into the dining room where Rachael sat shredding a newspaper, her hands and face covered with black ink, the barrette in her hair hanging at the end of a tangled, unkempt pigtail.

Music blared from the bedrooms in competition with the television, and as he stepped into the living room to rectify a dispute, his eyes followed a trail of toys and dirty laundry. Dishes stacked on the coffee table jiggled as he walked across the floor and turned off the TV that no one was watching.

"Boys!" he shouted up the stairway, guessing that the noise was coming from their bedroom. "Lower the volume!" No one heard him. "Shut that thing off!" he bellowed.

His order was followed by a hurried shuffling of feet and a long silence. He walked back into the kitchen, resigned to finding his own meal, when Hannah spoke up.

"You'll have to take Amos in hand," she informed him, not stopping in her rapid distribution of little squiggles across the tops of the truffles. "He ate an entire tray of chocolates while my back was turned. He's in his room."

Frank opened the refrigerator and took out what appeared to be an empty package of lunch meat. "I'll spank him *after* he throws up," he mumbled.

Hannah was not amused. "I would have done it myself, but as you can see, I'm too busy."

Hoping to soften her mood and erase the tired look in her eyes, Frank closed the refrigerator and placed his hand on her shoulder. "You've been too busy for a lot of things," he said gently. "Why don't we just leave this and go outside, get a breath of fresh air? The hills are actually green out there already."

Impatiently, she jerked his hand from her shoulder and continued to the next tray. "You have some fresh air for me," she retorted crisply. "I have an order to fill."

Frank stared at her momentarily. "Nope," he resolved, stepping behind her and literally lifting her off her feet. "You're the one who needs to cool off."

Hannah shrieked as he started toward the back door, her decorating tube leaving sugary pink icing along his arm where he held her by the waist.

He set her on her feet outside the porch, then quickly slipped back inside and locked the door behind him. He had no idea what she was saying, for she had slipped into a tirade of German-Dutch. Whatever it was, he imagined, it was probably best left untranslated.

Thirty-nine

*A*mos!" Frank called from the stairway. "You come down here."

Pale and sweaty, the seven-year-old boy came down the stairs, his features a picture of misery, his arms clasped to his stomach.

"Come here and take this," Frank told him, holding out a teaspoon of the clear liquid Hannah labeled "tonic."

"You have my sympathy," Frank said as he ladled the awful brew into the boy's mouth. "I'd rather take a whipping any day."

"Me, too," Amos agreed. He turned back toward his bedroom, then his eyes widened and he ran to the bathroom instead.

"I'll help him," Sam offered, having come downstairs to see what was going on.

Soon Frank had the entire family assembled in the living room—except for Amos, who'd been sent back to bed with a bucket and a box of tissues.

"I know these past few weeks have been tough on all of

us," Frank told his assembled guests. "And I guess I haven't been here much to help, either, what with irrigation and working at the Brownings.'" He looked them over. "It takes something like this to make us realize all the work your mother does around here every day, as a matter of routine."

The children were silent, their eyes fixed on the man they'd come to respect and trust. They waited anxiously for whatever was coming next.

"Now this baking thing," Frank said with some disgust, "has gotten way out of hand. But it means a lot to your mother. And knowing that she's the kind of woman who likes to finish what she starts, I figure we'd better all pitch in and help out before the house gets plumb tired of bein' dirty and walks off on us someday."

Giggles sputtered from the younger children, lessening the tension that had come upon the room.

"Now I don't have much time for cooking, but Emma, if you're game, I'll just put you in charge of whatever you think you can fix. You make me a list of the things you need, and I'll see to it that you get them. Just don't be serving candy for breakfast," he warned her with a wink.

"Rebecca," he continued, "I'm putting you in charge of laundry."

Samuel grinned, happy that someone else would be taking the responsibility of seeing to it that they had clean clothes.

"And after school, Becca, you help watch Rachael and Isaac. Make up a bath list and see to it that it's followed. Any shirkers," he announced for the benefit of the others, "will have to see me."

"Sam," he said next.

"Yes, Mr. Francis," he offered eagerly.

"Since you're such a smart aleck," Frank teased, "I'm putting you in charge of homework—all but Becca's and Ben's. And Ben, you're in charge of getting the boys' rooms clean."

"Aw, why can't Sam do that?" Benjamin complained.

"Because," Frank chided, "you have enough trouble getting *your* homework finished."

Disgruntled but subdued, Ben accepted his task as the others snickered.

"Malinda and Miriam," Frank said, "you wash and dry the dishes."

"But Mr. Francis," said Miriam, "we already wash the dishes."

"Yes," he stated, "but I want them done *well* from now on. I don't want to see Mama coming behind you to do them over."

Embarrassed, the little girls lowered their heads as their stepfather continued.

"Stephen and Henry, in addition to the chores you already do, I want you to get up early and take care of your mother's chores as well. Split them up between the two of you."

"Mr. Francis," Stephen objected boldly, rising to his feet.

"Yes, Mr. Stephen," Frank acknowledged with a smile. Without a doubt, he'd had more run-ins with Stephen than with any of the other children. Stephen was the instigator of the water balloon toss across the upstairs hallway last July, the one who painted the milk cow green on Saint Patrick's Day, the leader of the mutiny to make Friday night guaranteed movie night with popcorn and soda.

Yet, as many times as they had stepped into the mudroom for a "conference," Frank was that proud of Stephen, too. He was the one who had given his boots to a less fortunate boy to use on the playground each day last winter, never saying a word to anyone until the school called to complain that he was being sent to school "unprepared" each morning.

It was Stephen who always saw to it that the younger children had a share of his candy on allowance day, and that no one ever laughed at Gideon when he sometimes had an "accident" at school.

"Mr. Francis," Stephen said now, "chickens are women's work."

"Yeah," Henry agreed more timidly. "And feeding jerseys is, too."

Frank rubbed his hand across the stubble of his beard. "Well," he said thoughtfully, "I could give the job to Miriam and Malinda."

He watched their eyes brighten at the thought. "But then you'd have to do the dishes. The girls can't do everything."

"I'll do the calves," Henry countered quickly.

Frank turned to Stephen.

"Oh, I guess it'll be all right," the boy grumbled. "I just hope the kids at school don't find out."

"I'm sure they won't," Frank said with a chuckle. "Now Amos, when he's feeling better, can help you fill the wood box. We need a lot of wood for all this baking, and I don't want your mother to have to stop to fetch it. Is that understood?"

Leah was solemnly waiting her turn. As a wide-eyed baby she had looked so fragile that Frank had almost been afraid to hold her. Now at four she climbed trees with the others and stood unafraid beside old Caramel, eager to do her part in the milking.

"I want you to pick the toys up every day," he said to her. "Whatever Rachael and Isaac have played with down here, when you come home from school, you pick them up. And before you go to bed at night, I want you to check all over the downstairs and tidy up any toys. Can you do that, Leah?"

Her eyes sparkled, and she gave her stepfather a smile of admiration. "Yes, Mr. Francis," she promised.

"Well then," he concluded, slapping his hands against his knees and rising to his feet, "let's get started. And I'd better let your mother in," he said with a grimace, "before she takes an ax to the back door."

Hannah, of course, had long since left the backyard for the sanctuary of the barn. There, among the staring eyes of the barn cats and the gentle chewing of the cows, she had sorted through her anger and frustration.

Frank was right, she knew. She had lost sight of her priorities and overextended herself. But there was a part of her that really enjoyed what she was doing. She felt productive and important. Her baskets, her candies would be lining the shelves of bakeries and delis across southern Wyoming.

It felt good to have a craft that someone actually thought

was worthy of buying. There was little reward in washing diapers and folding clothes. Endlessly intervening in children's
squabbles and picking up other people's messes just didn't
stimulate personal growth.

Though she knew in her heart that her tasks as mother
and wife were far more important, the heady vanity within
her had caused her to make commitments she couldn't possibly keep. Perhaps, she justified, the long, cold winter had
deadened her senses toward more than mere survival.

But winter should have been when the fires burned
brightly in the stoves and she spent her days at the sewing
machine or the quilting hoops. It was a time of steaming hot
soups and chocolate with marshmallows.

The garden seed that she would normally have set in
starter cups was nearly forgotten, the chicks postponed for
another month. She had wanted to raise goats in the little
pen that once held her sheep, to fatten them on scraps so
they would be a supplement to their winter's venison. She
had wanted a little herd of nannies that the children could
milk by hand; she had planned, in the darkness of the winter
months, all the things that she would say to convince her husband of the wisdom of such a venture.

Now, she thought tearfully, she had let him down; she
had let them all down. How could she convince him that she
was capable of managing a herd of goats when she couldn't
even make a basketful of candy without neglecting her other
responsibilities?

She had meant for the candy making to be a family enter-
prise, a time when, side by side, they would make a product
to be proud of. But she hadn't helped them work together.

She had tried to do it all, to keep the house and the children and earn the money all on her own. She had shut them out in her pride to succeed.

"You still talkin' to me?" a voice questioned timidly from the doorway.

"Mr. Francis!" Hannah said. She ran to him, not worrying about her tears, and wrapped her arms around him.

Frank stumbled backward, barely able to keep his balance. "Hey, I'm going to have to shut you out of the house more often," he said, as he patted her lovingly on the back.

"Mr. Francis," Hannah said, drying her eyes on the sleeve of her blouse, "I'm so sorry. I didn't mean to get so— involved—"

"I know you didn't, Hannah," he said. "And—doggone," he mumbled, stepping from her to rub the back of his neck. "Doggone if I didn't get so all wrapped up myself."

"Oh, no, no," she argued. "It's your place to be in the fields now and at the Brownings'—not in the kitchen with me. I wouldn't hear of it."

"Well, you're gonna hear of it," he told her, "because now that the irrigation's done for a while, that's where I'm going to be."

"Mr. Francis!" Hannah gasped, raising her apron to her mouth.

"Oh, don't act so all-fired shocked," he said, wrapping his arm around her waist in an attempt to draw her toward the house.

But Hannah would not budge. "What exactly do you mean?" she demanded.

"I mean that while you're busy making tea cakes, or whatever else you're doing, the children and I will take care of the rest—the way we should have been all along, only we were too stupid to figure out."

"You're taking care of the house?" She was unable to disguise the amusement in her voice.

"That's right," he answered defensively, then wagged his finger at her in warning. "But if you ever once even *mention* making candy to me again, I'll— I'll—"

"Lock me out of the house," she answered for him.

Frank smiled as they started toward the warmth of the kitchen. "That's right," he agreed wholeheartedly.

Forty

*H*annah earned far more on her business venture than even she had anticipated. And Frank never did find the courage to tell her that Tom Carlson had been willing to wait for the money until after the sale of the cattle—nor did he offer any explanation to Tom as he dropped off his payment at the shop long before schedule.

A late snowfall marked the cattle drive to the mountain pasture that May. It was an adventure, not serious enough to be dangerous, that Sam and Ben thoroughly enjoyed. By the time they arrived home the sun had warmed the earth, creating a mire of mud that covered the horses, riders, and equipment.

Hannah refused to allow them in the house. She kept them on the back porch, handing them towels and rags and housecoats until enough mud was piled on the floor of the porch to suit her. Then she sent them single file to the shower and greeted them afterward with a steaming mug of coffee and a hot meal.

Frank weeded out his heftier steers and sold them at market. Though he made a considerably higher profit than he would have the past fall, the additional winter feed required to maintain weight had nibbled his profits down to a fourth of what he had hoped for. Still, he thought, it was enough to see them through the summer, pay for taxes and next year's bid on the mountain pasture and the seed he needed to improve grazing for the bulls, and still have a little extra to help the Brownings get a start. And, of course, to buy carpet for the upstairs. Next year, he vowed, their feet would not be cold when the winter winds blew.

It was the steers he'd sent up north to the feedlot, the ones he'd crossbred to produce a more compact, meatier body type than the lanky offspring they'd been working with, that really surprised them both.

It was late Saturday evening, and Hannah had gotten the last of the children from the tub into bed. Frank was standing outside the gate to the small pasture. The younger heifers, the ones he'd kept back from the herd, were just calving.

Hannah could see the outline of her husband clearly, leaning against the fence rail in the brightness of the moonlight, and she stepped from the house to join him, her black shawl draped across her shoulders.

He acknowledged her presence with a smile.

"Do you think any of them will calve tonight?" she asked.

Frank pointed to a heifer in the far right of the field. "That one," he said. "Tonight—maybe tomorrow."

In the distance, the coonhounds bayed restlessly at the oversized moon, and a cow lulled its calf to sleep with the quiet chewing that made her lullaby.

Hannah pulled the shawl more closely around her in the breeze of the cool night air, and Frank wrapped his arm around her shoulder to share the warmth of his body.

"It was surely a blessing," she said.

He nodded, knowing she referred to the choice steers he had sold that week through an electronic auction to a restaurant chain on the East Coast and in southern Europe. The steers, one-fourth of his herd, had brought not only double what his average beef earned above cost, but had landed him a contract for the following year as well. But custom feeding, he knew, was not a thing that one could count on. Markets fluctuated far too much to base one's living on. There were those who attempted it, but Frank had seen the damage of that sort of gambling too often to attempt it himself.

"It was a blessing," he agreed. "We can try it again, so long as we limit it to a fourth of the herd. Might not be a bad offshoot for Ben someday."

"Ben?" Hannah questioned. It was her eldest son she thought of as an avid rancher. "Not Sam?"

"We'll put Sam in charge of the meatpacking company—give old Pickett a little competition."

Hannah chuckled at his vision. "Well, maybe we'll let him get his driver's license before we throw him into the business world. See if he survives that, first."

Frank looked at her in surprise. "What?" he asked. "I taught Rebecca to drive, and she's done just fine. Don't you trust me?"

Hannah pulled him close to her once more, using his body as a shelter against the breeze. "I trust you, Mr. Francis," she told him, leaning against him as he draped his arms around her. "I've always trusted you."

She turned ever so slightly to look into the pale blue of his eyes. She had never told him in the year and a half they had been married, what had come to grow in her heart. "I trust you and I—I—I love you."

Frank leaned his head to kiss the softness of her hair. He closed his eyes, longing to hold onto the moment that he had feared might never come.

But the moment didn't last. Suddenly the sounds of the children's voices erupted from the upstairs windows.

Frank sighed as a frown riddled his brow. "Seems there's more than one herd needs settlin' down tonight."

Hannah smiled up at him. She had found a partner to share in the land she loved and the heart of her home as well.

Dear Reader:

We love to hear from our readers. Your response to the following questions will help us continue publishing the excellent Christian fiction that you enjoy.

1. What most influenced you to buy *Mr. Francis' Wife?*
   - ❑ Cover/title
   - ❑ Subject matter
   - ❑ Back cover copy
   - ❑ Author
   - ❑ Recommendation by friend
   - ❑ Recommendation by bookstore sales person

2. How would you rate this book?
   - ❑ Great
   - ❑ Good
   - ❑ Fair
   - ❑ Poor

Comments:

3. What did you like best about this book?
   - ❑ Characters
   - ❑ Plot
   - ❑ Setting
   - ❑ Inspirational theme
   - ❑ Other_____

4. Will you buy more novels in the **Promises** series?
   - ❑ Yes
   - ❑ No

Why?

5. Which do you prefer?
   - ❑ Historical romance
   - ❑ Contemporary romance
   - ❑ No preference

6. How many Christian novels do you buy per year?
   - ❑ Less than 3
   - ❑ 3-6
   - ❑ 7 or more

7. What is your age?
   - ❑ Under 18
   - ❑ 18-24
   - ❑ 25-34
   - ❑ 35-44
   - ❑ 45-54
   - ❑ Over 55

Please return to
ChariotVictor Publishing
Promises Editor
4050 Lee Vance View
Colorado Springs, CO 80918

If you liked this book,
check out these great *Promises* titles from
ChariotVICTOR Publishing . . .

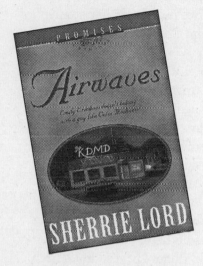

Airwaves
by Sherrie Lord
ISBN: 1-56476-706-X

H e was stunning. Flawless. Absolutely traffic-stopping gorgeous.

"Hello, Emily," he said—as if a sculptor's perfection should speak and smile like warm flesh. He held out his hand. "I'm Colin Michaels."

Inwardly Emily Erickson jumped, which must have been what jarred the heat loose to crawl up her neck.

"Hi," she replied, smiling as she pushed forward her hand, and not sounding a bit like a candidate for an FM studio. "Thanks for seeing me today."

"My pleasure. Sorry I'm late; I got tied up in production." He claimed the other chair on the interrogatee side of general manager Sterling Barclay's desk.

"We just got settled ourselves," Sterling assured him.

Colin nodded, then turned back to Emily. "How was the drive?"

"Beautiful, thanks."

It was only 180 miles from Coeur d'Alene, Idaho to Missoula,

Montana, but it was light years between the patched-together studio of KBTS, K-93, and Diamond Country KDMD. She'd been awake into the early morning polishing her résumé, after Sterling had phoned to request it. Two days later her stomach still effervesced in disbelief—Diamond Country's general manager liked the way she sounded.

She studied the portion of the station she'd heard first. Sterling Barclay was as tall as he sounded over the phone. His liquid brown eyes danced with a youthful mischief that said it was no imposition to attend to station business on a Saturday morning. He'd be here anyway, and besides, he was already sold—he'd invited her here. It was Colin Michaels, the station's PD—program director—she had to convince.

She turned to the younger man who supervised the broadcast side of the station, and who at the moment held her future in his hands. He sat in the chair beside hers, one ankle set on the opposite knee, elbow on the desk, fingers braced in an arch over his coffee mug. The mug didn't carry the Diamond Country logo, but only orange and gold block letters on a beige background, and for another station, KMLA. And the left hand arched over it wore no wedding ring—she definitely looked—but its owner sure was beautiful to look at.

Emily let her gaze lift from the dimples so prominently pressed into his cheeks to follow the strands of hair that were luxurious in both their thickness and color, so brown it was almost black. Parted off center, it lifted a little before it swept back in shorter wisps over his ears, then fell in lush volume, length, and gentle curl over his collar. He didn't tug creases into his blue-and-white Oxford, but neither did the shirt hang shapeless. He apparently didn't spend all his time at the station; it took more than standing at a microphone to produce bulk like that.

Only his eyes moved as he looked from the cup to Sterling, then to Emily. Their intensity, in mood as well as hue—navy blue and rimmed with dark lashes—threatened to puddle her blood, but this was a job interview, so she sat a little straighter for the sparring ahead, and prayed.

Make it okay. Daddy's wrong. I can handle this. I'll show him. I'll show You. I'll show everyone.

"Your résumé is a little thready," Colin said, his voice all-radio, all-professional, with a tone that promised perfect diction, inflection, and levels. "But your presence is strong—that is, your delivery is good, you're creative, and your voice carries well."

How does he know all that?

"I've heard your show," Colin added, as if he'd heard her thoughts.

Emily looked to Sterling, who explained, "I took the liberty of taping portions of it when I was in Coeur d'Alene. It's so much more like the real you than a spec tape you record yourself."

"You have nice pipes." This from Colin. "Good female voices—ones that have the depth to carry over a dusty speaker in the back of a muffler shop—are rare. But are you teachable?"

"How intelligent would I be if I said no?" Emily replied.

For a second Colin merely stared. Then he gave a full-dimpled chuckle. "Not very."

"Could you clarify what you mean by teachable?"

His stare shifted to his mug, and he narrowed his eyes, considering. "You have the personality for it, but it's obvious Kyle hasn't worked with you."

"You know Kyle?" she asked, referring to Kyle Larkin, her general manager at K-93.

Colin nodded. "Oh, sure."

This bedroom community called radio knew no geographic barriers such as Lookout Pass on the Idaho-Montana border.

"I worked with Kyle in a little AM station in Green River, Wyoming," Sterling added.

"You worked with Kyle? When was this?" Emily said.

Sterling rocked back in his chair. "Must have been the sixties. You weren't even born—but you don't have to respond to that. I'm not asking your age, you understand."

Emily laughed. The distinguished exterior and that dignified name carried no warning. It was the glint in his eyes that gave him away; Sterling's sense of mischief would find like company around a cowpoke campfire.

"I'm twenty-one, you didn't ask, and I'm not accusing you of discrimination," she replied.

To which Sterling smiled. "Good. Just wanted to make sure we understood each other." Then he looked to Colin as if to say he was finished with the detour.

Emily's thoughts raced. *Don't make me go back, begging for a job I just quit. Please give this to me. . . . I can do all things through Christ Who strengthens me. . . . Whatever things you ask in prayer, believing, you will receive.*

And these titles coming soon . . .

Alone. Without a job or money. This isn't what recent-
ly widowed Tabitha bargained for when she left
England for a new life in America. Now, in the pioneer
village of Waukegan, Illinois with just the clothes on
her back and a strong faith in God's provision for her,
how will she provide for herself?
Handsome, charming Etienne Rousseau
offers one solution to her loneliness, while
rough-edged Lucas Hayes offers another.
Can either of these men be God's provision for her when neither shares her faith?

Freedom's Promise
by Suzanne D. Hellman
ISBN: 1-56476-718-3

*September
1998*

Best friends—that's what Scott and Beth have been
since they were teens. Why is Beth blind to his desire
for more than friendship? "You'll make *somebody* a
good husband," she says. How can he make her see
that she's the *somebody*—especially when Michael, the
latest guest at her bed-and-breakfast, is a handsome,
debonair Englishman? Scott doesn't trust him or his
motives for romancing Beth. Could Michael's
presence have more to do with something valuable
hidden in the inn than with Beth?

Lord, where are You? Scott was so sure of God's plans
for him and Beth, but perhaps he didn't have a clue
about perceiving God's will. . . .

*January
1999*

Best Friends
by Debra White Smith
ISBN 1-56476-721-3